D0325669

THE EXTRA

THE EXTRA

MICHAEL SHEA

TOR®

A TOM DOHERTY ASSOCIATES BOOK
NEW YORK

THE EXTRA

Copyright © 2010 by Michael Shea

Edited by James Frenkel

A Tor Book
Published by Tom Doherty Associates, LLC
175 Fifth Avenue
New York, NY 10010

www.tor-forge.com

Tor® is a registered trademark of Tom Doherty Associates, LLC.

Library of Congress Cataloging-in-Publication Data

Shea, Michael, 1946–
  The extra / Michael Shea.—1st ed.
      p. cm.
  "A Tom Doherty Associates book."
  ISBN 978-0-7653-2435-1
 1. Motion pictures—Fiction.   2. Extras (Actors)—Fiction.   I. Title.
  PS3619.H3998S53 2010
  813'.6—dc22

                                        2009040676

First Edition: February 2010

Printed in the United States of America

0 9 8 7 6 5 4 3 2 1

Dedicated to my sweet Linda, Della, Jacob.
From the cave, I send my dearest love.

ACKNOWLEDGMENTS

The author most warmly acknowledges Jim Frenkel, the Black Prince of editors, and Lynn Cesar, who has been teaching the author to write for more than thirty years.

THE EXTRA

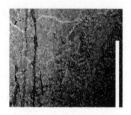

THE 'RISE

That's right, that was us. Amazing, how many people noticed, but then, for extras, we got a lotta screen time. Remember the big white guy with me after that running-down-the-fallen-skyscraper scene? He's my friend Japh. So. You wanted to know what drove me to make the leap into the movies. Well, it was this strange day the two of us had right before they started shooting *Alien Hunger*.

The first half of the day was like any other in the 'Rise. Japh and I had some courier work in the morning—which made us around 25 percent employed, about as good as it got for most guys our age. We'd arranged it so our last deliveries were both down on the thirty-sixth floor. Our 'Rise was fifty, and the new ones going up were taller, all towering along the north rim of the L.A. flatlands, known as the Zoo.

Like 'em all, our 'Rise was a cylinder, its axis a forty-floor Mall. There was a slideway, but it was always packed, and so were most of the walkways, so we used the walkway wrapped round the airshaft at the 'Rise's core. That's where all the Zoo wannabes hung out, so the rivers of shoppers, avoiding them, would make space there. With just a little dodging and shifting, we were able to jog at a good pace.

The wannabes rarely gave us trouble. Though we didn't dress Zoo, we couldn't entirely escape their culture. I had this neck scar—good blood drips doncha think?—and Japh had some ritual scars on his right cheek, from the I Ching, if you ever heard of that, the marks that mean "Tranquillity under Duress." But mainly, we didn't get much flack because being in good shape and knowing how to fight always shows. Japh's six-one with one of those little tough-mick faces. I'm smaller but these scars on my eyebrows and forehead show up pretty clear.

Anyway we split up on the thirty-sixth, our deliveries being on opposite sides of the floor. I dropped a cash deposit to a Merchant Bank branch and Japh some jewelry to an EarthWorks. We met up back on the fortieth. Japh had just thumbprinted the lock on our storage cell, and was rolling our book cart out when I got there.

Corporate retailers are the 'Rise's core. Pushcarters like us pay a big license fee, and then, have to find a space in the lobbies, solariums, or parks. The fat market of course is among the "upper" Middle Class down on the 'Rise's bottom third, but the best license we could afford was fortieth floor.

We took turns rolling our cart. We both liked doing it. Books from the past! I mean books more than like five years old. Real readers want the world, past, present, and future, and writers who really give it to them are always brand new, whatever century they wrote in. Meanwhile the Corps lists offer about the equivalent of vid programming.

Books, physically, are beautiful. There's lots of pod and vid books. But even the vids with all their holos will never shove real block-of-wood-pulp *books* off the shelves. Because it feels good to *hold* that paper, like a sandwich. One you can eat over and over, and nibble whenever and wherever you want. Japh and I rolled it with pride, that cart of ours, carrying the world to our friends and neighbors. Trouble was, we had less than forty books, because it was expensive to get out to the Zoo, where it was cheapest to restock. We still had some good stuff though, and a hope of profit.

The Commons, or greenbelt—each floor had four of them—was about a half acre of landscaped, bordered walkways with benches, and a bank of windows looking southeast out over the vast haze of the Zoo. Then, just as we were getting toward our corner, a booted leg kicked out of the plantings on my right, and slammed the cart so hard that half the top tray of books jumped out onto the flagstones.

Out they came, four wannabes—Middle Class goons dressed zoo. Lead rat was black—a human tattoo (full Maori swirls) on steroids. His three under-rats were white. It's me lead-rat confronts, to show he's the badder black. Everyone else vanished because looking like you're in trouble is a quick way to get solitude in the 'Rise. There were no Metro anywhere in sight. Japh and I didn't even have to trade a look to get ready.

"You black bitch," says big rat to me, "you work our turf here you pays us *rent*!"

"No prob, Bob!" I squeak. "We got clacks right here— easy! Easy! We chill!" Back-stepping scared, I made a production out of getting my right hand into my pocket, where I slipped it into my plastic knucks. Then I gripped my punching-slug, two pounds of lead molded to the *inside* of my fist. While I'm digging and back-stepping and he's stepping forward to keep me scared, Japh comes up and flanks the guy, hands-up, no trouble, but being big himself, he brings the guy's head around slightly, distracted, and I get my whole back into a straight punch to big rat's nose. His under-rats, close behind him, keep him propped up enough for me to get another one into his groin.

Japh picked up the nearest under-rat . . . guy had Day-Glo snakelocks and his head looked like a mop hanging sideways . . . and used him for a ram to jam the other two back into the bushes. The three of them were pretty strong guys, but we finally managed to hammer them into a squirmy little pile in the foliage and then jump up and down on them for a while, for maybe a little longer than we needed to. We heard a bone or two crack.

It leaves you shuddering and snorting, something like that, coming out of nowhere, but we had to pull ourselves and the cart together fast, because forget our spot here now. These guys would be full unemployeds still living off their families. They'd have parents with tech or service jobs who could and would hire lawyers to sue us for all we had, meaning our property, meaning my auntie's and Japh's parents' condos.

"Why? Oh man oh man *why*?" I kept saying as we trundled along. The day was shot—zip extra income to help out at home. Deeply bummed out, we lockered our cart, and decided to go down to the twenty-fifth to see Twig, the best Zoo merchandiser we knew.

It was more a gesture than anything—we couldn't buy much at Twig's prices. But just looking at new stock felt like a promise we would keep our cart rolling.

"Well," says Japh, "thank the lord at least that we're in the Middle Class, and not down in the Zoo." This was something my auntie Drew always said, not without irony, to keep herself going, keep putting in her ten hours a day at the keyboard. I smiled, but all the humor of this one had worn off a long time ago.

Twig's partner Zeena was Zoo. He'd had her non–Resident day-pass chip cut out (super expensive—'Rise techs really put it in deep) and for going in and out of the 'Rise she had an inhaler to pass the genetic Breathalyzer down at Entry. But did Zeena have great Zoo market connections! Thanks to her, Twig's crib was an Aladdin's Cave full of great wares: keys of the latest franken-weed fresh grown in Zoo nurseries, weapons, every kind of Zoo jewelry from nose-plugs to knucks, tat-kits, and mucho books, which Twig, that well-read bastard, knew how to value. His prices were far from wholesale.

Twig poured us some great dark-roast with cream, and gave us his little squirrelly laugh. "You look like you've been in it again." We'd both picked up some contusion and abrasion about the face. "I tell you that courier shit is too dangerous. You're mixing with the *public* every minute. Retail! Hang out your wares, let your buyers come to you."

"We were *hanging* out our wares," said Japh. "Got our cart jumped by Zoo-wannabes. You've got a whole crib here to sell from."

"You need a Zoo interface, dudes! You need to bond with a non-rez. Hook into the real economy. Link with some Zoo-meat, my bros!'

He liked to gloat about getting a smart babe like Zeena to shack trade with him. Twig was a tad fleshy, liked to share how smart he was with you. We were all old friends, but of course that meant he knew our buttons.

"Hey," I protested. "So you got Zeena! Had the clacks to cut her chip out! So you're slick. I sincerely congratulate you! Now you can get rich trading with your old friends here for plump prices!"

Got another rodent cackle from Twig with that one. "Speaking of which! Look what I got." He grabbed two, and put them in our hands. A Smith and a Barron. Good small-press hardback reprints. Japh and I checked them out all cool and skeptical—completely failing to hide our greed for them.

"We might be interested," Japh said at last, offhand. "If the price is right." Twig cackled again, and even I had to laugh. Japh and I are such failures at hiding our feelings about good books.

"Twig," I said. "We go back, man! I know you *love* to get top clack, even from friends. Especially from friends. We understand. You're slick, hats off to you, exsettera. But we just got nailed. We gotta work out a whole new spot for the cart and all. Cut us a break."

"Dudes. Look. This is bigger than just us! 'Rise and Zoo are *one economy*. And you gotta pay fair freight for what it takes to sneak Zoo goods up into the 'Rise."

"Don't run all this *again* on us, dog!"

"Truth! Millions out there"—and he waved at his nice run of windows overlooking the Flats, where the noon light was latening, growing more golden—"an' whadda they have for income? The Ag-workers come in from the Zone, buy Zoo rides, produce, recycle. A cupful of Social Services money trickles down in. Maybe half Metro and Maintenance paychecks get spent in the Zoo—and all that together is *half* a survival economy, dudes! They sell everything else they have in here. Basin-grown produce and meat, and the produce they process from the mountain towns comes into the 'Rises above board, but *most* of it has to be muled on the sly. Pirate-ware, books, music, exotics, weapons are all black-marketed here and all *together* it barely gives 'em a survival econ. You've gotta be cosmopolitan! I'm committed to my Zoo suppliers and to their rates of exchange! Even at these rates"—he gestured at his high-stacked wares—"the Zoo-meat just gets by."

"*Duhh!*" Japh said. "And my hat's off to 'em! We respect the Zoo. *You're* the one calls them Zoo-meat."

"Yeah," I chimed. "Sorry Twig, but that Zoo-meat shit's a little lame. It's like some white guys call me nigger as a sign of solidarity. They don't have the ear for it."

"Dudes. *Zeena* says Zoo-meat all the time! What can I do?"

"But Zeena *is* Zoo-meat."

A pause, and then we all laughed.

"Well," I said, "you're lucky to have her." And I meant it. We didn't need Twig's econ rundown. Zeena had plenty of company in here. Every 'Rise already had a good 15 percent non-rez pop smuggled into their genetic databases. These insiders smuggle in 70 percent of the Zoo merch sold in here. Even the Zoo-meat with real chips and Vendors' day passes take out three times the value of their declared goods every day in smuggled franken-herbs and bootleg tunes, vids, and games. The Zoo keeps the 'Rise alive culturally, and the 'Rise puts clacks in the Zoo's pockets.

We sipped coffee, smiley Twig waiting for us to ask him his price for the books we were still fondling. Japh said, "Why live in the 'Rise or the Zoo? There's a *world*, right? What about the Sierra foothills? What about the Trinities. The Sunrise Federation?"

He surprised me with that. It had been a long time since we'd talked about that dream. I realized we were getting worn down, worn into our crowded rut here. Time was slipping out of our hands. Neither one of us would ever see twenty-two again.

Well, we asked his price, and it was worse than we feared. We haggled and wheedled, and budged him . . . two clacks. If we bought even one of the books, it would cut our cash in half, and it would take even longer before we could hit the Zoo and restock more profitably. We sighed, and left.

"Fuck it," Japh said. "Let's buy a decade of vid and pork out."

"Why not?"

That's how down the 'Rise could get you. You'd just go cram some cheeseburgers, lay your clacks at the box office, and slam vids for eight hours, letting all the uproar and color pour through, washing over you, so you could stagger back to your crib and sleep like the dead.

"OK. So. At least let's clock some aerobes going back up."

So we ran the fifteen levels back up, doing some on the outer walkways, between the malls and the 'Rise's condo rim—pedestrians thick here but moving in currents you could thread. Then doing the rest on the airshaft walkway, enjoying the faster pace and not caring about the wannabes, feeling our worst encounter with the no-lifes was already behind us. Besides, Metro had just passed, a trio on their scooters, with Protoflex body armor, gaudy firearms, and high-volt prods that made perps soil themselves. Their patrols usually quieted things down for a while.

As we ran up into forty-three there was a more crowded stretch of walkway where a big department store was disgorging consumers. We saw a tattooed hand reach up from one of the ratpacks around the air-shaft. The hand sprouted a blue flame and melted a long slice down through the thick plastic netting that screened the gulf of the shaft. Some rockhead using his base-torch for random environmental modification.

You heard of this lately, goons feeding large debris down into the shaft and watching it dance on the air currents. The torch left two parted lips of melted plastic. Between them you could see the dark abyss, five hundred feet deep.

I can see so clearly now, how our whole future came flooding in on us through that sudden hole in the fence.

This little vandal's band of no-brainers wore the rag look, not actual Zoo at all, just made-up vid-Zoo they swallowed whole when they were cracked-out in some vid cave. They looked like they were covered with leaves of all different colors, had waxed baldies and spiked earrings. The guy with the torch was smaller than the others, a junior goon striving for status. He cut his slash in the fence, and then turned around and scoped for something to throw, something un-usual, to make a splash. His eyeballs were red. His face was grinned up so tight it kept clenching into a snarl.

"Man, check his veins," Japh says. We were slowing down before getting too close. "That guy's almost wired to death." Too true. His every vein was stark. It seemed to dawn on all three of us in the same instant, what he was going to do. And in the very next instant, he did it.

He pounced on the passing stream of shoppers, and snatched a small old man out of it. We had just a glimpse of him, slight and lean, his wispy weight too light to re-sist that quick strength. The ragged madman hauled him, hitched him up, and launched him—in one surging move—out through the scar in the shaft's netting.

We saw the old man sprawled midair for just an instant in the black gulf before it swallowed him. His neck was corded, his gaping mouth and his eyes were three smaller black gulfs . . .

You had to call it inspired: one single, insane dance move, mindlessly explosive, inhumanly accurate. A ten-second mur-der. There were hundreds of people within a twenty-yard radius, but the madman was whole heartbeats ahead of them all. His astonished packmates had barely begun to scatter as he plunged straight into the traffic stream. He was angling right toward us, and in seconds would be buried in people who had witnessed nothing. Japh and I traded a look.

It came to us in that instant. We just didn't yet know what it really meant. As he came, his nearness pulled the pair of us like triggers. We seized either side of him, and Japh, inspired, shouted, "No! No! Don't jump!"

"Life is still worth living!" I bellowed, catching on. We had his feet off the ground, and were rushing him back toward the shaft, though his struggles away from the shaft must have made the little fiction pretty obvious.

"Don't jump! Don't do it!"

"Life is still worth living!"

We surged up to the opening in the netting, and launched him through it. "NOOOOOO!" all three of us bellowed, but he bellowed longest. The vent drafts bumped him left and right as he dove. All his bright rags fluttering, he looked like he was on fire—a little rag fire, getting smaller fast in four hundred feet of empty air. . . .

"Metro! Metro!" we shouted, and, still yelling, pushed our way back into the stream. Once we were a few meters deep in the mass, we were as good as miles from the scene. Branching outward through the Mall's maze, we made our way to the 'Rise's rim without saying a word to each other.

Leaned at last against a window, and looked out.

Stunned. We looked and saw ourselves in each other's eyes: two guys with real blood on their hands. Not in self-defense! Manslaughter! God, to be out of this place! But out where? Cross the Zoo to the Ag-worker Zone? Live in a shack and pick crop in the Imperial Valley? There were other, realer places to live, but they all took clacks, and we had none. For us, those other lives might as well have been on the moon.

Japh said, "Thank the lord at least that we're in the Middle Class, and not out there."

We didn't even try to smile. "Let's get a drink," I said. Neither one of us drank. "Yeah," Japh said. "And then let's get the fuck outta here."

"Yeah. Let's go for a *ride*."

"We got the clacks?"

"Fuck it. Whatever we've got, we go."

The beer joint we found was near a cineplex, and when we sat out in its tiny courtyard, the 'plex's marquee sprayed out a swarm of holo-previews all around us, a kind of free cinematic scenery that came with your drink, poster-size shorts of new vids hanging in the air, tearing through their routines. Just behind Japh's head was a miniature car chase down a Zoo street, the chasing car getting its windshield melted by the flamethrower mounted on the pursuer's hood: *Rock Warriors*. I turned to see, and over my own right, two buffed young dudes were getting it on, oblivious to tentacles of smoking red jelly dangling toward them: *Unicellular*.

We looked at each other, no words needed to know we were both struggling for a grip on the fact that we had just killed someone. Japh gestured at the holos all around us. "We were gonna go drown our sorrows in some vids, remember? But damn, Curtis! We're *in* a vid, every minute of our pathetic lives! That nasty little rag-rat, *all* those no-lifes—what else are they doing but living a vid?"

I sat there nodding, letting him rant for the both of us. "So what vid are we in, Japh, you and me?"

"We're in *theirs*." He swept his hand, meaning our 'Rise and every other one, and the Zoo beyond them. "We're in the Mass Vid. Everyone's living it. The no-lifes just don't try to do anything *else*. That rag-man was playing *Max Bad* or some equally brain-dead shit. We walk into his scene and we're *cast*. We're the two good guys who"—a whisper here—"kill him for it. I mean, did you feel yourself weighing it before doing it? We were in *role*! We did what we were *written* to do."

"Yeah . . . Yeah, that's exactly it. Like I was just an actor. None of us was real in it."

"None of us but the old man, snatched right out of *his* script to die."

"I can't drink this slop. Let's go Outside, Japh. We need to go Outside."

We found we could buy just a couple hours of fuel and maybe a couple books. 'Nuff said. Just knowing we could manage even this tiny escape made us feel like we were dying for it.

THE ZOO

Schools were just out, kids flooding into the malls, making movement slow down to parking. Once there, another hour to fuel up and log out. Coming back in, the lines would be much slower, everyone getting scanned for drugs or weapons from the Zoo. We'd be longer in the return line than our escape outside might last, but didn't care.

Our ride was the bare minimal essence of vehicle, a tripod: three heavy treads, two big bucket seats, a windscreen, and a thumpin' four-stroke. Strapped in it at last, we roared it out onto the freeway, ramping up to eighty in sixty yards.

Space! Wind and sky! The sky was rich in UV and

monoxides, sure, but with the slanting sun an hour from setting, it was all reddish gold and glorious. An onshore wind rolled in at our backs from Santa Monica, and the freeway was pumping. The freeway system is truly the one great thing that Government did for us. Eight lanes all the way everywhere, with a Municipal Fleet of super-hueys with electro-mag danglers to pluck breakdowns and smashups right off the road quick-time. Everywhere the freeways ran, they stood knee-deep in the Zoo, and it was the wild, rockety rides of the Zoo that made up more than half the freeways' flow, caused most of the accidents, and left most of the wreckage. Even so, the Zoo rides were glorious, covered with wild art and *Road Warrior* body-work. On the freeways, you felt like you were really in space, flying among an alien fleet.

"There's a *world*, Curtis!" Japh howled. "A real world! Outside of walls!"

"Yo bro!"

To our left, 'Rise after 'Rise on the high ground at the feet of the Santa Monica Mountains and the Hollywood Hills. To the right, under the amber sky, the sparse neons and streetlights of the Zoo began to come on, making the whole plain gigantically glorious. As Twig had said, there was money and a livelihood to be had out there, but emigrants from the Middle Class survived the move to this place poorly. For born-Zoo, there *was* work if you were strong and patient. Recycle, photovoltaic harvesting, farms and orchards—a hundred and fifty square miles of cultivation puzzleworked in these Flats.

But that was it, short of armed robbery and weapons or

drug trafficking. It took work to secure those positions, and they paid a mean hard wage. 'Rise "drop-ins" worked starvation wage and, when young, got kidnapped by gangs for ransoming back to the 'Rise. . . .

But it felt big and wonderful to be speeding along out here. With all this possibility whirling around us right now, I felt like I was going to be spun up into the sky.

"Let's go for the La Brea off-ramp," said Japh. "Find that cute what's-her-name." Teasing me.

"Jool," I said, making him smile I had her name so ready. "She's got the best books of anywhere we've gone."

"Oh peace and love my bro, don't get defensive! And she's got those cute little *planes* in her Apache face!"

I'd let that slip a while back, about her ax-blade cheeks.

"Fuckya Japh, she's just got the best books."

"Yeah, yeah. Unbuckle, we're going down."

Diving down an off-ramp was always ticklish. Occasionally they were barricaded and bandidos would swarm out and steal your ride, and everything else you had worth taking. Nothing today, though, just a couple stalls down along the ramp's shoulder—and Jool's stand there among them, a pipe framework supporting open suitcases of books.

She didn't answer my wave—wearing her stoic show-me Zoo stare. Japh swung down to the street and into a vacant lot.

La Brea was pure Late Twentieth funk. Huge billboards with hand-lettered ads drowning in grafitti scabbed with ragged posters. And car lots! Half a mile of them on both sides of the street, all full of battered old boats parked on weed-cracked asphalt. Plenty of people in snakelocks or thornballs or umbrella-dos cruising these rides, a third of which would be electro-magged off the freeways within a month of sale. The customers looked like they might be offering crack, crystal, puff, or anything else in trade for the rides they liked, and the sales guys looked like they might take it. Meanwhile the street was full of roaring traffic, and the sidewalks were swarming with thugs, chimps, and turf-rats, all the real variety, many of them seriously armed, and workin' the whole sidewalk wherever there was a lamppost or powerpole for an axis they could cluster around. People just trying to get from point A to B had to flow into the street to get past them. In just the few seconds I'm scoping it all, I see a beat-up van slowing for a turn past a liquor store parking lot full of hardcases. A bottle comes tumbling through the air from the thugs and makes a bright little spray of glass on the side of the van. The van squeals to a stop, an arm comes out the driver's window, and fires four shots into the thugs. Thug pandemonium. Several crumple, and as the van pulls away, others start firing back. . . .

We got the tripod behind enough weeds not to strike the eye. Japh took out the shortsword we had stored in the undercarriage.

"Try not to spend too much time making goo-goo eyes at her, or someone might steal me before you get back."

I trotted back to the ramp. Goo-goo eyes not likely. Jool was frosty. She'd never even used our names, though I'd reminded her of mine a couple times. There she was, Apache with Mexican blood, small, dark, and tight, her hair in a prickly shag that made you think of a tough little porcupine.

"Hey, Jool. Remember me, Curtis?" I just couldn't let up—I had to make her call me Curtis.

"Yeah. You take forever to choose and you *dicker*. Scope the rack and state your case, I'm runnin' a business here."

"Dicker? The ramp's empty—you have no other customers! You get a customer you should let him hang around so he draws *other* customers."

"Look. Gimme a break. I've got my own *thoughts* to think. And 'scuse me but a 'Rise-ass shouldn't be hanging around where he can get his ass kicked. Didn't your momma tell you it's dangerous?"

"Damn right it's dangerous, and I'm into readin', not bleedin'."

Now she almost did smile—probably had expected me to come back with some swagger. "Well, your buddy's down there guarding your 'pod, so why don't you just shit or get off the pot for his sake?"

I had to laugh, but she was right. "OK. Got any Mitchell Smith?"

"Yeah. At least you got taste. I got *Reprisal*."

"You're shitting me."

She actually laughed at my sincerity. "You're a real smart one, aren'tcha? Trying to get me to lower the price?"

"JOOL! You sorry hole! You ducked on me for the last time, bitch-monkey!" This roar from down on the street. Out from under the overpass beside the ramp, a guy in a kilt and combat boots came stumping. He was big and wide, and apart from the kilt and boots, not wearing anything except a couple of spiked nipple rings and a sword on his hip. Heading for us in a fine rage, his scowl showing us that his teeth were dyed black, and his right hand drawing, not the sword, but a big nickel-plated pistol from behind his back.

My hand went into my pocket . . . and came out with my fist-slug. Useless. I'd never get to him in time to throw a punch. So I threw it at him, putting my whole back in it. Amazingly, *whack*—the slug hit him right in the jaw with a nasty bone-crunch sound, and pitched him back off his feet.

The guy must've had major control. He rolls back with his fall, somersaults, and comes right back up onto his feet, bringing the gun up. I sprint for him, knowing I don't have a prayer to tackle him before he fires. The girl behind me screams "Get down!" Right, I think, sprinting like mad—but then I trip, diving for the asphalt, and as I dive I hear a *smack*, deafening, and feel heavy air suck past my shoulder. I smash up my elbows saving my face, and when I can get my head up again, there's the Kilt on his back, and one of his shoulders is a mess of red meat, spouting blood, and white bone splinters.

"You asshole!" It's Jool. "You fire up your ride and you get me outta here *now*!" She's screaming and raving at me, her would-be savior. "If you'd got outta the way, 'Rise-ass, I wouldn't've missed! Get his piece! Move!" As she rants, she's unhooking the bookcases from the pipe, and slamming them shut. I run for the Kilt, thinking, *Missed?* Guy's groaning, but his eyes are clear and raging at me as I snatch his automatic from the pavement and shove it in my belt. And here's Jool, already hustling past me, her book-shelves latched together like two big suitcases that had to weigh half what she did.

"Gimme one!" I say, catching up.

"Fuck you! Watch our back and call your 'pod!"

And as we came down to the street—what else?—some ugly shapes in kilts rushed out of the shadow of the over-pass.

"Japh! Japh!" I screeched. "Fire it up!" I aimed the Kilt's piece back at his brothers, who were coming fast. What did I know about guns? You squeeze the trigger, right? I'm the guy in the vid making his getaway, so I follow the script, stick out my arm and *crack!*—I almost broke my wrist. Missed, but made them fall back and cover.

Japh came gunning right up the sidewalk, braking to squeal around in a one-eighty.

Jool jumped in the seat, boxes on her lap. "Make that on-ramp!" she shouted. No room for me, except on my knees right in front of her, my back crushed against the wind-screen. Japh launched the tripod off the curb and straight across the street into four lanes of oncoming Certain Death. Jool stuck an arm out past the screen and blew both my ears to shit. Brakes screamed, I heard a crash, our tires zigzagged across broken pavement, and then I felt smooth road as we climbed the on-ramp. I lifted my head to see behind Jool when half of our windscreen blew to spray. "Shoot 'em, ass-hole!" she shrieked. "What're you waiting for?!"

Past her shoulder was a pickup big as the sky right on our tail. I squeezed three rounds into its windshield, watching the glass cave in and the pickup veer into the guardrail. Japh hit fourth and wedged us at full howl into the freeway flow.

"God damn!" Japh shouted. "God *damn!*"

"Take the next off-ramp and break left at the foot of it!" And she added, an afterthought, "You fucking 'Rise-ass *ass-holes!*"

The sun was down. The eastern half of the sky was deep purple, and a last band of amber lay on the west. We were in a river of headlights, and the Zoo was a great plane of shadow on either side, with a thin sprinkling of neons and streetlights as far as you could see. It looked like the coals of a world fire that was almost burned out. Fifty years ago—the vids still love to remember it—those lights were like a pavement, thick as the stars in a galaxy. Now, all those people were out there, hunting and hustling and hiding to eke out a harder and harder living in the growing dark.

We exited down to a street a lot emptier than La Brea had been. Japh cut the engine to idle at the foot of the ramp.

"Left, I told you! What're you stoppin' for?"

"Just wait a minute," Japh told her. We looked around us. This street was definitely a different region of Zoo. No streetlights, and the nearest neon looked half a mile away. A little nearer, a big blue holo-board floated sixty feet in the air. It was the brightest thing around.

On both sides of the street there were old storefronts, their front windows boarded up, but some giving off glints of light from their back windows. Groups of people hung out in front here and there, with little drifts of tune-boxes turned low coming from them. These people didn't have the postures of thugs. Some were sitting on crates, and they seemed to be talking, I mean having actual conversations. Mainly watching, though, especially the cars that trickled past. You could see rifle barrels laid across their laps. In the growing dark you could just make out the next intersection: two other groups were stationed on the opposite corners. Quiet groups. Armed and watchful.

"You are taking me *home*, fools," said Jool. "I got no more time to waste with you, you have messed up my life big-time, and I have got to get busy fixin' things."

"Look," said Japh. "We got a fuel problem. If we take you much farther than this, we won't be able to get back home."

"Oh Christ. All right. Let's do some biz, an' maybe I can fill your tank. But get us off the fuckin' road—turn left on that street down there."

Japh and I traded a look. She was plenty pissed at us. She could gang shag us for our ride and be a lot richer. But I gave Japh a shrug. I just had to gamble that anyone who knew books couldn't be all bad.

One of three guys with shotguns stepped off the curb as we pulled up to the corner. "I'm OK, Wrench," said Jool. "These 'Rise-asses are my ride. They'll be comin' back out this way in a few ticks."

"You been chewin' on their windscreen, Jool?"

"Nah. We were the victims of road rage."

"OK. Say hi to your momma."

A short way down this narrower block, she had us turn onto a vacant lot and cut the engine. "OK, 'Rise-guys, here's the deal. I got fuel at my crib, but it ain't cheap. How many clacks you got?"

"Nineteen between us."

"Are you shittin' me? How were you gonna buy even one book from me?"

"Hey, we're not rich. I live in my auntie's crib, Japh in his parents'. We're lucky to get four months work a year. You can read, right? What do you think, the 'Rises are castles in the air? It took all we had to get this quarter tank we're almost out of. And what's this about us messing you up? What I remember, I was tryin' to save your life!"

"You were tryin' to save *your* life, an you over*reacted*! Fool was gonna wave his piece and strut an roar an' I was gonna chill him with some clacks! That's how protection's *done* down here in the real world, where you chumps have no business cruisin' around for the show. We're no vid, asshole!"

"Hey! I see a gun pointed at me, and adrenaline takes over! How did I know—"

"That's what I'm sayin'! Where you don't *know*, you shouldn't *go*!"

"Then you'd never know anything new! Fuck you! This is our world too. All of it. Is that your rule, just crouch down in the box you were put in?"

I could see that what I'd just said had moved her somehow, made something happen in her tight little face. Her eyes shifted toward something above and behind me. " 'Scuse me," I said. "I gotta stretch my legs."

I got out and stood in the weeds . . . and saw that Japh too, was looking up where Jool was looking. I turned. For a long minute, all three of us stared at it.

It was the holo-board, graffiti-proof advertising, hanging up there where it could be seen for miles from all directions. Simple and to the point, white block lettering on a blue rectangle maybe a hundred feet wide.

> **EXTRAS**
> *ALIEN HUNGER*
> **Tube Nine Six A.M. Panoply Studios**

And the bottom line was tomorrow's date.

Sometimes words—the simplest words, said at the right time—can change things forever. *Just crouch down in the box you were put in?* My own words, but I didn't really hear them till I saw the way Japh and Jool were looking at that ad. Because as I'd spoken them, they had heard them more clearly than I had. . . .

I regretted my words then. This Zoo-girl, given the big brutal box *she* was born in . . . well, the gamble advertised on that holo-board was something she had to consider a lot more seriously than I ever would. The thought shamed me.

. . . And then it registered how seriously *Japh* was staring at that holo.

I wasn't ready for this kind of thinking. "Look," I said. "I've got this gun. It's got to be worth a full tank."

She looked at me a minute, as if she'd forgotten the issue between us, and her mind was coming back from somewhere pretty far away. "*You* got the gun. All you woulda got was the short end of it, if I hadn't put him down." But she didn't give this much heat, said it almost absentmindedly. "I already got a piece," she added softly—and though it had saved us twice, I saw it now for the first time. She took it from her waist and looked at it like it was something new to her, holding it up and turning it this way and that in the dimness. It was a little handgrip with four inches of shotgun barrel. It didn't look like metal, more like dull black plastic. Jool twisted the grip, and it came free. Tilted it, and a shotgun shell slid out—the whole shell, even the casing, also plastic-looking.

"You see this?" she asked. It was almost a sweet voice she had when she wasn't using it to back you off, a velvety voice with a little grit to it, like superfine sandpaper. "And these, kind I use on the street?" She dug a couple other shells from her pocket. Brass casings on these. "I can get five pounds of *these* for your nineteen clacks. But *this* kind, with the hard carbon casing? I could trade that pistol for two, maybe three of these. Then I'd have two in the grip, one in the chamber, when I walk through the studio gate. Barrel up my ass, an' the grip . . ."

A hard-carbon weapon and ammo would be *concealable*—maybe—from the studio's detectors, if she went in to hire on as an extra. It stunned me a little, both that she'd reached this decision, and that she was telling us about it. Obviously she was her own woman and took her own risks. Telling us seemed more like telling herself what she'd decided to do. Maybe she needed to make us her witnesses—just to have that little moment of company before jumping off the edge.

She reassembled her little piece, put a "street" shell in the chamber—her moves getting brisker, her face getting harder as she snapped and clicked her kit back together.

"OK," she said. "Short and simple. You *did* mess me up. I had just one pack, the numb-nut Highlanders, leeching me, and they were bad enough to keep any others off me, and dumb enough for me to duck 'em and string 'em and keep 'em at bay at about half the going rate for protection. I was getting by, had control, and all the rest of that happy horse-shit we make do on down here in monkeyland. So *you* owe *me*, end of story. You butted in and you bitched me up.

"On the other hand, what you fucked up *was* fucked up. I'm writing you off as a wake-up call. You jammed me in a corner and forced me to grow some guts. You 'Rise-asses aren't the only ones can read. I know there's a real world out there, and *I* am gonna step out and *find* it. So. Take me home, give me all your clacks and that pistol, and I'll fill your tank. End of story."

". . . OK."

"Deal."

She looked from one to the other of us, nodding, scowling—till all at once, her scowl broke up, and she burst out laughing.

What a sound that was, what a wild song, that laughter! It was like gold coins flung up in the air, clattering down around us. We had to laugh too, but even while I was laughing I felt . . . envy. Sadness and envy. Because *her* laughter was wilder than ours, was totally free, that was it. Her laughter was freedom, the way you laugh when you've said good-bye in your heart to everything you treasure. Said good-bye, and jumped.

"And I gotta . . . I gotta say, guys . . ."—but Jool still had some more in there that had to be laughed out. At last she wiped her eyes and grinned. "What's your names? You're Curtis, what's yours again?"

"Japh."

"I gotta say Japh, Curtis . . ."—a few more giggles still in there—". . . I gotta say, you boys have some fair moves for 'Rise-asses. No time to think, and you do OK. And you're pretty cute, Curtis. Tell you what. You get back in here, lay your head back in my lap, you can whip some face on me on the way back to my place."

That set us all off again, but man, even while I was laughing, that sadness and envy was still there, right in the middle of my heart. I was in love with her. Completely in love with her.

"That's pretty bad odds in there," I blurted out, nodding up at the holo.

"Well, I'll tell you what Curtis," she said. "Thing you learn, living around here, is you never know what's gonna happen. I mean, rule of thumb, words to live by." She was almost solemn, looking around at the blocks huddled under their darkening trees. "Because if you don't keep that in mind," she seemed to come back to herself, smiled at us both, "what're you gonna *do*?"

She told us to keep the 'pod in second. "We're neighbors here," she said, "and we keep the noise down for each other." This, a unified neighborhood, was a side of the Zoo I never knew about. It was a residential neighborhood with all the vegetation run wild, houses totally swallowed in plantings and trees. Not so much run wild, you understand, as trained up into an outer shell for the houses. Streetlights around here were dead, but every block had at least four makeshift poles with antique kerosene lanterns mounted on them encased in bulletproof plexi, and two or three guys with rifles sitting around them on crates or chairs. They made a faint, old-timey kind of light, golden and fluttery, just enough to show you that the tree-sunk lots were sectioned into little compounds of three or four houses each with big chain-link fences crowned by razor wire.

"You like our coops?" Jool asked. "It's efficient. Each one maintains a generator, shares the power. Fuel, guard duty, plumbing repair—all a team effort. The scum factor can creep in, though. People go out, get dirty, get debts and trashy friends, and bring them home to their coop. Three or four houses to a coop works best, keeps infections small. . . ."

I could see she was growing more remote again. We were now in the middle of everything and everyone she was saying good-bye to. She had us stop midway down a particularly tree-thick block. "Here. Wait at the gate." We killed the motor. Jool opened a heavy padlock, locked it behind her, and disappeared through the foliage inside. I didn't talk to Japh. I was already afraid of what I thought *he* might have decided.

Jool came back out with a fuel can. Took our clacks and the automatic, and started filling our tank. Avoiding our eyes, and avoiding talk too—holding on to her hard decision, preparing herself already. All I had to do was lean forward. I didn't let myself think about it. I kissed her cheek.

She looked at me with complete surprise. It was already

tomorrow morning for her—she was on Tube Nine, heading out to Panoply Studios, steeling herself for it—and suddenly she's kissed. "Good luck," I said.

She blinked, and gave me a little smile. Capped our tank, and turned away without a word. Slipped back through the gate. A whisper of leaves swallowed her, and she was gone.

Full dark now, in the river of headlights. This night was wild and sweet! We hit the freeway, and westwards we went, the black night above us tearing our hair back. I was getting a lot of wind on my side where the windscreen wasn't. "Smell the ocean?" Japh shouted.

"Yeah!" I shouted back.

At the coast we pulled off to the Palisades, and parked on the clifftop. Watched the view a while, not talking. There was a piece of moon up there that put a pale varnish on the sea and made it look cold as ice and wide as the sky. Down under the corpse-piers little campfires winked out from between the pilings, and glinted from the midst of dark knots of people all along the beach, miles and miles of nomads camping on the sand. There was even someone swimming, or drowning, a pale foamy commotion out past the break, someone desperate enough for escape to swim in those toxins. Or maybe just jubilating in the water's cool grip. People come to the sea to remember the earth, see proof of the size of it. As I looked at it I really believed there was a whole continent at my back . . . and it made me ashamed. I should be straining every nerve to enter that continent, to take my auntie into some freedom, some beauty. . . .

Japh's silence was getting louder by the minute. I already

knew he'd decided what Jool had. I'd never felt so alone in my life.

"Hey. Curtis."

"I know, man. I *know*. But I just can't do it. Your mom and dad have each other. I'm all my auntie's got."

"You think I don't *know* that, Curtis? Hey. The way I see it, I'm getting up early tomorrow morning, and I'm comin' back rich enough for all five of us."

"I don't even wanna think about you doing it. I don't wanna talk about it."

He gripped my shoulder. " 'Nuff said, my brother. 'Nuff said. Just be ready to be rich by this time tomorrow."

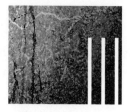

THE SET

Sunset laid its glory on the set below them—the grandest set Panoply Studios had built to date. The burnished office buildings flashed copper and gold above the wide crazy puzzle of rooftops, streets, and the green clouds of tree-filled parks—all of it gorgeously half-lit in gold, half-etched in jet-black shadow. Their hover-raft hung about ten stories above its highest buildings, and from here every mega-clack spent on this set was visible: a Late Twentieth city in flawless detail, right down to the graffitied phone booths, the dogshit on the sidewalks, the animatronic drunks sleeping in alleys under blankets of newspapers—right down to the zits on the drunks' cheeks and the headlines on those newspapers.

Kate could not help feeling a thrill of ownership. Well, *membership* at least. She knew she hadn't risen above the pack yet, knew that assistant directors were legion. But she had at last arrived in the ranks of those who actually worked on the shoot. More than that, she was gazing on the set from the raft of Val Margolian, King of Panoply, and the greatest living vid director.

There he sat in the pilot's chair, checking the feeds from the on-set cameras. Tanned, handsome, lean, a vigorous sixty, he looked from time to time at the set itself, as she was doing, seeming to savor it, as she did. His fine, strong jaw in profile had a little flaw, a dent in the bone on its left side, maybe an old fracture. She knew in his youth he'd taught in the Zoo, had stepped out of his Middle-Class safety to help the poor. His first films—his social realism phase— were all set down there in the Flats. She felt the old wound, that crack in the line of his strongly chiseled profile, per- fected Val Margolian's beauty. It was a mark of struggle, and thus a mark of honor.

Her peers saw her friendship with Val as Success itself, but Kate's pride insisted on more: that her rise in the stu- dios be her own, be earned by her proven talent. Still, it was hard to repress the euphoria of riding in the raft of the man who could put her in a director's chair with a single word.

"It's beyond praise, Val," she said, gesturing at the prospect. "It's the grandest, most realized work of art I've ever seen." Kate could say this as she felt it, easy and warm. Ass-kissing was not a factor between them.

Val smiled gratefully. Kate's praise was a gift he knew he could savor, not just another blowjob from young ambition.

"Thank you, dear. It's . . . true, isn't it? It is grand. It's absolutely complete."

"And made for destruction. I think somehow that's the finest thing of—"

"Made for *immortality*!" This interruption came from Rod, who lay in the lounge at the stern. A buffed young man, his dad a big stockholder in Panoply. "Its destruction will live forever in the minds of our viewers."

Kate bedded Rod, he was good in the sack. He had an enthusiastic nature, but he wasn't the sharpest knife in the drawer, and his personality needed work. *"Forever?"* She smiled. She didn't usually taunt Rod when he was schmoozing. He'd irritated her.

"Hey." Rod raised a solemn, prophetic finger. *"All* Val's work is supreme, but this one is epochal. I hope I'm not being arrogant here, Val, since I pitched the concept. Because what's an idea? You're the one who made it reality, Val, and that's what's going to live forever, the reality you've made of it right here, the greatest live-action vid of the century."

Kate was amused by a certain tension in Rod's profile. She could see he was a little afraid that she might speak up here. The "concept"—i.e., the monster in *Alien Hunger*—had in fact been Kate's. Rod, one night, sitting in a recliner with a legal pad and an expensive pen, scowling with thought, had asked her: "Kate, what's the most horrible way you can think of to be killed?" She'd given it a moment's thought, and told him.

Rod hadn't copied it down right away. He'd sat there brooding and pondering for another hour, as if his creativity were transforming her banal notion into something more, something with depth and meaning. *Then* he'd copied it down. Pitched it at Panoply the next morning.

Rod needn't worry. Kate felt certain that Val, not just indifferent to the death machines in his live-action vids, was actually more repelled by them than anything. She was sure that the APPs in his vids, the Anti-Personnel Properties, were if anything distasteful to a man whose mastery of his art was so complete. Kate herself was well-read and gifted enough to see, on every shoot, his angel's eye for weaving gigabytes of detail into an irresistible reality.

As if in confirmation of her thought, Val reached out to the controls and wafted their raft twenty stories higher. He punched his com button. "Willy? Let's see the first wave over Sectors A and B. Deflect the collisions by a nice wide margin, please."

An answering chuckle. "You don't wanna see a smashup or two, boss?"

Smiling tiredly, Val said, "No thanks, Willy—let's save those for immortalizing tomorrow."

That tipped Rod to the Big Guy's mood. He stood up and got absorbed in the air show, the robot alien craft arrowing down across the city below them. They were gorgeous in the gold light. And then here came the intercepting wave of our guys—bright knives parrying the lethal onslaught from a distant star. Some breathtaking close passes between craft scheduled for collision during the shoot, while they all traded harmless red bolts of laser light to test the programs that would join them with bolts of live cannon fire tomorrow. With her excellent visual memory, Kate could isolate from the swift melee just which craft would erupt in a spew of deadly, building-smashing debris on the city below. It was harder to calk out casualties from impacts and explosions than the probable kills of the aliens themselves on the sidewalks and in the buildings. . . . Panoply had budgeted for a huge draft of extras—just about everyone who showed up would be taken on. Bread for the masses.

So many of these would die tomorrow—here, of course, was the hard thing about this work. Val had been the pioneer of "live action," the euphemism his own. But hadn't the global economy thrust it on him? Would he ever have brought it to birth, if the swarms of extras who answered the first call hadn't made it plain? That if this genre would feed a need in its audience, it would feed an equally urgent one in its actors?

At the outset, there had been stormy weather from the bleeding hearts within the industry, but Val already had the whip hand at Panoply, and once it was known he was going through with it, all the other majors kept their people in line until *Last Gasp* hit the screens, and they could see how it grossed. They were poised either to send their politicians in baying like wolves for Panoply's blood, or to jump on the bandwagon. The Zoo was gung-ho from the first. Already hardened to a dangerous environment, they went for the lottery aspect of the arrangement. The macho glory angle too, like going to war, except that from this kind of war you could come back rich.

Last Gasp grossed off the charts. Val, by grit and gall and a young genius's drive to make his visions real, had created a whole new entertainment genre. He had grasped the need of the billions, seen that all the tube-suckers were galled by the guilt of synthetic lives. Live action put substance back into vid-sucking, because the people you were *watching* were having life as real as it got, dancing on the border between life and death. . . .

In the decades since *Last Gasp*, Val and all his imitators had . . . *made possible* hundreds of thousands of deaths. How that must weigh on a brilliant, humane man like Val, though he would never express these thoughts, not by the slightest flicker of his tanned, handsomely lined face.

Kate gazed out over the vast basin to the south: Zoo without end! Six tenths of the world's population in perilous poverty. She'd been born to Uptown here—Pasadena, Burbank, Hollywood, and all along the hills west to the sea. There ought to have been a wall like the set wall, but running all along the skirts of the hills to the Pacific. There *was* a wall of course, not visible from up here. Uptown's wall was Metro, practically a cop per block throughout this lofty zone. Half their cruisers were Mercedes, so as not to damage Uptowners' self-esteem.

It *did* hurt to know you were eating the poor. But throughout history, the elites had taken the world as it was left to them. She at least was part of an industry that created a fiscally viable way to put hundreds of millions into the Zoo economy.

Rod, still restive at Val's quiet irony about immortalizing, was looking around for some thought to repair his standing. He took a cue from where Kate was looking.

Waved at the Zoo. "Well, we're giving them a day off to-morrow, Val. All that talk about social programs for the lowlifes, *we're* the ones, *you're* the one who cuts their crime rate in half for weeks after every extra call. They oughtta do a study about *that* when they whine about live action."

Val went absolutely still. So did Kate. Dear god, the arrogant carelessness! Rod had gone beyond digging just his own grave. He had seriously insulted one of the most powerful men in the vid industry. Called him an executioner of the poor. When you put hurt on a man that size, put him in a mood to lash out, every lesser being in his immediate neighborhood was likely to go flying. Kate's heart was hammering. Even Rod was alerted by Val's stillness.

"Actually, Rod," Val said pleasantly, "I think your study would disappoint you. The lowlifes who live by crime tend to be more secure. It's likely to be their *victims*, desperate for escape from them, who'll crowd the tubes tomorrow morning to come here."

"And we're giving them something real!" blurted Kate. She instantly knew the error of saying anything at all at this juncture, but she had to speak, had to separate herself from Rod, who stood blinking, struggling to process Val's words. "Aside from their bounties, I mean. We're giving them a kind of quest, glory, a chance to be heroes right there on the screen for billions to see!"

Oh Christ, how lame it sounded in her own ears! The tone of it was worst of all, protesting Val's innocence. She had made as grave an error as Rod had made. She had tried to *excuse* Val Margolian!

She watched Val take it in, saw him discover in the

words her intent to ease his conscience, and discover in this her belief in his guilt. And she knew at once that those few reckless words were a major disaster for her career.

Val touched his com again. "Willy."

"Yeah, boss."

"Get me the Showboat up here, would you?"

"Comin' up."

For a few heartbeats Kate thought that awful moment would be forgotten. The Showboat was the director's throne, a raft with massive banks of monitors accessing every camera in the set. Since about 25 percent of the doors in this little city accessed actual interior sets, and every room of every interior was multiply camera-ed, the Showboat monitored more than ten thousand video feeds—and this wasn't counting the cameras mounted on all the APPs, whose camera eyes recorded their own footage as they pursued and killed the extras. Val had taken his pet assistants aboard the Showboat on previous shoots. But when the big boat hovered near, and extended its gangway, and they turned to follow him aboard, Val turned to them with a gentle, detaining gesture.

"Kate. Rod. I want to tell you how much I value your directing skills. Real talent there. *Real* talent. I want to nurture that talent. But there's a danger in rising too swiftly, too smoothly to the top, as both of you are, perhaps, in danger of doing. A director needs to *feel* the action, the flow of a production, from the ground up, from the front lines, as it were. I've been remiss, too busy to really monitor your training. But live action is explosive, it's dangerously fluid, and subject to catastrophic shifts. This is actual war after all."

He let that hang there a moment, watching them. They nodded gravely. Kate didn't worry about Rod speaking—he was utterly clueless at this moment—but her own heart was hammering away.

"You'll both get directors' credits, draw your checks per contract, but on this shoot I've decided I want to repair the deficiencies in your training. I want the two of you flying a payraft. Please tell me now if this isn't acceptable."

"Val," Kate blurted out, glad the suspense was ended at least. "I'm grateful. To put me . . . this close to the biggest live action ever shot. . . . If I'd been smart enough, I would have thought to ask it of you. I'd be proud to do it, Val."

His smile still had a touch of frost to it. "That's my Kate. Rod?"

"Why sure, Val . . ." He sounded like he'd been stomach-punched. "I'd be glad to. I'm grateful too!"

"Outstanding. Take the raft down to Accounting. I'll com them, and I'll tell Payboats to prep you a raft. Good luck. I know you'll make the most out of this priceless experience."

Kate piloted them down toward the hotel rooftop at center-set, beneath which Panoply's administrative offices were concealed. "What the—" Rod began.

"Don't say a word. Not a word." She struggled for composure. If only Rod had fallen out of the raft while he'd stood there, pronouncing the fatal words. If only she'd pushed him out while Val wasn't looking, before he'd had a chance to open his mouth!

"Just listen, OK? Val doesn't gloat over how quiet the

Zoo will be after the deaths of ten thousand lowlifes tomorrow. You congratulated him on being a mass killer. The result? We're going to fly a payboat tomorrow. If you have any reservations about doing it, leave me when we land. If you have any *thoughts* about flying a payboat, other than just *flying* the fucking thing and doing your job, do not give those thoughts the form of speech. I don't want to trade another unnecessary word with you."

She'd ended a lot angrier than she'd started. Saw his stunned face, and struggled to soften it. "Rod, you've—we've both offended him. You've got to get used to it. If we run the raft well, he might decide that's enough." (Not likely!) "We've just got to focus, follow his orders, and concentrate on doing a good job."

As they landed on the hotel roof, and entered the elevator down to Accounting, Rod was quiet. But as they approached the teller's window, he got his back up again, for the grittiness of tomorrow's work was coming home to him. They were picking up payboxes of four million clacks because they would be making payouts to extras who made kills during the shoot. And the raft they would be doing this from would be a far bleaker, more serious little craft than Val's luxury ride. This little raft's banks of monitors would, tomorrow morning, be swarming with shots of mayhem and death, and its cruise level would be scarcely six stories, on average, above all that mayhem and death, into which the raft must plunge, again and again, to drop killbonuses. Naked-eye and -ear work all shoot long, carnage at close range, the raft's high-powered engines and hissing vents growling and gasping with the work. Poor Rod's jaw clenched tighter and tighter. His dad was a major Panoply stockholder! This couldn't really be happening to him.

No breakfast tomorrow, Kate thought grimly, and not just because of the rough riding. She was already realizing how her customary director's perspective had sanitized death—and tomorrow it would be *her* choice of death she'd be seeing so close! Who would have dreamed Rod would sell it to Development? Would actually get thousands of people killed in that unspeakable way? Till this moment, she'd imagined it through monitors, through a kind of glass condom! But tomorrow there would be nothing but a short stretch of empty air between her eyeballs and their dying, and their screams would reach her ears.

Rod erupted as they emerged from the elevator doors. "I can't do this! That bitch Roz in Accounting! She won't say anything—she wouldn't dare to actually *say* a word! She won't have to, though. She'll just look at me, say it all with her eyes! I can't do this!"

Kate stared at him. He still had the power to astonish her. She burst out laughing. "You were screwing her, right? You were a godlike assistant director, and she was a lowly worm who'd topped out in Accounting? I can just imagine how you condescended to her, even *while* you were screwing her. Rod, wake *up*! You're not even thinking about what we'll be *doing* tomorrow. All this means to you is status loss!"

Down in Accounting, Kate almost enjoyed herself. While one of the clerks was counting out their bonus cash, Kate chatted amiably with Roz. "Look at him," she said. Rod turned his back on them. "You know, his absolute singleness of purpose looks like strength at first."

"Yes! That was it!" said Roz. "And then you realized that he only had *one thought*, his image. That's what made him seem so focused."

Kate laughed. "I wish we'd talked sooner. Now we're both pay-techs. It was inevitable he would say something to dig his own grave. Why didn't I *see* that?"

"Well . . ." Roz was more solemn now. "You'll be seeing something tomorrow, honey. . . ."

"I know. But you know, suddenly . . . I feel I deserve to. And it kind of helps."

Roz nodded gravely. "Hold on to that, Kate. Just remember that staying focused is the way to give them the best break you can."

"Thanks, dear. I'm holding on to that."

LEAVE-TAKINGS

Jool paused awhile amid the trees inside her compound, listening to the leaves whisper in a light breeze from the west. She could smell the jasmine, and the earthy scent of geraniums Momma cultivated close to the house, the spicy pepper tree, the carob with its faint semen scent, honeysuckle and passion flower vines that everywhere added their delicate tang, and all the shrubs and grasses their pleasant bitterness.

But the monoxide-and-asphalt smells of the Zoo overlaid it all. That's what you did here, you dug the sweetness out of the pollution, the tranquillity out of the danger. Even as she took in the whisper of greenery, she listened for the sound of stealthy feet betrayed by the deep dead leaves left lying everywhere, a natural alarm system. . . .

Inland lay the west foothills of the Sierras, and upland, the Trinities . . . broad stretches of Oregon and Washington. There were a lot of vital little towns, whole counties of working towns out there. A quarter mil in the municipal account made you a taxpayer in good standing with five years' credit and bought you some decent fire and law enforcement protection; another quarter mil bought you up to twenty acres of plantable soil, water. A hundred grand more would buy your vehicle, tools, and building materials besides whatever stone and lumber you harvested on your acres.

Over a million, that was the reality, the hard figures. And what did extras really walk out with, those who did walk out? They got a quarter mil survival fee, flat rate. If you just found a place to hide on the set, and lived, you could come back here and be taken care of for years, except that people would know you had that cash, and you'd be doing double-compound guard shifts the whole time. You could put it in a bank, and then risk a hundred separate trips for cash over those years, because checks were a joke in the Zoo.

But if you had a weapon, or found one on the set, you could hope for kill-bonuses. Street word put bonuses around a hundred, a hundred-plus K, but who knew? And what were the odds of bonusing big, big *enough*? You heard this and that, but people who bonused big and hung around here afterward rarely told the straight story, which would basically be telling people *This is how much you could rob me for*. She just had no way to guess the odds.

But if you *could* make it out into a town? Even if you had the entry clacks, nothing would be really settled till you'd worked, planted, and helped your neighbors, and everyone knew that you were gonna make something solid, pull your own weight. Oh how happy Momma would be if Jool could set them up in a place like that!

Her jaw was trembling! She was blinded by the tears streaming down her face. Get a grip, you silly bitch! Stow these feelings, fool! You can have them when you get out and have a life. Then you can bawl your stupid head off. You can cover Momma's face with kisses and get her bawling too.

She scrubbed her face with her sleeve, and took deep, shuddering breaths, and squatted down on the path in the dark under a bush until her eyes were clear and she could see properly. It wasn't her guard shift, but she was always on full alert when she was out on the grounds. Whacks on dust, once they got into a compound, could sit as still as stones for hours under cover till they saw the moment to move in on your house.

All four houses had twenty-five watters mounted outside above windows and doors. It gave you a shot at anyone who got close enough for a break-in attempt. Her own front porch had a heavy grill across it—she could just make out Momma's armchair inside it, in the shadow of the bougainvillea. Could see the neighboring wall of Chops's place next door, and farther in the shadow glimpses of the back porches of Millie's and Rick's places, and centered between all four the locked steel shed that housed the generator they all shared. They'd just had Gas Bill come by last week, so the generator's tank was topped off, a hundred gallons. The pump for the water tank ran off the same gas, and the water tank was full, five hundred gallons—that was water for dishes and cooking. City water was still OK for toilets and watering and baths if you didn't get it in your mouth.

Everything was topped off, and Momma's cupboard was full. Jool hadn't planned it, so this readiness seemed like an omen, a sign that tomorrow was meant to be.

There was a stealthy step from around a bend in the path. About time Chops showed up. Softly she spoke: "Proclivity."

"An inclination to. Exiguous."

"Extremely slight or small." Invader scum tended to have small vocabularies.

He stepped into view, his sawed-off at port arms, wiry, bald little Chops, all tattoos.

"All cool, Chops?"

"All cool, Jool."

"C'mere a second."

When he got close she wrapped a hug around him. He was startled, but after a second got his shotgun out of the way and hugged her back. Very shy, Chops, even after their years as neighbors and friends. He'd been fucked with in prison. A couple years back, she'd finally managed to get him into bed with her, and with a tender, relentless patience, had made love to him, and made him happy. Started some healing going, got some of the poison out of him. He would never become a lover, be someone who *had* a lover, but since that first time, every so often she dragged him to bed, sometimes just holding him, sometimes making him more completely happy again. "Just so you don't forget," she'd scowl at him afterward. "Deal is, as long as we're partners, you're gonna have to pay up." Lately, she'd been getting a real smile out of him. Smiles and personal communication weren't Chops's thing. But he really surprised her one morning a while back.

"Jool . . . ," he'd said, looking miserable and uncomfortable, visibly wondering what he was doing opening his mouth like this.

" 'Jool' what?"

"Jool . . . My life for yours, Jool. Any time, always. My life for yours."

She'd had to hug him then, completing his discomfort. "I love you too, Chops." And understanding how this would scare him, she added, with an impish smile, "Look, Chops. You gotta pay up, but what we're about is an always thing. Like we're family. My life for yours too. Always."

And Chops, solemnly, relieved, "Yes. That's right. Always."

But this last hug was something different, and she could tell he sensed it. No point in beating around the bush with Chops. She had to hit him with it quick before he made up his mind he was coming with her. Held him at arm's length. "I'm tubing to Panoply tomorrow morning, brother, and the day after tomorrow we're all heading out of here. Don't say anything. You told me your life for mine, right? Well, I can't do this without you here to take care of Momma. No way. It's got to be me, *got* to, I decided first, so I take the turn. And I'll die for sure in there if I think that Momma's unprotected. Don't let me down, Chops."

Silence. Not a word for the longest time, his eyes working darkly. ". . . OK. I take your patrol tonight. You sleep."

She gave him the clacks and the piece from the two 'Rise-asses, and that was that.

Jool went through her door as quiet as a housebreaker, and her prayers were answered. Momma was snoring in her recliner, a book on her ample bosom. Jool sneaked out onto the porch, and settled into the armchair for some sleep. She'd be gone before Momma woke.

Thinking about all they'd done to this place, her mind strayed through the compound around her, home to her since Momma'd moved in with Aunt Mae when Jool was ten. That very same year, Aunt Mae had stepped out of Punjab's Mini-Mart with some groceries, and died instantly, a "bonus" casualty of a drive-by. Then the house was just hers and Momma's, who gave reading lessons there to support them—there was some market for them, the schools being the hardscrabble operations they were.

Jool got her first job at thirteen. She might have gone the safe, dirt-work route—an Ag job was always easy to find. Half the L.A. Basin had reverted to the gardens and groves of its earlier era, with the population cut in half and half its sea of houses burned away, and with the soil and sun as good as it ever was. Picking, trimming, tractoring— for a tight, tough little thing as she already was, she could have had full-time work right out of the gate. Or, well-read as she was, could have joined one of the many Literacy Co-ops running all over the Basin.

She chose instead to make real money, and so her first gig—never described to Momma, who thought she *was* Ag-working—she got from the dad of one of Momma's pupils. That income had put up the house's fireproof siding and roofing. She'd been so proud of that job, riding shotgun for Snakepit on his regular route as a crystal courier from Sanberdoo, been so proud of encasing Momma in extra safety earned by her own wits, her own nerve!

The generator shed was bought with more shotgun money, this from Spade Trade on his in-City smack route. Spade was a sweet guy, a nonstop talker, who believed in "adequate *precautions*, not fuckin' *luck.*" He had steel plate instead of side windows, but they'd got him through the supposedly bulletproof windshield. Jool had grabbed his bag, tucked and rolled out, ducked and run. She got away and wholesaled it to a dealer the next day. You did what you had to do to protect your own. . . .

After Spade Trade's death, she had managed survival more skillfully. She turned to firearms, which seemed less evil than drugs, and worked out a delivery job for A-Rab. A-Rab's flea market down in Culver City was a collection point for—among other under-the-counter items—handguns. His site was an ancient drive-in theater where the huge screen had been cut into six-foot slices to fence the lot, and the old speaker posts supported the long tables.

A-Rab sold all his pieces for later delivery. What little was left of Metro patrols in the Zoo gave most of their attention to gun trafficking. No one, especially A-rab, wanted a flow of happy new gun owners circulating in his immediate neighborhood. He said he would give her thirty clacks for each piece delivered, and the more she carried per trip, the better. Jool had a gutsy scooter with a stout tail-box, so she'd said yes, and headed down to Culver City to pick up her first run one midmorning in summer.

Her way lay through a zone she liked, northern C.C. around the old MGM studios between Culver and Washington Boulevards. There'd been a lot of destruction there in the first years of Metro downsizing, the patrol fleet down to 15 percent within the decade. Gang wars had raged around the studio, its useful soundstages and set hangars. Fire had razed a thousand acres of old suburbs south of Culver.

In the twenty years since, bougainvillea and passion flower vine had clothed this mile of charred hulks. Everything was waist-deep in grass, and all the trees, untopped for a generation, towered, their leaves rippled in the breeze. She sometimes came down here to stroll around this place she called the Woodlands. In the summer the bougainvillea was beautiful, like lush pink and lavender leopard skin draping the burned stud bones, morning glory running in rivulets of sky-blue around chimneys, along fences, ice plant's succulent spikes overflowing like green barnacles—and once as she sat in the grass savoring all this, she turned and saw a young coyote, his rufous throat fur and silver back taking the sun, standing in the grass watching her shyly. Seeming to give her a little nod of greeting, he'd trotted off down the cracked and weed-tufted asphalt.

On the way to that first run for A-Rab, Jool drove

through here, and had the idle thought that some of these hulks, looking as demolished as they did, might have unscavenged basements. It was a notion that was shortly to save her ass. Coming back from A-Rab's with six handguns in her tail-box and a thin layer of books he'd thrown on top for cover, she was carrying her delivery addresses and her cash on her person. Then, just ahead, Metro flashed past on Culver, and she spooked.

Veering sharply off into the Woodlands lanes, she pulled her scooter up off the curb, and climbed up to the nearest green-furred hulk, trying to look like a scavenger, just in case they whipped back this way . . . and saw, under the collapsed studs and sheeting, an empty space. Tugging up the charred lumber and breaking the weeds' grip, Jool found a basement workshop, practically untouched. A bench, shelves of hand tools—and a big shelf of books.

And, when she came up, charcoal-smeared, with her first armload of books, there was the Metro, bigger than shit, pulled right up beside her scooter. They gave her the bug-eyes, flipped a bitch, and sped away.

A dozen visits, and she'd mined all the tools, and thirty cubic feet of books. Thereafter, she went *to* A-Rab's with a full load of books. She would sell him just a few, and ride back out with fifteen handguns under a large, convincing load of reads, and have besides a convincing cover for visiting the flea market so often. Jool sold the tools and bought another forty cubic feet of books from all the cheap wholesalers her momma was friends with.

She stayed with the gunrunning almost two years because

the money really made the homestead secure, and paid for the state-of-the-art chain-link and razor-wire perimeter, their nice new water tank, and a new, efficient generator.

She checked out the rest of the Woodlands too, finding other basements, tools, and more books. And would sometimes steal a few hours relaxing there, watching fox kits playing, a red-tail nail a rabbit, the waterbirds wheel above La Ballona Creek. On these dangerous gains of hers, she and Momma were making do quite well, but her first real thoughts of escaping the Zoo had come to her there on those Woodlands afternoons—dreams of living somewhere where there were deer on the hillsides. . . .

She'd been just a book dealer now, these last three years. Seemed she'd settled in, buying Momma bigger and more solid furniture to give her comfort as she grew slower and achier with chronic fear and despair. Jool had had an older sister she didn't remember, Kamesha, who was gunned down back in their old neighborhood, along with their daddy, whom she didn't remember either. . . .

So much done, and the work here still not finished. It scared her to remember all the close calls she'd had, just getting by down here. When you've used up so much luck, you worry if you have enough left for tomorrow. But no way out of it, all this carefully constructed security around her, all to be left unfinished, whether she came back rich, or didn't come back at all. Because look at her now. Actually going to step *out*. Panoply tomorrow, and the next day, if she lived, the world.

She thought of that 'Rise-ass boy today, that Curtis. He'd launched her on all this, had been that little touch of bad luck that changes everything. Out of nowhere. The boy had liked her, was kinda cute too. If it hadn't all blown up, he would have come back, looking for more books . . . and for her. Funny boy. Had some nerve on him, for a 'Rise-ass. Chops would've liked him, a serious, sweet boy like that. . . .

You couldn't hold on to anything. Shit dropped on you, and you just had to hit the ground running and pray for a way out. That would be tomorrow—hit the ground running. It would hurt, but she was gonna hide her piece, with the help of plenty of grease, and hope to make it past the detectors, then pray she could get it *out* before she had to start running. Even a little gat like that would seriously cramp her sprint if she couldn't. Hit the ground, girl . . . all you can do. She saw herself running down the streets of an endless set, saw herself dodging, though she couldn't see what it was she dodged. . . .

She was asleep. Chops patrolled by her every ten minutes to check on her. Toward dawn he noticed that she must be dreaming—her legs were giving little twitches. He understood. Dreaming of running.

"Curtis. What are you lookin' at? You been starin' out that window a solid hour! It's midnight, boy!"

"What if it is, you crusty old shrew?" I got up to kiss her. My auntie Drew had shuffled out in her slippers and robe. She wore her hair in a shiny processed conk that she dyed snow-white. That was just like her. No way she was going to pretend she wasn't getting old. First signs of gray, bam, she went solid white, and proud of it, thank you.

With her sharp eyes and her shrewd little chocolate face, she looked like what she was: one bad-ass little lady.

She liked me to call her names, to spar with her. My auntie was kindness right to the bone, but the only way she could handle it was to bark and snap. She'd never let me call her Momma, though I kept doing it when I was little. When she figured I was old enough to understand, she sat me down about it.

"I'm not your momma, Curtis. I'm your momma Lee's big sister, and you save that Momma for her if you ever meet her, 'cause she's not dead, boy. She just . . . left you, Curtis. She was sorry about it, real sorry, but she was always an adventurer, not a workhorse like me. She could never settle in after your daddy got killed, sat staring out my window for the longest time, thinking about where else she might go. She knew I liked you just fine and I would be glad to have you with me right up to the day I died. I wanted your company, you little devil—so that I'd never get lonely, long as I had you with me."

I'd never needed her to come out and say she loved me—I'd always known it. "I'm gonna make you some of your tea, Auntie. You sit right here."

But she stood behind me, looking out with me. "That used to be *all* lights. Just a sea of them. I ever show you where I went to work, just out of college?"

"You know you have." I smiled. "Right down over there. Hamilton High where you saved up the down on this place."

"You *had* to move up here, into one of these"—gesturing at the other 'Rises around us—"It was just getting too rough down there, but Curtis, I've always missed it. The trees. The crazy sidewalks buckled by their roots. Walking down them under the *sky*. Even the *traffic* was pretty at night. All those headlights and taillights an' signals rippling colors. But they *designed* it, you see, pulling all jobs in here, in the 'Rises. And now . . . well, I hear they're still teaching classes over at my old school. Private contractors, couple dozen or so doing the best they can, using not even half the rooms, barely keeps the building maintained."

"I know, Auntie. We were down on La Brea today, buying some books. There's still good people down there . . . keeping things alive. Now *sit* here, witch-lady an' I'll make you some tea. It's got the good vitamins in it."

I spied on her from the kitchen while I made it—and caught her at just what I was watching for, those little movements of her shoulders that told me she was rubbing her hands together, working in that arthritis cream of hers with the steroids in it. When she'd realized I could smell it, she'd started paying extra for an odorless mixture . . . but how could she hide anything from me?

She was a keyboard demon—had a brain like a calculator for figures, and hands that could almost keep up with it, but she was losing those hands fast. Casualty Credit, which also held the note on our home here, gave her Gold Star Employee Status for the load she pulled, with a .5 percent break on the interest on her loan. Last year she'd reached the equity level for a straight trade to a paid-off place in from the rim. Not good enough. She was going to own *her* place, with *windows*. Whenever she had some free time she'd sit by them and read. Read, and look up from the pages every now and then, out at the world, where there was room to spread out the imagination her book was feeding. . . .

It almost brought tears to my eyes, seeing her there secretly massaging her hands. I'd tried to make her give me some of her load, had done a couple hours after she knocked off tonight, as I always did, and was OK at it, but compared to her, I was slow as molasses. She knew she had to get this place paid off for me—I'd never make it on the board myself.

I'd argued with her about taking me on as a full-time helper. "Full time, I could cut your load by a *quarter* anyway."

This would always get her going. "I don't want you workin' for 'em! I want you to develop something of your own, Curtis, merchanting. I like that book cart of yours. Why don't you boys push it into something big enough to live on? If you work directly for the Corps, they lock you in. They start you in debt, and keep you there. Let *me* pay off the windows."

That's what she called our condo, the windows. I imagined my mother staring out of them years ago, me a toddler nearby, Auntie Drew watching both of us. Maybe Auntie had flashed on the same picture, seeing me sitting there just now. My momma Lee, an adventurer. That was my whole inheritance from her, it seemed. Just that word. That idea.

When I brought Auntie her tea, it was like two people were doing it, me and this Curtis dude, me watching him putting the cup in her hands, in her fingers that already looked a little twisted. And I was thinking: Look at this guy, putting tea in those hands of hers that she's twisted up working to buy him a house! What a useless asshole!

We looked out over the Zoo, so darkened from its days of glory, which the vids still remembered—a pavement of stars, a bed of white embers and gems, threaded with the freeways' corpuscular rivers, their murmur like a great beast purring.

Once the Corps got full globalization, had bought all the governments and staffed them with Corps, what *had* to happen? So many poor in the world, *all* wages sank. That Zoo was a Malthus zone now. It *had* to be a place where many died every day, just like the Ag-worker Zone, miles and miles of it to the east and south. Because to run the world smoothly, the Corps only needed enough people to buy their products, and enough of the desperate to fill their hard and high-risk jobs. Just enough to nourish a seed crop of the poor.

My auntie got up to go back to bed. After he hugged her and kissed her, I watched this useless Curtis dude smile, and I heard him say, "I'm goin' out early tomorrow, Auntie, and try to scare up some work. I'll get my breakfast out." His voice sounded wrong, the guy screwed it up, because Auntie gave him a sharp, almost a scared look.

"What're you talkin' about, Curtis? How early?"

"Early enough to beat the crowds on the ramps. I need to move my limbs, run a little, Auntie. Fact, maybe you want to come with me—we'll go slow, get you up a nice power-walking sweat before you sit down to the board."

Best to put her on the defensive, distract her. But she said, "Well, I'm sorry, but I got *real* work to do, and I wanna see you here when I sit down to the board, you hear me? You can give me a hand tomorrow. I got some . . . spreads you can help me with. Eight sharp, you understand?" She sensed something, no doubt about it.

"OK, eight sharp. I'll be here. You just take your tea here to bed now—please? We both gotta get some z's."

She looked back at me from the door of her room, something I couldn't quite read in her eyes. Her white hair made her eyes dark as night to me. Quietly, at last, she said, "You a good boy, Curtis," and went inside.

Both of us sat down by the window alone again—me and this new, somewhere-outside-himself Curtis, the Curtis who was going out there as soon as Auntie was asleep, and hoofing it down to Tube Nine. Was *I* really going out there with this guy?

I nearly puked with fear when I had to admit that I was.

Then I was just me, one scared 'Rise-ass who'd stepped out of his 'Rise and fallen down into a whole new world— that one out there.

My eye picked out something blue—beyond the freeway, floating just above the flatland of the Zoo, above the faint freckling of weak streetlights and spiky shadows of powerpoles, trees, billboards: a little luminous blue rectangle. I'd been brooding on it when Auntie came out. Had she noticed what I was looking at? You couldn't read it from here, but maybe she knew what an extra notice looked like.

I stayed there at the window, like a guy shaking at the bars of his cage I guess, asking myself if there was no other way to make money . . . and I knew there wasn't.

Shit. She'd be alone the rest of her life if I didn't come back . . . and her hands would shrink into knots if I let this go on.

But even if I came back alive, loaded with clacks, where exactly would we be *going*? The Trinities. The Sierra foothills. The Land of Oz! What if these mountain communities were just fictions? You drove in, met with the Town Council, and found a bunch of crackers with shotguns who took your cash and buried you in the hills?

I couldn't believe it. I *wouldn't* believe it. A big chunk of the best produce and meat that fed L.A. was trucked into the Zoo wholesalers and processors from the mountains to augment their own Basin-grown goods. The best tomatoes, the best canteloupes—my own personal favorite—were stickered Moonrise, from the Trinities. And Wolverton, in the Sierras, ran a damn good reprints press. All my Shakespeare, my Dickens, my whole collection of Raymond Chandler were Wolverton Offset Books—scarcely a misprint in any of them! No, there were real people up in them there hills, running real communities.

The bottom line was, if there was even a chance of something better, we had to take it. Because not to take it was to surrender, and live the rest of our crowded lives without self-respect.

After a bit, I peeked in Auntie's room, and saw her asleep. At her workstation I left her a note—not a lie: *Sorry, Auntie. I found some work. I'll see you later.* At least I hoped that last sentence wasn't a lie. Then I slipped out our door, and headed for the street.

THE TUBE

Tube Nine. The gangways converging from the streets were jammed, the vast platform packed right up to the fence erected for this extra call. I'd come straight from the 'Rise six hours early and gotten this frontline spot, but was wedged in tight within minutes of arrival. I stuck my hands in my pockets so no one else would. I dozed standing up, supported by the fence and the crowd, and woke to a lively roar. The multitude seethed. It must be getting close to loading time.

Forget finding Japh. Anyway, the word was that they filtered people apart as they came on-set to separate anyone who arrived buddied up. When the shoot started they wanted friends scrambling to find each other, to give things that realistic air of catastrophe, people searching, calling out names.

The people packed in this chute couldn't turn easily to face each other, so they just shouted out what they had to say, everyone trading rumors.

"They say the APPs are giant dogs, bigger'n people. That true? Anyone hear that?"

"Fuck no! These APPs half rat an' half bug. Big ol' bug jaws on 'em. Bug-rats, Fool! Everyone knows that!"

"Fool *you*! My man *works* at Pimply, crotch-weed. APPs're *reptiles* wit' poison tongues whip out an' stab right through you. Poison melts you an' then they lick you *up*!"

"Hey, what kinda detectors Pimply got? They go off on tempered plastic an' shit?"

"They got staydade*art* scans, whaddaya, simple? They go off you even *thinkin'* 'bout sneakin' a blade in!"

"Hey, whaddabout Kevlar undies?"

There was a lot of laughing going on, the crowing kind, people showing off that they *could* laugh. Just then, somewhere in the crowd behind me, a shrill voice said " 'Rise-ass!" There was a hubub of voices, and then a defiant "Fuck you" in a voice I could have sworn was Japh's! Could I be so lucky? It seemed an omen of survival if I was.

We were all crammed way too tight for any serious fighting to break out, but if that was Japh I wanted him to know he had backup, know I was here. At the top of my lungs I roared:

" 'RISE-ASS RULES!"

Boy, did that raise a storm around me: "Who said that where he at you looking to die 'fore you even get to the set hey we gotta 'Rise-ass here your candy-ass is mine I got him first who said that where he at?" No one could even turn around but everyone was trying at once and it felt like being inside a huge snake trying to digest you. That was good. The upheaval snuffed itself right out, everyone equally hurt by it.

But what was this? Echoes? All through the crowd I was hearing it: " 'Rise-ass rules. 'Rise-ass *kicks* ass! Fuck you, Zoo-meat!" The Middle Class was here in force!

What a revelation. While it angered the Zoo-meat, it seemed to impress them too. Going extra was a Zoo thing— the whole world knew that, right? But subtracting for the ones who kept silent, the Middle Class was here in the hundreds at least!

The crowd was roaring louder now—not violence, but fierce conversation.

"Ho, 'Rise-meat."

Somebody close by in the chute was pitching this at me. I couldn't spot him, so I threw back in his general direction, "Yeah, Zoo-ass?"

"Hey, just a friendly question. I'm against the fence like you—see me?"

I pressed my face sideways against the mesh at my back. Two heads down, a short guy with a waxed baldy was doing the same. Coal-black eyes, a wide rubbery face, amiable grin. All his teeth were gold. "I'm Capyerass—call me Cap, bro."

"Cap. I'm Curtis. Call me Curtis." I gave him a little bit of his smile back.

"How many 'Risers you think be down here?"

"Hey, I got to guess just like you. I figure less than half of them would shout it out."

"Yeah . . . Man, I thought it was cherries an' berries up there in 'Rise-land."

"Think again."

"I am, I am. You people *know* the odds up there? On the set?"

"I heard twenty, thirty percent survival."

This got a roar of laughter from everyone listening. "Fool!" someone brayed. "Twenny-thirty percent of every-one's *ass* be survivin's what that means!"

"Check it out, Cherry," someone else hooted. "Bonus on a APP's a hundred seventy-five K for this vid. Whatchoo think that means about survivin'?"

I couldn't process this one, and Cap could see it. "Standard kill-payout's around a hundred K per tag most vids," he said. The tag would be the token you took off any APP you managed to kill.

"So these APPs are extra bad?"

"Way. An' as for the odds?" Cap grinned wider and put on the voice of a smooth suit. "Studio law says you gotta have at least eighteen and a half percent walkin' back out of the set alive." Everyone laughed the louder because no one liked being reminded. "Man!" added Cap in his own voice.

"I love that *half*! They musta felt really *good* about themselves when they tossed *that* in! On this shoot I'm bettin' it works out more like *seventeen*."

"That's like . . . one out of six!"

Everyone chimed in at this in furious irony:

"Hey! This vid's gotta net two hundred bil, baby, or they won't be able to hold their heads up!"

"Yeah, it'll be a flop!"

"The stock'll take a dive!"

"The board'll shit its pants!"

"One hundred ninety-nine point nine bil won't *do*, Cherry!"

I realized that actually these Zoo thugs *liked* my being here. It eased their bitterness to pump some of it into a newbie. And it staggered me. Four to one odds against surviving.

Cap was watching it sink in. I looked up into his grin— his biggest yet. "Scope this, Curtis my brother. Far as I'm concerned, when that gate opens, there ain't no 'Risers. We all just Zoo."

The train's doors slid open, and Metro stepped out and flanked them. As the gates of the chutes slid aside, something like a moan went through the multitude. We surged into the train like a fluid. My feet were on the ground, but just barely, and they were carrying only a fraction of my weight. I was in a giant's fist that gripped and shoved me straight into the car.

We filled the car like a piston. Cap and I were side-by-side now, and we were pushed against the barred enclosure behind which the Metro had retreated. Holding their prods and shields, they stared stonily out through the bars at the human mass.

The train started moving. I locked my arms against the bars, but the crush of acceleration felt like it would break them. When we hit cruise at two hundred klicks, the pressure eased off. The roar of the rails steadied down, and everyone started talking at a shout. We were on our way, committed, and the adrenaline set in.

Cap started ragging one of the Metros facing us from behind the bars.

"Hey Metro-meat! I know you, man! Used to be with the South Central Savages—called yourself Popper. Hey Pops! Ain't that right?"

The Met, like his partners, stood stony, his eyes staring over our heads.

"I'd know you anywhere," Cap crowed, getting an audience now. "My, my, you moved on *up*, didn't you? Into a Met compound. I bet you live right by the wall though, can hear the Zoo on the other side, all night long! Hey! I'm talkin' to you!"

The guy's face was red; you could see Cap had scored. Most of the Metro, in their compounds, *were* right out of the Zoo.

"I'm *talkin'* to you, Pops! That stone-face shit don't fly with me. What, you think you *transformed*? You a higher class of being now? Your shit don't stink?"

I began to sense that Cap, who had the whole car for an audience now, wasn't just playing, but playing for something. "Hey, you *still* Zoo, fool! You can't get away from us, you neck-deep in us! *We* the ones goin' somewhere—you stuck right where you started, just another turd in the pipe!"

"Fuck you! You going somewhere! I'll tell you where you're goin'!" Cap had that Metro now. The guy was beet-red. His squad mates went double-stony, obviously wanted him to clam up but were afraid to get sucked into the exchange. "Where *you're* goin'," hissed Pops, "is to *die*! With *these* APPs, fool, you be lucky if'n fifteen percent a you walk. These are the baddest APPs of all time! And bonuses? You'll be so fuckin' scared, you won't even try to kill 'em. You *find* a dead one, you won't even touch it to get the tag!"

The Metro next to him had enough, and rammed the butt of his prod into Popper's ribs without looking, without changing expression. Popper doubled up, but came to his senses. Straightened, and stared ahead.

The whole car was quiet. Cap had been playing the guy for information, and now we all had it.

Extra-extra-extra-extra-extra—the rails were roaring it. A whole train packed tight with extra human beings, surplus lives that could be spent for entertainment purposes. Wouldn't be missed, not one of them—plenty more where they came from. We were all packed in here in a desperate bid to get out of this part of the world, but in that moment everyone was thinking, that almost all of us were on our way out of the world period.

We'd known it, but we hadn't *known* it, right? People started struggling to put their attitudes back on. "Fuck yous" were shouted here and there, and some people started trying to rev up some large talk, but it sounded pretty thin, subdued . . . and then we started to decelerate.

Panoply. Already.

We poured out of the car, and into a tunnel lined with . . . trees! And distant mountains, ceilinged with blue sky and fat white clouds!

It was a stunning effect, and it was cruel and unusual in the extreme, this tube of holo-wall maybe a quarter mile long. At the far end you could see an arch of actual sky, yellow-orange with the first sun, see lots of fencing strung in chutes, a maze of them ending in a whole array of little gateways. . . .

But in this tunnel, this cheap trick of the studio's . . . well, the trick really worked. None of us as we shuffled ahead could stop gaping at the phony great outdoors all around us. It was just too beautiful. There were little cabins on the far hills, nestled in the pines—the visibility was incredible! The air was like crystal. There, maybe a mile away, was a homestead where you could even make out the garden, huge red tomatoes, the yellow tassels of almost-ripe corn like gold dust on the rows. Along one slope of a little valley you could see a breeze kick up, see the trees shiver with it, their needles like licked fur. . . .

We were a quiet crowd in that tunnel. We wanted to mock it, because it was such an obvious ploy. It told us, *Remember what you've come for—keep your eyes on the prize and don't back down from the swearing-in.* It reminded us all of our dream, and our desperation.

This *was* our dream, surrounding us. The fucking

studios! People's dreams were their business, and they knew their business. They had us by the heart, and we just walked, and looked around, and longed, all the way to the cattle chutes.

TWO NEW PAYBOAT TECHS

Just after sunrise, Kate and Rod met outside the set wall. They climbed onto a crew shuttle and rode down the wide concrete ramp, into a vast basement bazaar of maintenance vehicles, prop shops, and materials yards underneath the set.

The place swarmed, and their shuttle hit stop lights at every intersection. Waiting beside a five-acre lot of alien spacecraft, they watched three huge flatbeds roll past with tarped loads. APPs—Anti-Personnel Properties.

"Your inspiration," Kate murmured. Rod scarcely registered the sarcasm. His body was stiff, and he had a stony stare for all the intricately organized turmoil around them. It wasn't hard to read his mind, for only one thought consumed it: He, Rod Richmond, a goddamned assistant *director*, his father a personal friend of *Val Margolian* himself, was sitting in a crew shuttle, elbow to elbow with *techs*, for christ's sake!

Rod was aggressively—even belligerently—spiffed out. He was wearing a kilo-clack Italian cashmere sport coat. What ate at him was that no one among these drones would *realize* just how much it cost. He was visibly stiff with indignation.

Just looking at his smoldering profile gave Kate some comic relief. It even helped with her own anxiety. OK, with her *terror*, and not just the terror of her morning's work ahead. This was a pivotal moment. This was *career* terror. Already at his meager talent's pinnacle, Rod had very little to lose—he just didn't know it. But Kate had the intelligence, the imagination, the guts to direct. And she had offended Val Margolian, a king.

Well, vain and ambitious she might be, but she was going to survive this setback. Look at Rod with his status rags and disdainful air. *Kate* was starting out on the right foot. Even though she'd be issued the standard jumpsuit before the shoot, she'd dressed functionally this morning to show her readiness: khakis, with lots of utility pockets and Velcro flaps.

Paymasters watched people die, and today she would be watching them die a death she herself had thought the most dreadful of all. And not from a godlike director's distance, where everything was monitors, nothing eyeball-to-eyeball, but from close at hand—from hover-level, all day long. . . .

How did the raft crews handle it, shoot after shoot? This woman on her right, for example—was one, wearing the blue jumpsuit with shoulder chevrons that showed her to be not only a pilot, but a sector chief, in charge of a whole squadron of payboats.

"Excuse me. You're piloting a payboat, right?"

The woman didn't return Kate's smile, just a sharp, cold look. She was slight and pale, had faint freckles and sandy eyelashes, blue eyes so keen they seemed to bite. She just stared at Kate, while the shuttle hit another stop, and an electric tractor hummed past, towing a large cage shrouded in a tarp. More APPs, these on their way topside for the demonstration to the extras, once they'd been sworn in and processed. The blue-eyed pilot gave that cage a look, and then her eyes switched back to Kate, but only continued to stare.

"I'm paymastering," Kate tried again. "My first time out."

Now the woman smiled unpleasantly. "Is that a fact? *I* thought you were Kate Harlow, one of Margolian's annointed." So cold, those blue eyes! Kate had to smile herself a bitter little smile. Didn't she know about studio gossip *yet*? Always assume that everyone knew everything.

"Yes, I am."

"So to what do we owe the honor?"

She'd know this too, of course. "I've offended the King, and I'm being punished with grunt duty. So. What's it like, watching people die for money?"

This got a smile. "Do you mean, what's it like getting paid to watch people die, or what's it like watching people die to get paid?" Trading punches was obviously what this little freckled bitch liked best.

"Both."

"You'll know in a couple hours, Kate. Tell me though. What's it like getting paid to *arrange* people's deaths?"

"Up yours."

"Oooh. Sensitive, are we? I'd advise you to get over that ASAP, Katie. Because you're gonna have to catch those tags and drop those bonuses with a steady hand. And I hope your boy Rod the Bod there is half as good at punching a raft as he is at thinking up ways for other people to die."

Well. At least one of Kate's secrets was safe. They had slid into the curved drive fronting the basement lobby of HQ. Rod, during this conversation, had gone so rigid ignoring the little pilot, that he stumbled stepping off the shuttle. Kate tactfully took his arm and steered him through the crowd.

But inside, when she headed them toward the slideway up to the techs' canteen, he balked, and turned to face the bank of code-operated elevators, which were the gateways to the upper floors.

"Hey!" She had to struggle to keep her voice down. "Rod. Listen to me. Today, you're a tech. Go with it. Accept it. The Big Guy's whim is our command. Rod?"

He shook off her hand and smoothed his cashmere. He gave her a cool, pitying look. "You know, there's a difference, Kate, between obeying orders and . . . cowering. I'll punch raft, fine! And I'll show that little bitch how it's done. Meanwhile, I'm still an assistant director, and I've had a few thoughts that Val might find useful before we jump off, and I'm gonna share them with him. The bottom line, Kate, is that if you don't know your own worth, then nobody else is gonna know it for you. So. I'll find you in the canteen, or I'll meet you at Payout."

She watched him walk to the elevators and punch in his code, every inch an upper-floor man. The elevator door closed behind him, *sealing his fate* Kate thought. That would surely be the last time his code worked.

She took the slideway up to the canteen, more afraid for herself than sorry for Rod. Little Blue Eyes' smiling malice had left her wide awake to the horror ahead. Even the extras would be readier than she was for it because they were going to get a demonstration. But she, in two hours, would be right in the middle of it, with Rod for her pilot—and how tweaked would he be by the time Val got through with him up there?

The slideway stopped at the sixth floor, four floors above the street level of the set itself. HQ was housed in a twenty-story building that, seen from outside, was a hotel on the set's upscale Wiltshore Avenue. It was one of a number of "dummy" buildings—it couldn't actually be entered by extras seeking a refuge from the APPs. All of its windows were holo-screens, presenting to the cameras outside the attack of aliens on hotel guests in their posh suites. From inside, the holos produced a rainbow sheen that obscured Kate's view of the surrounding set.

She had half-expected a funereal gloom in the canteen, and was relieved by the roar of conversation. Sickened by the smell of food, her stomach let her know she was even more frightened than she had thought.

She took strong black coffee, and sat at a little table by herself. She took disciplined sips, concentrating on steadiness of hand, firmness of posture, and a calm expression. If Blue Eyes recognized her, who else here did?

Well, to hell with feeling watched. She should be the watcher, the listener. She would take this opportunity to glean what she could. Everywhere she noticed pilots in close conversation with their paymasters, partners digesting the task at hand. Teamwork. With her own teammate twelve stories overhead attempting a last-ditch blowjob on Val Margolian, and likely to be in total denial once Val brushed him off, Kate saw that managing a competent performance on her raft might be largely in her own hands.

So she forced herself to focus. Learn from the pros around her. For instance, those gizmos on the paymasters' belts. Those little keypads would be the APP scans, controls for punching up on the raft's monitors the input from the cameras mounted on the APPs in her payboat's sector. Kate remembered that these were standard issue on all Margolian's live-action shoots, a humane touch. With them, payboat pilots could scan what the APPs in their sectors were seeing, and thus they could be forewarned if one of their APPs was getting killed by some extra.

Other studios equipped their payrafts only with tag sensors. If an extra killed an APP, only then would the rafts sense its tag being taken, and only then would they head toward it to pay off the lucky extra. But with Panoply's scans, the payboats could know in advance that an APP was in trouble, and they could get there quicker for the payout. Because, through the twenty-year history of live action, plenty of extras had been killed with a kill-tag in hand, scanning the sky for a payout, while another APP nailed them from behind.

"Most crews don't use those scans nearly as much as we're supposed to." Here was Blue Eyes, taking a seat at Kate's table, smiling nastily. The woman was unnaturally acute—how could she have known what Kate was looking at? Kate held her gaze, sipped some coffee.

"Why's that?"

"Because more than half the time, when you punch up an APP's cams, you're going to get an extreme close-up of some poor fucker that the thing is *eating*. Why else do they mount the cams on the APPs in the first place, Katie? For white-knuckle close-ups! And most of us feel it's bad enough watching that kind of shit from twenty or thirty meters."

"Oooh. Sensitive. You're such a humanitarian, you'd rather reach the lucky ones late than watch the unlucky ones dying."

Blue Eyes was still smiling, unfazed. "I didn't say *I* didn't use the scans. And most of the others are so damn quick on the tag sensors that it doesn't make much difference.

"So. I've handed you some funk on us payboaters. Are you going to run squealing it to Margolian? Worm back into his good graces?"

"What's your name?"

"Sandra Devlin."

"Well first, Sandy, up yours again."

Big smile now. Those blue eyes had been reading Kate closely when Sandra had delivered that taunt about squealing. It seemed Kate had passed the test. "That's first. And second, Katie?"

"Well, second, since I assume you care about the extras getting paid off efficiently, why not help me out? I'm a novice at payboating. Tell me things I need to know, techniques, dos and don'ts."

"I sense, Katie, that you've got balls. I like balls on a rich bitch. Tell you what. Let's see how big they are. You were checking out our gear . . . You know what this is?" Sandy indicated a touch pad on her belt that looked a little more complex than the APP scan next to it.

"Emergency override? That whaddayacallit . . . ?"

"The APP driver. It's an override in a limited sense only. It's more an interference tool. If you find yourself crashed, which does happen, and you're on the ground facing an APP, this won't change its basic program, which is to eat you. But it can override the APP's movements, one body part at a time—as long as you hit the keys right. If you key it right, you can turn the thing around and walk it away from you. But if you stop keying, back it comes. And if you key wrong, then it's right on you, munching away. And let me tell you, when you're facing an APP on the ground, like one of the extras, then it's easy to get the shakes and screw up your keying. I've seen it happen."

"You mean you've seen a payraft go down?"

"Hey, that happens a lot more than they tell you, every other shoot, practically." It seemed Sandra got more conversational the more frightening her topic might be to Kate.

"See, the big problem, until they beefed up the rafts' cooling systems, used to be overheating in the raft drive. Melt down even one of your anti-grav coils and bam, you drop like a rock. I saw that happen to a friend of mine. The crash tumbled her out on the street into heavy APP traffic. Well, she got her feet under her quick. It broke her pilot's back and by the time she was up, *he* was lunched. The APPs were those things with the three-part jaws and needle teeth?"

"Right. *Altair Invaders.*"

"That was the vid! Well, my friend, *she* had another APP hopping right toward her, but had thirty yards clearance. She'd Maydayed, and Metro was rushing to her sector, and I scanned the APP after her onto my monitor. I saw her in detail through that APP's eyes. There was my friend, a few yards off, keying her driver like mad. The APP stops short, it turns this way, turns that way, then it spins all the way around—and there she is again on cam, my friend, keying like crazy, obviously panicked, but she's still got the APP coming straight for her. Then it launches, lands right on her. I watched her head bitten off as close as you are to me right now. She fumbled the keys, see? Lost the pattern, and brought it right on herself."

A comfortable silence, Sandy gazing at Kate, taking in her reactions. All this had been by way of proposing some kind of challenge to Kate. Sandy was waiting for Kate to pick up the thread herself. "OK . . . so . . . you want to find out if I've got nerve."

Sandy's smile looked genuine. "Thanks—I lost my train of thought there, recalling old times." (Right.) "So. One of Panoply's thoughtful provisions for its payboat union's safety is a driver run-through. They put you in a pen with a live APP, set the APP at three-quarters speed, and you get a chance to make sure you don't succumb to the Sweaty Fingers Syndrome on your driver keyboard—in case you crash, I mean. It's totally optional, this run-through. You have to request it, in fact, and sign a waiver too. There's handlers watching with manual override, but a wrong touch on your driver can totally fake them out and beat them to the draw, and you can still get lunched. Well? Whaddaya say?"

Kate wanted to snap her answer back, but her throat clenched up and, to her fury, she had to swallow before answering. "I'll do it if you will."

"If I do it? Katie honey, I *always* do it, every fucking flick I raft, and I don't do any of that candy-ass three-quarter speed shit either. Set it high and send it in, I tell 'em. Every single flick I raft."

Kate had her hands on her lap now, afraid they might betray a tremor, though she thought that her face was OK, meeting Sandy's stare. But what in Christ's name had she just talked herself into? Damn this freckled bitch! She'd marked Kate out, moved in, and backed her into a corner, one-two-three, as easy as if Kate were a month-old kitten. The revenge of the Lower Orders. Kate was had, and had cold, because there was no way she was going to back out. No way she would let those malicious blue eyes gloat over her.

"OK. I'll do it."

"Good for you. The way I see it, it's not just a precaution. It's a kind of dues thing—face what the Zoo-meat's facing before I go out and play god over them. 'Course, their lives aren't nearly so significant as yours is, but they're still human in a technical sense, belong to the same species and all."

"Hey, bitch. Enough. I said I'd do it. And, besides, you're living off their blood as much as I am."

"Yes. I suck their blood for a little house in the lower Hills just as much as you suck it for your manse in the Heights. Whoa! What have we here? Behold, the gods walk among us."

Kate followed her eyes. Val Margolian had come into the canteen with Rod. Val had a friendly hand on Rod's shoulder, seemed to be chatting with him, at the same time turning a smile to the people staring at him, returning a wave here and there. Rod looked fully inflated, lofty, speaking earnestly to his mentor and ecstatic to be seen by all these drones as he did so. Look who he'd brought to *his* table! Was Val actually going to sit down with them?

"Hi, Kate. You look rarin' to go."

"Hi, Val."

"Hi, Sandra!"

"Good morning, Mr. Margolian."

Val was famous for his democratic touch, a real name-rememberer, but there was an undercurrent of something in his greeting to the pilot. And did Sandy's reply have a touch of irony? Val was pulling out a chair . . . and pressing Rod down into it. Remained standing himself.

"Val? Aren't you going to . . . ?" Rod—surprised.

"I have a million things to see to upstairs. Kate, you let Sandra show you the ropes. She's an ace."

"She's taught me plenty already, Val."

"Go get 'em girls, Rod."

He went out easy and amiable, dispensing more waves, pausing at a table of APP techs for a brief exchange.

Rod looked disoriented, as if waking from a dream. It was dawning on him how his little entry scene had played. Val had brought him back downstairs . . . and sat him down at a canteen table. Put him in his place. He looked around him, and you could see how conspicuous he felt here, a guy in a kilo-clack sport coat, marooned in a sea of jumpsuits.

The man had actually thought Val Margolian was going to eat with him down here! Kate's urge to laugh died. This man was going to be sharing her raft in less than two hours. And Kate knew instinctively the horror that now consumed him, and it had nothing to do with the real horror of today's business. What galled Rod Richmond at this moment was that, just like all these people around him, he himself would shortly be wearing a blue jumpsuit.

It dawned on Kate that she was seeing Rod in this moment in much the same way that Sandy saw her.

"So!" Sandy brightly piped. "You're gonna be a payboat pilot, Rod? I was just telling Katie here about our rafts' coil meltdown problem—over twenty crashes in the last five years. I don't think I mentioned to her, though, that they solved that little glitch just this year. They enlarged the suck-vents to cool the coils better, and we haven't had a single meltdown since. We *have* had five more crashes though. Another pesky little glitch. It seems that the beefed-up vents will occasionally suck in airborne debris from explosions and such. Makes the engines seize up. You don't just drop, you tend to *flip*. Well, come on, kids, let's get you suited up."

Sprightly Sandy was on her feet now. "Sorry we don't have any cashmere jumpsuits for you, Rod."

"Why don't you just fuck off?" Rod's face was red beneath his tan, his shoulders swelling in his suit.

"Why don't I fuck off, Rod? I'll tell you. Because I'm the union rep, and the chief of your sector, and I'm your fucking *boss* today. I'm personally assigned to your case by the great god Margolian. If you don't feel like doing your job, or perhaps just don't have the balls for it, I'll be happy to have security throw you off the set right now."

Rod's shoulders slumped. He wouldn't meet her eyes, and Sandy, apparently, was above extorting a spoken surrender. She merely smiled and nodded, and led them out.

As they followed Sandra out of the canteen, Kate felt an unexpected gratitude to the woman. She might rough up Rod's ego enough to focus him for the work ahead. "Hey, Rod," Kate said. "Sandy has a great, like, warm-up activity for us, kind of a practice run with our APP drivers. Interested?"

"APP drivers?" Rod asked. "What are those?"

because she couldn't even bend over without something peeking out.

She did a second pirouette, reverse direction . . . and the studio tech impatiently waved her through. Bless the inventor of hard-carbon firearms! Ahead, beyond further chutes and arrays of booths, she could see the set wall, and within it, the jumbled architecture of the place designed to kill her. "Up yours," she muttered. "Loom as large as you want— I'm goin' *in* you, and I'm comin' *outta* you." She was armed against three tight spots. Had the means for three *kills*, if her aim was true. Three tags, 525 K. Just hold on to that thought.

At the contract stations, a fleshy, heavily made-up woman sat at the console of Jool's. "Can you read the contract on the display?"

"Damn straight I can."

The woman kept talking as if Jool hadn't answered, her spiel dropping out of her mouth without inflection, a verbal leakage she had nothing to do with. Jool understood the fat and the makeup: insulation, a sheath to hide in. "You are contracting to participate as an extra in the filming of *Alien Hunger* if you default on this agreement at any point subsequent to entering it you will immediately begin serving a ten-year prison term for fraud you will immediately receive a hundred and seventy-five thousand dollars cash for each Anti-Personnel Property you disable or destroy and whose paytag you remove and render to one of the payrafts you will receive a survival bonus of two hundred and fifty thousand dollars on exiting the set at the conclusion of the filming any and all monies on your person at that time will be legally yours and tax-exempt do you accept these terms."

"I'm sorry, my mind wandered—would you repeat that please?"

The woman's eyes had never left her console, and did not now. "You are allowed one repetition you are contracting to participate as an extra in the filming of—"

"That was what they call a joke. I accept the terms."

"Please place your left hand palm-down on the hand-shaped depression in the console in front of you doing so will legally constitute your binding entry into this contract with Panoply Studios Incorporated."

"You mean this hand-shaped depression here?" The woman's eyes remained fixed on her screen. Jool pressed her palm down.

"Thank you please follow the green line to Makeup and Costume."

At Makeup, hundreds of chairs were manned by techs in smocks and work aprons, all bulging with pockets. They wore bandoliers of pencils, brushes, combs, and scissors, and wielded little latex spray guns. The skinny guy at Jool's chair wore plenty of makeup himself, and was definitely not the impersonal type. "No tats?" he enthused. "Real unprocessed *hair*? Gracious, sweetie, are you a 'Riser?"

"Naw, I'm rich, got a house in the Hills—I'm just addicted to thrills."

"Chin up, please." He was lipsticking her, applying mascara and eyeshadow. Quick deft strokes on her lips and eyelids felt like affection, those gentle, unaccustomed touches.

"What's my look?" she asked. "Feels like you hoin' me up."

"No, you're a dish, sweetie, in lavender sweats and

Nikes, out jogging—an uptown babe who dolls up for her workout."

"Hey. Thanks." She meant it. All the extras' footgear, whatever the apparent style, was supposed to be good running gear in disguise, but he was typing her for the real thing.

"And of course you'll have a fanny pack."

"What's that?"

"You'll see. Let's put some rhinestone studs on your little elfin ears." As he leaned close to apply the studs, he murmured, his voice covered by the whine of a latex spray gun masking the barbed-wire neck tat of a bruiser in the next chair, "You'll have just enough time to get it out of you and slip it into the pack in the changing booth."

Jool's startled eyes met the tech's smiling green ones. He kissed her cheek and grinned. "I'm an expert observer of all the nuances of a woman's walk, dear. You've got balls, honey. Godspeed."

Jool's eyes filled with tears—actual tears again! He patted her shoulder, pointed out the booth, and called, "Next!"

All through the queasy calisthenics of extracting and assembling her weapon and stowing it in the fanny pack, Jool felt that light, feathery kiss on her cheek. A tingly little spot of luck. She kept resisting the impulse to touch it, because she was afraid of rubbing it off. And it was the *second* kiss, the second *kiss-out-of-nowhere* that she'd received in the last twelve hours. That funny boy Curtis, last night . . . What was going on?

Jool had, especially at moments of great risk, a sort of

cosmic turn of mind, because where else would luck be, if not in the great starry gears of the universe? So. Was the universe trying to tell her that today some major luck was on her way? Or was the universe kissing her good-bye, because today, her ass was toast?

Beyond Makeup, a high fence crowned with razor wire. Through a gate in this, she emerged into the perimeter of the set wall. Arrayed here were banks of bleachers facing that gray barrier. These bleachers stretched at least a quarter-mile. Climbing to a seat in one of the upper tiers, Jool felt ridiculously gaudy and flamboyant in her purple sweats and makeup. It went against all her instincts to go into danger so brightly flagged. The other extras seemed to feel the same, looking a little stunned in their new identities, tat-less and wigged, stripped of the selves they'd evolved for survival in the Zoo. Their insignias, scars, and badges of toughness all latexed and tinted and glad-ragged away.

The scale of this whole operation made it more frightening. The set was a city, nothing less. Heavy traffic ran along outside the wall: tech crews in electric carts, tractors hauling flatbeds heaped with props, maintenance trucks with booms or cherry-pickers or painters' spray tanks tentacled with multicolored hoses—all streamed in and out of ports in the vast set basement. Along the front of the bleachers, four little platforms, and beside each platform was a tractor coupled to a big cage shrouded in tarps—an arrangement that doubtless had to do with the demonstration of the APPs they would be facing during the shoot.

Big prison vans were parked at either end of the bleachers,

flanked by squadrons of heavily armed Metro. Once the APPs were revealed, defectors from the contract were to be expected.

"That there's one humongous hellhole to be goin' into wit' no one to stand your back, babe." This from the guy beside her in a suit and a blow-dried head of black hair. She had to squint to recognize the goon who'd sat in the makeup chair next to hers, getting his neck tat latexed over. "I mean I'm bad," he said, "but even *I* would'n' mind havin a' ally in *there*."

Had this guy caught the makeup man's murmur, or read Jool's walk in the same way?

"Really?" She batted mascaraed eyelashes innocently. "So why you wanna team up with someone small like me?"

"Hey. You look sharp, quick. It's about speed in there, *alertness*."

"Oh! And here I was thinking it was about havin' someone handy you could throw to an APP to get yourself out of a tight spot. Or havin' someone team with you for a bonus that you could rob for her share."

"Hey, you a real cynical nasty ho, you know that?"

"Whatever. Just run your scam on someone else an' stop talkin' to me, fuckhead—I'm tryin' to concentrate here."

"Hey, dude, *I'll* take you for an ally." Something familiar about that voice. It was a guy on the other side of the goon, another white guy of about the same size, but even stronger looking. She blinked when he winked at her, and then recognized him. Under the green spike hair and earring of an early punk, it was one of those 'Risers from last night— Japh.

"First, though," he was telling the goon, "you gotta show me you know somethin' besides shit. See those big metal armatures mounted on that set wall every hundred yards or so?"

"Metal *what*?"

"Like big metal plates with bulges on them?"

"Yeah. So?"

"You know what they are?"

"Damn if I know, an' damn if you know either."

"I do know, 'cause I *read*. See, reading is this thing where you run your eyes across printed words and get *information* from them."

"Hey, listen you fuggin' sissy—"

The goon had lifted his fist, but suddenly it was bent high up between his shoulder blades, and his torqued joints were emitting grinding sounds. "Whaddaya think," Japh asked conversationally, "should I cripple this for you?"

"No." A muffled groan.

"You sure?" A slight increase in the grinding noises.

"Yes!" Much shriller.

"OK, but since you insulted me, find a different seat when I let you go."

The guy had to sit way down front—the bleachers were almost full now.

Jool asked Japh, "So what are they? Those armatures?"

"They're holo-generators. All the set's streets dead-end at the wall, which has got to spoil a lot of the camera shots. So at the dead ends, all the streets are continued in holo out to a vanishing point. This is very bad news for an extra with an APP on his tail, booking it for that next cross street and bam! The holo won't fool the APP, it's on infrared. The APP just jumps in and chows down. And the studio still gets the close-ups from the APP's cameras."

"Great. So what's the defense?"

"I dunno. I'm hoping on the run-through to stay near the perimeter, and identify the streets that have to be dead ends. Try to memorize the holos."

This sounded smart enough. But the run-through, they knew, lasted forty-five minutes, and there loomed the set in its hugeness. Jool considered this big white guy. He could handle himself—he'd shown that last night, as well as just now. Seemed sharp and informed. Could she trust him? She'd known him for a total of maybe an hour. What were the odds that he was just a much smarter version of the thug he'd just ousted? She felt no vibe of this off him. . . . On the other hand, he *did* know that she was probably armed with a micro twelve-gauge. . . .

Thing was, as she studied his eyes, she found she just couldn't distrust them. What lay behind this instinct? Wasn't it precisely . . . the kiss that Curtis planted on her cheek? It seemed so stupid, but there it was, and somehow it felt absolutely sure to her. No goon could fake a kiss like that, or would even think to, and Japh here seemed truly tight with Curtis. . . .

The demonstration was at hand: little go-carts were bringing studio personnel to the speaker platforms next to the shrouded cages

"So," said Jool, "did your friend make it here? Curtis?"

Japh grinned at her. Something in his eyes joshing Jool

about her and Curtis. "You know, he didn't tell me he was coming, but I think he's here."

"You spot him?"

"No, though I've been looking. But I think I heard him—down at the tube station."

"*Heard* him?"

"Yep. I'd know old Curtis's voice anywhere."

"So you're gonna try to find him."

"You bet I am. We're natural-born allies. Wanna join us?"

I **stood up** in the bleachers—a lot of people were standing, looking for partners they'd got separated from—but I couldn't spot Japh. Damn small chance anyway in a crowd of thousands, and who knew how they'd dressed him? They'd put me in a security guard's uniform, but they hadn't messed with my hair, so he might be able to spot me, if he knew I was here. Had that really been him I heard, and had he recognized *my* voice?

All these stacked heads, acres of them in strange wigs and hats. I felt sorry for them, sorry for us all. All studio property now. There were plenty of thieving, even murderous scumbags here, but the vast majority of them were people who just hustled any way they had to just to stay alive. Now they were about to do the most desperate hustling they'd ever done.

But here came those good folks on *our* side, the Actors' Union reps in their little go-carts. Our rep was a babe, dressed very Zoo to show she was one of us. In fact all four of the reps who climbed onto the platforms were just about the only ones who did look Zoo here, and they probably had houses in the foothills. Our honey wore oiled snake-locks bagged in a sheer sheath and dragon tats coiling down her one bare arm. I could see her tinting them up in the mirror this morning in her house in the hills.

"Are you down widdit, players? Ready to get rich?" A real cheerleader, this one. Her voice came out of speakers embedded in the bleachers, so that while there were four simultaneous spiels going on, hers was easy to follow. Her rah-rah pitch roused some sneers from our sector.

"Hey Zoo-momma, what's *your* hood?"

"You a ho fo' sho, Hill-meat!"

"Walk us the walk an' *then* talk us the talk!"

Well, she'd *tried* to be nice. Now she got out her script and started to read, chilly and brisk. "You are entitled to one read-through. No information will be repeated." That produced a perfect silence—awesome in a crowd so huge.

"First, note the following characteristics of the set, which we have examined and found to meet contract specifications. Eighty-five percent of the street doors will open to you. Forty-five percent of *these* offer a viable form of refuge, though you may be required to *secure* these refuges.

"A wide variety of structural elements in the set—trees, fire escapes, powerpoles etcetera—may appear to offer a means of escape from pursuit. Forty percent of said props have less load-bearing capacity than they appear to have. Be warned, that the Anti-Personnel Properties, hereafter termed APPs, in *Alien Hunger* are, despite their mass, very effective climbers.

"The set's props include a large number of tools, implements, and furnishings that appear *usable* as defensive or offensive weapons. Only thirty-three percent of these will stand up to the stress of actual use against the APPs. The set contains more than nine thousand *actual* weapons, most of them firearms. Fifty percent of these are viable, but only fifty percent of *these* can be considered adequate for defensive or offensive use against an APP with regard to their caliber and/or the number of rounds they contain."

The bleachers were quiet as a tomb through all of this. Practically no one here had sat through a lecture half this long in his whole life, but right now we were all a bunch of straight-A students. The three identical but slightly out-of-sync spiels running to either side of us gave eerie emphasis to each dismal stat. Thousands of street-smart brains were rabidly tearing down the numbers. Doors: most would open, one out of three were dead-end traps. Climbing: don't do it unless you flat out have to. Grabbing things to fight back with: test them first, except guns, which might have only one round if they aren't dummies.

"You must be cautioned regarding the set's many *vehicular* props. The set contains more than eight thousand motor vehicles, of which four thousand are robot vehicles, identifiable by the animatronic drivers behind their wheels. . . ."

It went on. You could take refuge in a robot vehicle, but at some point it was going to start up and get into a wreck. Other vehicles you could actually drive, even kill APPs with, but none of these had much gas. Meanwhile, a live ammo air battle would be in full swing and falling structures, crashing planes, and major explosive debris would be everywhere.

"Now we come to the APPs. The Anti—"

"Wait! What about questions!?"

"Yeah, I wanna ax about—"

A general roar of urgent queries erupted. Each rep touched her wrist-pad, and they resumed their readings at an increased volume. Everyone went dead quiet—no one dared to miss any information.

"The APPs also meet contract specifications. They are no faster than a healthy human being running at full sprint. They *are* capable of five-meter leaps, ground to ground, though they can change direction only slightly in midleap. They . . ."

The tarp at one end of the shrouded cage parked beside our rep began to bulge from within, and there was a muffled scuffling sound. It wasn't planned, because our rep broke off and looked around, while the other three kept talking.

"Each APP weighs one hundred and sixty kilos," she resumed, "so while they are well adapted for climbing, even up some sheer surfaces, their climbing speed does not greatly exceed that of an agile human being."

The tarp swelled, strained, and burst open, and out jumped—a dog.

A big shaggy blond one, really big, with a yard of pink tongue hanging out and a seriously wagging tail. He took one look at our bank of bleachers, and sprinted right toward it.

Pandemonium. Screams at first, and then roars of laughter as it climbed into laps and started licking every face within reach. All the other spiels stopped, while a touseled-looking tech in a blue jumpsuit hopped out of the same cage. The union reps started conferring on their wrist-coms, which the speakers still broadcast:

"What the—?"

"Hold up till they quiet down."

"Tell Bill to get that sonofabitch—"

Then the speakers cut off, while good old Bill waved his apology at the reps and went after the dog.

The whole crowd, a quarter mile of people, was howling: "Come on Bowser, show us a five-meter leap! Hey Fido, climb up a wall for us! Whadda they do when they catch ya, tongue ya to death?"—while the handler produced a leash and threaded his way up through the tumultuous crowd.

The dog had waded halfway up the benches, taking a full bath in all the pets and hugs. He was in dog heaven, a hundred hands patting him at once, kisses and baby talk, people touching noses with him. Bill was having a hell of a time reaching him, and nobody in the bleachers was helping any.

We were *all* taking a bath in it, this comedy, this total harmlessness. We were milking it for all it was worth. But the chill was already coming back on me. This little moment of doggy warmth belonged to a world different from the one we were about to step into.

It was fine for old Bill. He'd have a nice little breakfast after the demo was done, slip Bowser some of his bacon under the canteen table, get ribbed about the comic incident, and laugh sheepishly. Just another day at work for him. Christ, a *job*. If any of us meat-sticks had a job, we wouldn't be here.

Bill caught Bowser at last, excuse-me-ing his way back down the bleachers, everyone giving him plenty of humorous mauling and obstruction on the way. He dragged the dog back into the shrouded cage.

The bleachers were still alive with a soft roar of talk. A mishap. Fallibility in the mighty studio. Could it mean there would be other chinks in the studio's arrangements? We'd just seen they could drop the ball, right? Any gaps in the grid of their iron percentages were gaps we might dodge through.

All the speakers came back on, and the reps were four-barrelling us with the same almost synced message. "Attention. Attention, extras. The presentation will now continue without repetitions. The APPs detect you by infrared sensors of considerable efficiency."

Utter, instantaneous silence in the bleachers. Utter attention.

"Eighty percent of set walls, partitions, and doors are penetrable to their sensors to a degree that allows them to detect you through three layers of cover. If, for example, you have placed a street door and two additional interior walls between yourself and any APP, your signal will still be readable, though at a reduced intensity. A given APP will always pursue the strongest signal within its radius. Bear in mind too, that APPs are distributed throughout the set, and an APP may be present that is separated from the position you have chosen by fewer partitions than those you have put between yourself and your point of entry."

Our rep gave a little unconscious preening pat to her snakelocks here, pleased by how well she had delivered those complex clauses. What a cutie! A world away from the world she was sending us into.

"The APPs are also equipped with vibrational sensors. In sectors of high activity, they are relatively ineffective. If you take refuge in quieter areas, however, you are advised to be mindful of your movements and their impacts against floors and walls.

"Now, as per our contract with Panoply Studios, you will be given a chance to view the Anti-Personnel Properties with which you will be dealing today."

Another flutter and bulge of the tarp covering the cage. The silence of the bleachers was like a hole in space, the vacuum sound of thousands of people not breathing.

And out from behind the tarp jumped . . . Bowser again! On his leash still, with Bill at the other end. Wagging his tail in joy at rejoining all his new friends.

There was a gasp and a growl from the crowd, almost the beginning of new laughter, but it was swallowed in silence once more. Because all down the line, *other* Bowsers jumped out of the other cages, all on leashes to guys jumpsuited just like Bill here.

The silence was getting deeper, as understanding dawned. All four handlers clipped their ends of the leashes to little ring bolts set in the runway, and stepped back—well back—from the tethered animals.

For a long moment the dogs sat there obediently on the pavement, their tails wagging, their noses glinting hopefully toward the crowd staring down at them. And then, the tarps on the cages bulged again.

TWO RAFTS, TWO PILOTS

Panoply had a basement arena—a sizable sunken concrete pit—where payboat techs could practice the use of their APP drivers on "live" specimens. Kate came staggering out of it after her near-death confrontation with one of *Alien Hunger*'s robotronic nightmares. She limped out toward the locker room, head down, face burning with shame. Sandra Devlin watched her go . . .

. . . and a short time later, stepped quietly into the locker room doorway, and stood watching Kate as she showered. A graceful, long-limbed, athletic woman, crouched and huddling in the hot water's stream.

Physical daring came naturally to Sandy, but she understood this woman's shock. Kate had been raped by terror—had been pinned beneath death, and had clenched herself so tight and small in her desperation, struggled so hard to vanish, that her body was no longer her own when she returned to it. That complete cowering had metamorphosed her into someone who now felt too large, too awkward to move normally.

Sandy felt a touch of remorse, but she'd *had* to push her hard, had to know. Margolian was putting two assistant directors into a boat in her sector. They could well be a plant, and there was just too much riding on this shoot for her and her allies.

It was pretty quickly clear that Rod couldn't be acting—he was just too transparent. And as soon as Kate agreed to the APP driver test, she was cleared too, to Sandy's way of thinking. Only someone genuinely demoted and dispossessed could be so easily stung by Sandy's challenge. No director still sure of her job would get into the pit with an APP.

The test had gone just as Sandy thought it most likely would. While explaining the driver's patterns to her, she could feel Kate wasn't really absorbing it, was too hypnotized by the confrontation just ahead. When she stepped into the pit, and the steel door closed behind her—when the *other* door opened and the APP rushed out, Kate lost almost all self-command. Keying wrongly from the first, she made it rear back, but then immediately launch forward—made it pause, but then accelerate toward her. When it charged, she panicked, and fumbled the driver till it jumped out of her hands. Desperate, she fled to the wall, ran into it hard, slid down and cringed. If the guy at Control had been half a beat slower . . .

Sandy approached the shower. "Lighten up, Kate. So you pissed yourself. So what? It just shows you were paying attention."

Kate straightened, and stared at her. Sandy found herself liking her stubbornness. "You've got nerve, Kate. You stepped in there. You faced it. And you *know* something now, don't you? With nerve you purchased knowledge. You know what it's like, or some of what it's like, to die that way."

"Do you . . . Do you think I need *you* to tell me that?"

"OK then. You know, and what you do with it . . . that's your business. But I'm your sector chief, and I take that seriously. You're one of mine, and I *protect* every one of mine, but—"

"Do you mind if I get dressed . . . *Chief*?"

Sandy laughed. "Sure. I get carried away . . . not that you're not cute like that, Harlow."

"Fuck you, Devlin," said Kate—but with the hint of a smile.

Sandy got her a jumpsuit while she toweled off. "I've got your back every second I can spare, just like all my pilots. But Margolian's *batshit* to be putting you two down here untrained. You've got to be alert every microsecond to everything at once, including air-battle debris."

"I will. Believe me I will. I don't think Rod will be much help."

"Exactly. You've got to be the brains for you both. Like that jumpsuit?"

"Yes." And Kate did like it—light, flexible, as tough as hide, limberly padded at elbow and knee. "It feels like you could take a tumble, dive, and roll in this thing."

"Now you're thinking right. Now you're thinking crash, and it does happen, Miz Harlow."

Kate found there was another thing she liked: Sandy's icy blue eyes. They looked straight at you, and if they liked you back, they showed you that just as plainly as they showed their anger. "I think," she said, "that I owe you a thank-you."

Sandy smiled. "You're welcome. You know some shit now, because you had the spine to look."

"There's one thing I do know. I haven't been demoted. I *quit*."

A big grin from Sandy. She looked like she was just about to tell Kate something, but thought better of it.

They slidewayed up to the top of the payboat techs' compound, the roof of which was a flight deck covered with payboats and prep crews. Rod was waiting for them by their raft. His antidote for the humiliation of wearing a pilot's jumpsuit was to scan the set with an abstract, critical air, scowling at this or that imperfection, and to pay as little attention as possible to the two women. He'd rejected with scorn the idea of getting into an arena with an APP, recoiling even more from the affront to his dignity than from fear, Kate suspected. She jabbed his arm, and announced, on impulse, "Hey, Rod. I blew it on the driver. APP almost nailed me. I was so scared, I pissed myself."

She asked herself why it felt so good to tell him this. She watched the changes his face went through. He looked of-

fended, then looked as if she were insane, and then looked
. . . irritated. *He* hadn't done anything scary enough to
make someone piss themselves.

Rod got in the pilot's chair, the women standing on either side of him. Sandy gave them a rundown on the pilot's
console, with its battery of monitors and control panel.
"This is your hover ceiling, key's flagged, see? Hit it and
you jump vertically to ceiling at a hundred klicks per.

"When you want to surface fast at an angle, say you got
some air battle debris, a chunk of a building slanting down
at you, you hit one of these vector keys at the same time
and angle out at max speed."

"Spare me your bullshit," said Rod. "You're not scaring
me. We have the blast schedules for our sector. Random debris hits don't happen."

"Wrong. Industry-wide, a total of seventeen boats went
down last year as a result of debris, and three were Panoply's.
Eighty percent tech fatalities for those crashes too. Let's hit
ceiling and scope your sector. Run-through's in less than
twenty minutes, and then we can practice pay-dives with
people on the ground.

"Fire up the monitors, Kate. We'll practice correlating
interior shots with the buildings."

Rod hit the ceiling key, giving them a taste of the boat's
impressive acceleration. This craft made a bit more noise
than Kate usually associated with payrafts; the enlarged
suck-vents for counteracting anti-grav meltdowns hissed no-
ticeably.

The whole set was a huge eye, designed to suck up, from
every angle, the mayhem that was going to fill it during the

shoot. Payboaters, besides watching the streets and rooftops for tag wavers, had to comb all this footage on the monitors for kills in progress indoors and out, so they could *anticipate* tag wavers, and shorten payout time.

It was tricky, integrating close shots on the monitors with the big physical sprawl beneath them, but Kate quickly developed the knack, her director's overview of the set a big help.

Rod wouldn't play. When Sandy tapped an image, and said, "Show me," he would point somewhere at random, sullenly refusing to be tested by his social inferior.

"Roddy," Sandra said briskly, "let's have you practice pay-dives while Kate keeps working the monitors. Hit that skinny sucker, mid-block." She was referring to a narrow street dead-ending at the set wall and flanked by six-story apartment buildings.

Just as they dove toward it, all the set wall holos came on, and suddenly the cul-de-sac stretched on for miles, over-arched by freeways in the middle distance. Unfazed, Rod smoothly hit hover at payout height, seven meters. "Good, Roddy! Little bit more of a swerve as you go down, though. Tuck into the street more lengthwise—it gives you more approach to the guy on the ground. Now dip your prow at least fifteen degrees, otherwise those guys down there are lobbing their tags straight up. Good. It gives them more to aim for, see?"

"Hi, kids!" It was Val Margolian, on the console's com. They all looked around, then up. There was his big director's raft, the Showboat, way up there, maybe two hundred meters above them. "Sandra," he smiled from the com, "I'd like you to give Kate some time on the stick too. Let them both get the whole experience."

"Oh, I'm testin' 'em both, Mr. Margolian. Best man pilots!"

"Great! Enjoy, guys!" His raft banked slightly so they could see him wave down at them, and he moved off toward center-set. They all traded a look.

Sandy smiled. "I guess he wants you to really get into the part. Once run-through starts, we'll practice zeroing down on a running target—an essential skill. Having the extras on set is a big help, helps you time your moves just right."

Was Kate actually going to be *doing* this? Catching tags and dropping cash into the carnage? Here she sat practicing for it, like one of those animatronics in the robot vehicles, an automatically responsive cog in Panoply's huge apparatus.

Why didn't she just com Val and tell him? She quit! Willingly renounce all her ambitions. She'd seen, and felt, the extras' side, and suddenly saw her whole ten years' climb within Panoply's hierarchy as a fly's ascent of a great corpse.

But she'd already closed to herself that quick escape; she'd already embarked on the only kind of reparation she could ever make. *These* extras she could join on the front lines. These she could struggle to serve and share risk with, for the first and last time in her career.

She thought of the kindness she'd always seen in Val, his infallible gentleness with every one of his army of subordinates. He had risen by his own guts and vision through nearly forty years' absorption in his art, and his thoughtful respect for all around him never flagged.

But how did he *process* what he was doing? What did he

think at heart about paying a volunteer army to fight death on camera? He had hurled her down from heaven for daring to excuse him but—amazing this had never come to her before—how did he excuse himself?

And in that parting smile of his . . . hadn't there been a touch of merry malice?

Val Margolian's monitor console had ten times the spread of Kate's. Its arc of screens wrapped around both sides of him in his pilot's chair. He liked to do here—and was a wizard at doing—exactly what Kate was practicing on her much smaller console. He liked to give just the briefest glance at one of the hundreds of interior cam displays before him, and then instantly pick out below him the building that housed it. For him, the point was his complete mental possession of the set. The self-testing never found him at a loss. He reveled in his mastery of this intricacy. It was like having X-ray vision.

His creation! This whole huge fate machine! He went up to the air-battle ceiling, four hundred meters. All the tech rafts were beneath his survey now—little swarming chips threading the black rivers of the streets, as busy as pond life under a microscope. Up in this slice of the sky, Val's only company were the widely deployed robot aircraft, home team and aliens, parked here and there in the air: Val's pets. His hurlers of thunder and lightning.

Kate Harlow. Amazing, how deeply she'd galled him with her *forgiveness*. The moronic Rod's crudity meant less than nothing. But Kate. If he hadn't seen her talent, her unerring editor's touch with a scene of any kind, she could never have stung him so. She was gifted, but she was old Hill money, and she had squeaked at him from her hilltop of social ignorance. *He* was Zoo.

Oh yes, born to the Upper Middle, a tax attorney's son in one of the first 'Rises—but thanks to that classic strong father–artistic son clash, he'd rebelliously entered the real world, and *possessed* it. Was one of the first private-contractor teachers serving the Zoo's ambitious youth, taught a screen-writing class in the old Dorsey High campus deep in the Flats. At night he worked on his own scripts with unremitting self-discipline. The income was "derisory"—his father's word—but it didn't matter to Val. He wanted to share the world's horizons with the trapped, the embattled.

But it wasn't his three years teaching that truly made him Zoo. That solemn initiation came one night, when a street gang set upon him and another teacher as they walked from the classroom to their cars.

His colleague was crippled for life. Val received five broken bones, the most severely damaged of these was his jaw. Received too, throughout this skillful, *studious* mauling, a sneering sermon on 'Rise-meat arrogance, and a merry prospectus of each break before they inflicted it.

That terrible beating had made him an artist, an acolyte no longer—that beating, and his father's look of pity and disgust on his one visit to Val's hospital room. He began a new work, his devotion to it absolute. He wrote it left-handed, lying in traction. Abandoning all the trendy themes he'd tackled theretofore, he wrote the life he himself had chosen, wrote himself and his fellow teachers, wrote the good, brave, uncomplaining students who sought light in the dangerous wilderness around them, wrote the demons of ignorance and hate that assailed them. *School's Out*, he called it. In the penultimate battle—a siege of the school by a street gang—one teacher strode out to the barricade, and dared to preach light and compassion and community to the wolves. This speech, and his violent death by beating that followed, were still, a whole generation later, called classic by the critics.

Val's uncle had a friend in the studios, Jack Tyrone, then Panoply's head. There was the luck that rewarded true art, art from the guts. Tyrone, an exquisitely cultured gay man, instantly recognized in *School's Out* the birth of a whole new genre of compassionate social realism. He lifted Val straight up to writer-director before shooting even started. *School* exploded the charts. And Val never forgot, through all the chart-breakers that followed, what Tyrone had said to him after they'd viewed its rough cut.

"It's perfectly, powerfully balanced art, Val. That last act!" In this, the surviving teachers, with their fight-savvy students, daringly penetrated the gangs' infernal compound, and in blistering battle, slaughtered its troops to the last man. "That last act is flawless," Tyrone told him. "It will be utterly seductive to the privileged sector of the audience, which will recoil from the populist compassion of the first two acts. It will completely win them to the picture."

Jack Tyrone, at his death, left Val a significant shareholder in Panoply, and the six-hundred-pound gorilla of its writer-directors. By this time Val had made four more record-breaking SCATs—Social Compassion Action Thrillers, all of which bled for the Zoo, and made the Zoo bleed in beautifully balanced measure.

But Val nourished a growing grievance with the genre he'd invented. In his vids, the retribution on the killer class was merely wishful, and wholly impotent. In the real Zoo, the gunmen always had their way. The good could escape them, but never beat them in battle. His work celebrated nobility, but left broken justice in its grave. . . .

Then, one afternoon, on the set of *Chop Shop*, a crash-cage broke loose in one of the vehicles of the big road-war closing scene, and the stunt driver was killed. The driver was a big, smilingly insolent man named Crack. His face was reminiscent of a profile Val had glimpsed among his assailants, on that long-ago night.

Crack was Zoo, like most stuntmen, and as they gurneyed the corpse past Val, he thought of the scuttlebut that Crack, on his own time, drove for the Ag Raiders—wheeled convoys of plunderers who raided and robbed the Ag-worker Zone. So. This one film of his, at least, had literally killed one of the criminals who made life hell for the rest of the poor.

Like an electric current, inspiration entered Val. Fatality releases were a common instrument in the new corporate globe. They were practically universal for the armies of Ag-workers surrounding L.A., who glutted the labor market, making them powerless to resist the new "liberalization" of labor law. Employer liability for disease, damage, or death incurred in the course of voluntarily undertaken employment was now nonexistent. Meanwhile, Panoply had just inaugurated its first squadron of anti-grav camera rafts with the shooting of *Chop Shop*. These might allow the filming of an *actually* lethal conflict on the set. . . .

So what about a real Zoo shoot-out on his next flick? "Live action" he could bill it. All volunteer, and who else *would* volunteer, even for big survivor bonuses, but gunmen and killers? Film a hermetically sealed kill-off of the worst of the worst? Cleanse the Zoo, even as he chronicled it.

Turf War was two years in the making, two years in which Val grew at last into himself: a world changer. He'd had to shoot three wars before he was done. In the first, his rafts received so much fire from the extras themselves, that the whole fleet had to be armored and armed. After the second shoot, the deficiency of camera angles was revealed, to be solved with more sophisticated in-set cameras. . . .

They went three hundred percent over budget, and netted three billion in the first two weeks of release.

Long before *Turf War* was in the can, Val had jettisoned the self-deception that only the violent would die in it. All three extra calls had brought hordes. He'd studied every frame of every shoot: half the extras were just terrified amateurs gambling for a better life.

He'd grasped the true scope of his discovery, and in *Last Gasp* had wholly embraced it. No social theme was needed— that was embodied in the extras themselves. They were themselves the global truth he brought to every screen: a standing army that would run for its life, would kill and be killed, for a place in the sun. He was able to turn to sci-fi, because the story scarcely mattered, save for its skill in evoking passion in the viewers, and desperate ingenuity in the extras. From then on, his story was always the world itself, to which he held up a mirror.

As now he gazed across the set of *Alien Hunger*, Val's

heart exulted. "Just look at it, Kate, you silly dilettante! Don't you *see*?" How could the woman praise this set as rightly as she had, and not grasp what it was? World changers always reshaped what lay to hand. For Alexander, it had been the phalanx, for Caesar, the legions. For us, it's the media, and the mass mind it creates. The awfulness that was about to fill this set would add one more nightmare to that mass mind, plant one more seed of outrage at injustice. And Val would keep on planting nightmares till they shocked the world awake.

The blameless always died. Within the legions and among their foes, the guiltless abounded. Whole hosts of them fell in every battle. Kate hadn't been wrong when she said he gave them a quest and a glory. For the fated ones, death was not met in some squalid alley out there in the endless Flats. Here the Zoo's long hardship was accelerated into one swift delirium of risk and reward, their deaths gathered into a cultural happening, their souls sent up like incense from an altar of truth.

But *glory*? Did she think him so self-deluded that he didn't know death was just death? A terrible wrenching-out? He gave them a chance to die in an ecstasy of awareness and effort—to die at full throttle. That was all.

Kate had actually gone down into the APP driver test pit—they'd commed Val the vid of it. Did she still think of glory, now that she'd huddled beneath that monster? Before he'd learned that, he'd toyed with repatriating her to the director's sphere. But she'd chosen to embrace the extras' point of view. She had betrayed the sacred directorial objectivity he had particularly schooled her in.

THE RUN-THROUGH

The bulge in the tarp was pointed, and brief, like someone in the cage was poking it with a stick and then retracting it. "The Anti-Personnel Properties are set at full speed for this demonstration," our rep was saying. "You will see them execute two short runs, and two leaps. Notice the arching of the rear legs for the leaps—if you have an APP in pursuit, it's a useful cue to change direction, as the APPs can change their own direction only slightly in midleap."

Again that pointed bulge in the tarp, a testing touch. And then the tarp exploded, and out jumped a spider bigger than a man.

It stood poised on the pavement, bobbing slightly on the crooked cage of its legs, looking tight with power as a steel spring. The sunlight glinted on its spiky fur, on the cluster of its black eyeknobs, on the black fangs beneath them. Flanking the fangs were two shorter legs that dabbed at the air like hideous fingers twiddling, palpitating the heat signal from the tethered dog.

It rushed forward, tickle-footed, light as a dancer. Fast! About fifteen feet from the dog—now yelping and straining at the end of his tether, nails scrabbling on the concrete to get away—came the bowing of the back four legs, and the leap.

It was a shiny blur in midair, and then it was on top of Bowser, seizing him in its front four legs, sinking its fangs into his spine.

A bulge formed under the fur around the fangs. Bowser struggled wildly, until the bulge spread out over his back and he stopped moving.

"The APP injects a paralytic combined with a powerful solvent, which is quite rapid in its action, and then drains out the solute. The entire operation takes less than five minutes."

Bowser hung there tremoring slightly—and then began to swell, and the tremors died out. The spider shifted its grip, and sank its fangs into his midsection.

"Please take note of the APP's eye cluster. All the eyes are camera lenses, and any one of them is a valid tag that can be immediately redeemed by any payraft in the sector for a hundred and seventy-five thousand dollars in cash. They are detachable with a firm pull. The studio recommends selecting one of the larger eyes as being easier to toss more accurately up to a raft. All the eyes are coded, so don't bother trying to get paid for a tag from someone else's already-killed APP."

Bowser wasn't swelling now. He was beginning to shrink back down as the spider tilted him this way and that, inserting its fangs now here, now there, the fangs sucking, not pumping.

"The studio advises you that if you manage to strip a tag from a still functioning APP, it is redeemable at full value. For your own safety, though, they remind you that these are not the APP's actual eyes. They are merely recorders of pursuit footage, and feeding close-ups, and stripping them in no way impairs the APP's infrared or vibrational detectors."

Bowser was shrinking faster and faster, shriveling right before our eyes. All his bones showed now, he was a skeleton tightly wrapped in fur, his lips shrunk back from a grin of stark teeth. The spider turned him once, twice more, as if testing his weight, and then dropped him. His husk made a dry, rattling sound on the concrete. The spider spun, and rushed back toward the cage.

"You will note a slightly diminished speed. After repeated feedings, an APP's feed-load reduces its speed significantly, though it remains quite dangerous at close quarters."

It leaped back in through the tarp. If that jump was any slower than the first one, I couldn't see it.

"You will now have your run-through of the set." The speakers sounded in the deepest silence yet. All of us were far inside ourselves, asking ourselves *Am I really going to do this?* "Please enter the coaches now pulling up to take you inside. Good luck to all."

But another movement had already begun in the bleachers. Everywhere, people were standing up, working their way down through the crowd, and heading to the left or the right down the runway, toward whichever cluster of police vans was closest—surrendering themselves for arrest, climbing aboard the paddy wagons for their ride to prison. Hundreds of them!

"Ten years, my ass! They'll do two or three max—all the joints are too jammed." I recognized the voice of Cap, my tube buddy. There he was, sitting just below me. He was wigged in a 'fro, and his wide, rubbery grin showed white teeth now.

"They must be losing five, six hundred people here," I said.

"Yeah. Biggest walk-off I ever heard of."

"Hey," said a woman in a fast-food uniform next to me, "they turned away people at the gate, but not before they took in a thousand meat-sticks more than they needed. They planned for this, man."

"Yep," said Cap. "Extra extras. Makes you feel down-right *superfluous*, don't it?"

We tried to be cool. Tough talk like ours was going on all around us, but there was a second conversation raging in the bleachers at the same time, a shadow conversation of silences, pauses, hesitations, a layer of dead air pressing down on us, always on the brink of snuffing out our voices. And in this unspoken conversation, all of us were asking the same questions: *Why am I still sitting here, not running for my life* now, *before it's too late?*

I don't know about everyone else, but what I held on to was Japh and Jool. When the coaches pulled up, and we were told to board them for the run-through of the set, I knew that wherever in this mass those two were, they weren't backing out. They were getting up and filing down into their rides, and that was the only reason I did the same, the only thing that made it possible for me to move my legs in that direction.

On my coach, everyone scrambled for window seats as we got on, thinking we'd go straight on the set and get some orientation, see where the walls were, have some shred of preparation for when we were all brought back for the shoot. But we drove down a ramp into a tunnel under the set, and followed a long curving course between concrete walls.

"You didn't think they were gonna let you get *oriented*, did you?" Cap sneered.

The driver kept varying the coach's speed too. We weren't even sure how far in we were, let alone the direction we'd followed, when we took a branch ramp upward, and rolled onto the set from the exit of a parking structure.

I don't think any of us had ever seen such a silent city before. All around us it towered motionless, its windows flashing in the sun. Robot cars and robot people were everywhere, their frozen faces grimacing behind windshields . . . frozen, yet seeming as charged with potential motion as dynamite. Because once they were all switched on, we, the hired population and the city's only true life, would begin struggling tooth and nail to stay alive in this giant machine constructed expressly to kill us.

Roman gladiators might have felt something like this when they first stepped into the Coliseum. Brought in from some desert on the edge of the empire, how they must have stood staring up at the grand high walls. All this, built to catch our deaths!

We stood there gaping at the sky. Its upper reaches were densely populated with aircraft. Nearest was a big raft maybe twenty meters up, which began to lay down a mellow voice upon us, a canned spiel in a suave, laid-back tone that said we were all in this together.

"Good morning, extras, and welcome to the set of *Alien Hunger*. Here are the rules governing all Panoply set runthroughs. Violation of any one of them is punished by an automatic five in slam, we repeat, a half decade in state walls."

Other sectors of the set were getting a synced readout from similar rafts—you could hear a faint overlapping of echoes. Everywhere, between the burnished glass towers, down the wide streets glittering with frozen cars, we, the brand-new population of this brand-new place, were hearing its laws.

"You were all subcutaneously tagged with micro-emitters during makeup. If you try to hide on-set after run-through, your hiding place will be instantly known on our monitors and you'll be taken straight to the prison vans. Immediately at regroup, you must step into the nearest street or boulevard for raft-guidance back to a transport. Here is the regroup signal."

A long stately trumpet riff rang through the golden air—

it was baroque trumpets, like something from Handel, incongruously beautiful. It seemed to be . . . a kind of mockery, considering what we were going to do here.

"At that sound, robot traffic will be stopped and you must come into the streets at once. If on the run-through you find useful implements or weapons, you may smuggle them off set with you if you use reasonable discretion. If we don't see it on a visual search, you can keep it. But you may not do visible damage to the set property to obtain something. You can do that during the shoot itself, so make a mental note of what you want to come back for.

"During run-through, the robot traffic will be running at full speed. It won't be set on collision, just circulating, to give you a realistic preparation for the street hazards you'll face, but it *will* collide with you if you step into its path. . . ."

As we looked up at the speaker raft we also studied all the layered air traffic above it. Lowest were the payrafts, most at about seven stories height—trim little boats, most at hover, but one of them practicing approaches and shallow dives. "Practicing pay-dives," said Cap. Quite a few of them up there, and millions in cash aboard each one—each one a quick-flying wedge of the proverbial Pie in the Sky.

Above the payboats was a more ragged layer of tech rafts scooting back and forth for last minute touch-ups and adjustments to the set—these were bigger boats, some with jutting tow bars and hoses and hydraulic arms, fixing a wall with a burst of spray-crete, touching up signs with airless rigs. . . .

Highest of all were the robot fightercraft at hover. This layer represented a potential avalanche of hot debris, cannon-bolts and building wreckage, random death-from-above while you were busy ducking and dodging the death on the streets. Some of these were squadrons of Late Twentieth jet fighters, and others sleek, scythe-winged rigs that had to be the alien forces.

All that lofty traffic up there, their ventilators humming just barely audible, all of them bathed in the morning light! Lord, I yearned to be up there, to belong to that high sunlit part of the world. Oh, to be able to fly above these streets, to be part of the crew! Oh, not to be down here on these mean, *mean* streets!

And as I stood looking up into the sun, it occurred to me that the wall holos might not have this early morning sunlight in them—might be lighted for an hour later, when the shoot would be full pitch. "Hey, Cap. Maybe the sunlight in the wall holos is out of sync with this stuff."

He looked down at our long shadows, and caught on instantly. "Look down there. There maybe?"

Down one of the streets radiating from the park, the more distant blocks did seem to be bathed in a more vertical light than the early sun was actually radiating. . . .

Suddenly a semi-tractor hauled a huge cage on a flatbed out of the same parking structure we'd emerged from. And the laid-back voice from the sky was saying, "Please don't be alarmed if you see any APPs being brought topside. They will of course remain caged throughout the run-through. We wish you now a profitable tour of the set you'll be working in today. Please do be alert to that robot traffic. Run-through will commence in ten . . . nine . . ."

Through the countdown we were all silent, staring at that cage, which the tractor drove onto the raft pad and parked in one corner of it. Fifty of the huge spiders swarmed all over the floor and the chrome mesh walls of the cage. The sunlight flashed on their polished black fangs, on the black diamond knobs of their eyes. From their seething restlessness it seemed they were set on search and destroy. Why? Why were they trucked out here at all, except to rattle us right down to our bones for the run-through? Get us shook and spoil our look at the set.

God how I hated the studio shits who had worked out all these details, these little touches—because some suit *had*, had suggested them to his suited chief who said, *Yeah Ralph, I think that's a great idea!*

Man, those spiders were real—nothing mechanical about them. Or rather, they had exactly that hideous fluid mechanicalness of real bugs, all those joints rippling in sequence, all that springy power. . . . One thing that looked familiar from nature vids was a greeting ritual they kept going through whenever two of them confronted each other. They immediately started wiggling their short legs, touching their palp-tips together when they faced off, and after a few seconds of this communication, wheeled away from each other. It made sense. If these were set on hunt to scare us more, and their motors gave each of them an infrared signal, then they did this identifying riff to avert mutual attacks.

". . . two . . . one, go!"

The noble trumpets sounded, the frozen traffic in the streets roared to life, and we all scattered—Cap and I sprinting down the street whose more distant blocks looked wrongly lighted.

. . .

Kate was piloting now, finding the raft very satisfying to drive, much more acceleration than she'd ever handled, very tight on turns. When the horn sounded, they watched a flood of extras radiating from the plaza below.

"Slant down to ten meters along Division there," Sandy told her. "Slant down fast and glide to stop just short of that wall holo."

As Kate swooped down to the hoverpoint, two black extras—one in a security uniform, one in a 'fro—ran right through the holo and vanished inside it. After a moment, they came running back out, looking purposeful. They'd found the wall, and now were going to run to the next street parallel and follow *it* back to the wall, memorizing as many as possible of the holos that hid the fatal dead ends.

"Poor fuckers," said Sandy cheerfully. "How have you suits calked it out again? The odds against their finding their way back during the shoot to the area they ran through are thirty to one, is that right?"

"Higher than that, I think."

"Oh, what a miracle you have wrought!"

"Enough with the bad mouth!" barked Rod.

"Shut up, Roddy. Do pay-dives for me, Katie. Go up to hover and we'll practice fast deliveries at my call."

"If you think," Rod persisted. "I'm not gonna be in a position to pay you back for your—"

Sandy's reaction so startled Kate that she almost yawed the raft going up to hover. The wiry little pilot sprang like a cat at Rod and with a roundhouse swing clanged him in the face with something she'd snatched from her belt. Knocked him right off his feet with the unexpectedness of it.

"You will *shut—the—fuck—up*! Or I will Tase your ass right off the edge of this raft and say you jumped! I will land us right now and fire your ass and have you dragged off set by security! I will stomp your face to oatmeal! You will shut the fuck up and do exactly what I *tell* you to do! You get up here, stand your station, and *mark* me." Slow and sullen, Rod took his post at the bow.

"That light there's your blip. Green flash tells you the tag's real as it's tossed aboard. You mark?"

"Mark."

"You drop your packet the *instant* it blips, and you drop it accurately. You mark?"

"Mark." A stubborn growl. A total kid here, thirty-five years old. You could *see* him thinking it: *I'm gonna get even with you for this*. Not getting it. The freckles were like fire on Sandy's face, her pallor almost incandescent with anger. She got an inch closer to his face, Kate holding them at hover, feeling the air as brittle as glass around the three of them.

"I hope you do mark, because if you don't do exactly what I tell you, I am going to . . ." A longish pause, in which both Kate and Rod heard her unstated threat as clear as a bell: *I am going to kill you*.

Sandy took a deep breath, marched back to Kate. "Dives, woman! Slant me down to that bag lady, sharp and tight. Paymaster, stand post!"

Kate stopped almost dead above the animatronic street-person, and got even tighter with each succeeding dive, beginning to feel a comfort in slinging the raft. It was a total concentration kind of task, and she welcomed the distraction it offered from what, all too soon, was coming.

"You're the shoot pilot, Kate," Sandy said after a couple more dives. "That's final. You pay out, Rod, and pay out right. Pick your own targets and practice at will now."

A murderous look from Rod at this decision. He was denied even the manly job of piloting!

For Kate, the assignment gave her something to hold on to. She could channel the horror of the shoot through her task. While this calmed her a little, she was beginning to feel a new anxiety. Sandra Devlin. For all this sector chief's cool irony and control, it was dawning on Kate that the woman was vibrating close to homicidal frequency. She was radically enraged, and barely masking it.

I'm going to kill you.

Not said, because it didn't need to be.

Sandy made Kate do dive after dive, then pull up to hover, then speed to a distant street and dive again. It was hypnotic, with all those crowds swarming the sidewalks and darting through the robot traffic. Every street was seething, people searching and probing—all this onrush, while everywhere Kate looked in this landscape, her director's overview recalled to her the precise survival projections and all the little death traps in detail. Her empathy went out to Zoo-bred toughs, so nimble at darting around corners, at shinning up powerpoles and fire escapes, diving into hardware stores for weapons, checking car doors for refuges. All that nerve and agility. All that doomed energy!

. . .

Jool and Japh worked down opposite sides of each block, checking doors, scoping interiors. As a team they could process a lot more environment. The odds were low that on the shoot they would find their way back to anything here, but they could learn at least the kinds of possibilities and traps the set offered, could find weapons they might smuggle back onto the transport, and just might find Curtis too. They shouted out his name at every new turn. They took turns ducking through the traffic to regroup at the end of each block.

Dodging between these cars, Jool noticed, behind the oncoming windshields, that the faces of the animatronic drivers were grimacing, contorting in expressions of terror and panic. Because, of course, they'd only be filmed for close-ups just before they crashed.

"An apartment building lobby," she panted to Japh when she gained the opposite curb. "No catch on the street door; you'd have to brace it with your body to keep something out. Staircase leading up to a walled dead end. The door to that deli would shatter at one good hit, but there's solid chairs in there you could club with." As she spoke they both stared at the building in question, struggling to imprint it on the long shot they'd find it again.

Japh reported in turn. "A whole floor of opening rooms in that hotel, but all the furniture and doors are balsa wood. The tools in that hardware store look real but the door's a dummy—maybe the plate-glass window will break."

He darted through the traffic, and they started working down the next block. Amazing how few voices they heard— the talk of teams like theirs so rare. In their silence the roar of the traffic and the hum of the rafts' ventilators overhead loomed too large, as if the living people were already ghosts, and only the set's mechanism was alive.

And when they came to the end of another block, Jool, catching Japh's eye across the street, shouted her report to him for all to hear, pointing back at the two buildings she'd just checked out: "Four inside rooms with good doors and solid furniture! That other one's a death trap!"

He caught on, bellowed back, "First two floors of these apartments are real, but no catches on the doors. Some metal lampstands heavy enough to fight with! Liquor store's a death trap—blind walls and no solid props!"

And they kept doing it, not crossing the streets between them anymore, shouting stats at top volume, trying to get something going.

Come on people, let's share a little, it's us against them.

And it *did* begin to catch on. Here and there people coming out of doors shouted out what they'd found to the street at large. You wouldn't say it caught *fire*. Everyone was still thinking Zoo, and several times after someone had called out a death trap, they saw other people rushing right in, assuming that the call was a ruse to keep others from finding a good refuge or a cache of possible weapons. The stupid assholes! Given the odds, what could they *lose* by sharing? Better to be somewhat *together* when the shit hit the fan.

Before too long though, as they were all getting down to short time, the shouts began rising thick and fast. People just trumpeted everything they found to the sidewalks at large. An embryonic sense of cooperation began to spread. It gave

Jool an inspiration, and at the next crossing, she shouted out, "Japh! Japh! Curtis! Curtis!"

Across the street, Japh caught on instantly. "Jool!" he bellowed, "Jool! Curtis! Curtis!" Why not increase the signal, in case Curtis caught only part of it?

Curtis didn't catch it. But when Japh roared Jool's name twice, someone else stopped in his tracks: a small, toughly skinny extra, dressed as a gangbanger in Nikes, baggies, basketball shirt, and sideways baseball cap. Chops froze like a hunting dog, his ears seizing the sound. *His* Jool? And more than that, he thought he'd heard, just before, the fragment of a *woman's* voice that might have been hers. . . .

Chops hadn't wasted a minute of the run-through on anything but scanning the other extras, and then finding other groups of them, and again, scanning faces, profiles, postures. . . . As the run-through clock ran down he'd been fighting desperation. If he didn't find her now, he *would* find her during the shoot, but it would be so much better if he could find her *now*. *My life for yours*. His heart beat it out.

Chops sprinted across the street, hooked over a block . . .

There! It was her hair that snagged his eye—they hadn't disguised it! That was Jool's hair, beyond a doubt! Lavender sweats, a little belted pack on her butt.

Five seconds later, Chops was twenty feet behind her, and tailing. If she knew he was with her, she would be watching out for *him*, which was the opposite of what he wanted. He was going to be the angel at her shoulder, scoping the whole zone around her at all times; hanging back to cover her. If she knew he was there, she'd increase her danger by worrying about him. . . .

The mellow trumpets of recall made their regal music. The robot traffic froze in the streets, and the rafts dropped down low and began shepherding the extras toward their collection points, where the studio transports awaited them. A digital display of pulsating arrows lit the flanks of the raft above. Japh, Jool, and the unsuspected Chops followed its promptings. Its pilot's amped voice welled out above them: "Please proceed at once to the blue beacon for re-loading. Exit all buildings at once, and proceed to the blue beacon." One of the lampposts by a small park two blocks down bore another pulsating a bright blue light.

As the crowd converged, Chops, not to lose her in the thickening crowd, got within ten feet of Jool. A big white guy was conferring intently with her as they walked.

Jool was sharp, but in case she'd picked a treacherous friend, Chops was going to be watching this guy very closely—and he was going to be watching *out* for him too, if it turned out that he really *was* standing Jool's back.

A big section of the park's lawn slid back, and three transports emerged from a tunnel mouth. People began boarding. All Chops had to do was stay close enough to her, now a couple of people ahead.

She and her friend were up the steps . . . then Chops was up behind her. He kept his face turned away as he sidled to a seat just back of her and her partner. He'd done it! Against long odds, Chops was where he'd prayed to get to by this point.

Chops knew a shoot survivor. The poor woman was still

in the Zoo, her nerve to get kill tags had failed, and she'd survived by hiding out. Her survivor's bonus wasn't enough to get her away to the mountains. From her, Chops had learned that after the run-through there was no more shuffling, that the transports went under-set, circulated, and came back up to deliver their loads at new locations for the shoot. So he *had* Jool now, and from this moment on, nothing on earth was going to make him lose her. *My life for yours.*

And then, Chops saw a tall skinny man in a suit and tie sit down two seats ahead of him, and he caught a flash of profile that made his heart stop cold.

Was that . . . ?

Here came another flash of profile: the squashed nose and little knobby cheekbones, the spit-pale eyes that makeup hadn't changed. . . .

It *was*. It was Kite.

Chops himself had squashed that nose with a desperate kick. In a dark dirty corner of the laundry room in City. The smells of detergent and bleach and stale sweat and stinking breath flooded back into Chops's nose. The kick hadn't done Chops any good, because of the three other guys holding on to him. Hadn't done him any good at all, hadn't kept them from clubbing him half-senseless, from ripping his jeans off. . . .

Chops's heart was beating now, all right, each beat hammering his ribs like that kick with which he had hammered Kite's face, that kick that Kite had made him pay so dearly for.

It was terror that drove Chops now. The sudden terror that, after all his desperate effort, he might fail Jool. He'd thought that nothing on earth could separate him from her, now that he'd found her. But how could he have imagined *this*? Because now, if he followed *Kite*, Chops had the chance for a revenge he had been craving for five long years. If he followed *Kite* instead of Jool, he had the chance to feed Kite to a spider.

Chops had a carbon knife taped to the inside of his thigh. Once he'd seen the APPs, he'd all but forgotten it, and thought it hardly worth untaping. But now . . . Now the knife burned his skin. He wouldn't kill Kite with it—that would be too merciful. But he could *capture* him with it.

All Chops could do now was pray that when the shoot started, Kite would run in the same direction as Jool and her partner. Because if they ran in different directions, then Chops, God help him, wasn't sure it was Jool that he would follow.

The transport's door hissed shut. A moment later, they were humming through the fluorescent light of the tunnel under the set.

LAST-MINUTE PREPARATIONS

"**Shoot minus ten** minutes," said the console.

"Sector-boat C, roger that, mark shoot minus ten minutes," responded Trek, wiggling two fingers at Lance. Lance, his co-captain, licked down the joint of tobacco he was rolling, and fired it up. A few tokes were Lance and Trek's preshoot ritual. In the roofed sector airboat, these indiscretions were safe—and likely tolerated if they were seen. Sector-boat captains tended to be young hotdogs—former payboat or Metro pilots upgraded by Val Margolian for their expert judgment of anti-grav piloting. They watched their sectors for rafts in trouble, spotted incompetence in payboat, tech, or

Metro flight performance, and lately, were particularly on watch for what Val called "sabotage."

Trek hit the com button to the Metro rafts. These were Lance and Trek's minions for sector control during the shoot. They hung in the air, six little Metro cruisers to each side of their command boat. The whole formation hung just above and outside the set wall at the edge of Sector C. "Attention Sector C Metro," Trek transmitted to his minions. "Shoot minus nine minutes, fifty-seven seconds, mark."

Their com crackled back: "Metro Alpha. Roger that, mark shoot minus nine minutes, fifty-five seconds."

Trek clicked off, took the reefer from Lance, and sucked in the healing nicotine fumes. Lance pointed to one of their screens. "Here she comes."

That screen was focused on an empty payboat, into which Sandy Devlin had just stepped. She cocked back on one leg and, with offhand accuracy, threw a slow sidekick at her console, punching the needed buttons with the tip of her moccasin, while beckoning impatiently to someone off-screen. "Man," said Lance. "She's a vid to watch. All 'tude. Pull back."

Trek clicked the screen to a longer shot, now showing them a piece of the pad, several other payrafts prepping for launch, and Sandra's paymaster stepping on board her raft with his hefty payout satchel in one hand.

"She's using Radner this time," mused Trek, exhaling thoughtfully. "If she was runnin' something, you'd think she'd keep the same partner."

"Hey. It just means there's a *lot* of people in on it, and

she can rotate her partners in crime." Lance said this in the tone of one who presses a long-standing argument.

They both watched Radner set the satchel on the counter in front of the raft's monitor banks, and begin counting out the cash in front of Trek and Lance's cams. Neither young man paid the least attention to this close-up count-out, standard operating procedure. They were watching their other screens focused on Devlin who was boredly disattending to the whole transaction, and—still from a sidekick stance, was activating the readouts for her systems check with the darting tip of her foot.

"Man," chuckled Trek. "She must have thighs like rocks. So what's your call? I think she's definitely dirty."

"Yeah, she's laying the casual on too thick. She's amped, and she intends to kick some serious ass once the APPs come on and the rafts hit air."

"Absolute. So I just gotta ask. How's she *doin'* it?

"Look at that balance!" enthused Lance. "See that jump-turn? She's a belt for sure."

"Could kick *your* ass sideways."

"Only because I couldn't bring myself to hit her!"

"You *know* she's runnin' something—just look at her body language. She's telling the cams, like, *Up yours, Panoply! Eat my feet!*"

Now Sandy recounted the stacked packets back into the satchel—all this for the HQ screens that the co-captains weren't bothering to look at.

Trek and Lance were buff, in tan HQ jumpsuits, with the rad barbering of the young. Trek's baldie was waxed, and his only hair was his 'bones, two precise triangles of beard on his cheekbones, dyed orange. Lance's hair was trim except where it was pomaded into a short-horn, a three-inch spike projecting above his forehead. They sat smoking, enjoying Sandy Devlin.

"What'd her file say?" asked Lance, their eyes not leaving the screen.

"She's thirty-five, gay, made sector chief in two years. Best fuckin' rafter in *any* studio."

"That's a hot thirty-five. And all nerve, if they're right."

"If it was just the stats, I'd say *if*. But look at her! She's a flamehead. Born to make trouble."

"Hey. You gotta admire that."

"Absolute."

Sandy's raft, and two dozen others on their screens, were now lifting off and moving toward shoot formation above the sizable wedge of the set that was Sector C. Lance hit drive, and their boat rose straight up to hang a hundred meters above the set wall. Their dog packs of Metro rafts rose in unison with them.

Sector-boats stayed off camera to monitor their payrafts, and sent in Metro at need. They only entered set air on code reds. The set was a minefield of cameras; roofs, walls, lampposts, pavement were studded with them. The bottoms of the payrafts, which had to stay above the set at all times, generated a microwave shield that made them just blips in the video record, which were easily edited out. The HQ sector-boats got all the rafts' input on their screens, so they could almost always hang offsides and avoid adding their mite to the editing chore.

"Trek? Lance? Val here, guys."

Trek thumbed the com. "Hi, boss. We're locked and loaded, Val." Val Margolian indulged a special informality with his watchdogs. HeadQuarters sector-boat crews weren't union—they traded that for their much higher salaries. They had the same balls-out ethic as the pilots they policed, and Val liked to flatter them with a Special Forces kind of patter. He called them his top guns.

"I want you boys really bird-dogging Sandy Devlin on this shoot now, even if it means neglecting the others a bit."

The young men traded a grin. "We're doing it already, Val, as per your memo. She's a piece of work at the controls, boss—we've never seen slicker flying. So far everything's SOP—systems check, payout count. She's at position now, and is taking reports from her fleet."

"That's a point of particular interest, guys," urged Val. "Every communication she has with the other rafts is important. Keep her on zoom, and at max volume—put a dozen monitors on it. Every move her hands make, every word she coms to another pilot. We're looking for sabotage, and if you watch her closely, you're going to find it."

"Copy that, chief. We've got her scoped to the eyelash. If she kills any APPs, we've gotta see it."

"You're my fastest guns, guys—that's why you're on her sector. I'll leave you to it."

"Roger that, Val."

"See?" said Lance, when Trek had clicked off. "Val thinks what I do—she's got a lot of people runnin' this with her."

"Hey. How not? Average length of employment here is five point two years for those rafters. Five years watchin' people die for a living." A pause here, a quick slanted glance at Lance before adding, "It's gotta get to you."

Lance gazed blandly through the windscreen out over the set, absently sharpening his horn with tugs of his circled thumb and forefinger. "Five years at that pay, a lot of them must already have the down on a nice little house in the Hills. It's a good fuckin' job. *This* is a good fuckin' job. You and me could put together the down in another two years." He was still gazing out over the set, grooming his horn.

"Whatever," said Trek after a pause. "So. How the hell is she *doing* it?"

"However she's doin' it"—they had not ceased to watch Sandra Devlin on their monitors as they talked—"it's something slick and bitchin'. Look at her. Pure 'tude."

High above everything, even the poised robot fighters, Val Margolian began guiding his raft through a complex horizontal pattern. Convoluted curves, loops, spikes . . .

Val was skywriting. His keel was inscribing invisible letters on a big page of sky.

His whole body knew the moves as if he were a single stylus inscribing the atmosphere, and a clock in the back of his mind timed the turns flawlessly. He knew that an actual smoke trail would show his letters to be perfectly sized and spaced.

Val *knew* what Devlin was doing. Did she think that even the tiniest detail of his productions, his vast canvases, escaped his eye? That she thought she could deceive him simply proved that all fanatics were ultimately stupid. They believed that sabotaging achievement bestowed achievement on themselves. Had Devlin been capable of grasping what art was, she would never have dared to betray him. Art was nothing if not a mastery of detail, a capacity to possess it, comb it, weave it.

Performance stats. Val had first detected Devlin's subversions in the performance stats—in a statistical desert she could never have imagined him personally exploring, would have assumed he left to some drudge in Human Resources. Reviewing these, Val had noticed that for the last four shoots running, Devlin's raft had the shortest kill-to-payout interval in the whole payboat fleet. Two shoots out of four might just be talent. Four out of four was passion, obsession. There was no pay-grade reward for this kind of obsession with paying extras fast. Everyone hustled, but if an occasional extra with a tag happened to get APPed before he could redeem it, it was, after all, just the gamble of the genre.

So Devlin's passion, obviously, was to minimize the risk extras ran coming out into the open to get paid. Her passion was intense *com*passion for the extras, a very problematical symptom in a payboat sector chief, especially one who was, like Devlin, a habitual union troublemaker. She had that something hard and ironic in her eyes, her combative face long a standout in Val's encyclopedic memory.

It set Val's intuition humming. The on-shoot destruction of APPs and gross payouts to extras had been on the rise for a while, nothing major, but definite. Val told Properties to work up a profile on APP kills by set sector. . . .

Bingo. In the last two shoots, Devlin's sectors' kills were the highest by 12 and 17 percent, respectively. He was both angered and intrigued. It had never occurred to Val that payboats might start *helping* the extras kill APPs.

If Val had bothered to share his conclusion with any of his upper management, they would have thought it—though not dared to call it—a pretty wild conjecture. But Val had only to picture Devlin's ironic eyes, that grim little smile of hers, to know otherwise. He had told only the two HQ captains of sector-boat C. Those cheerful young yahoos wouldn't question it an instant—it was too much fun to believe it.

Once they did nail Devlin, they would have to be terminated. Val didn't want the details circulating in the studio. Devlin would of course be terminated and jailed, once her method and her accomplices had been discovered.

Val steered through the double arch of the last letter, a cursive "n."

It was written—a vast, invisible "Margolian." It was what he always did just before the shoot—sign his canvas. It was arguably more logical to do it just *after* the shoot, but then there would be far too much uproar, too much to oversee. This moment of serene exaltation was better. The shoot *was* accomplished, after all, had all been foreordained by the intricacy of his design.

ACTION!

When the transport techs ushered us aboard after the run-through, there was no way they didn't notice me limping, or notice what looked like a spare tire wrapped around Cap's middle under his shirt. Studio seemed to think whatever weapons we smuggled off set wouldn't make much difference on the shoot. Or maybe it was policy to let some of us come out armed, make some of the opening shots more interesting.

The transport hummed through fluorescent-lit tunnels. I felt a lot of eyeball on me. Anyone who looked like he was luckily armed drew that. My right leg stuck out the slightest bit into the aisle because I had the haft of a fire ax down my pantleg.

The fire ax had a spur on the back of the bit that kept digging into my hip under my uniform's tunic. I didn't mind the pain at all. I felt more than lucky. This ax could chop the legs right off an APP.

Cap and I had been leapfrogging interiors right at the end of the run-through. In the lobby of an apartment building, I saw that I'd run right past the glass case with hose and ax. I high-kicked that glass to pieces, and seized the ax, feeling its blessed weight. I ran out and called Cap. He unspooled some of that hose—thick canvas, heavy brass nozzle—and I chopped off twelve feet of it. My ax bit through the canvas and *thunk*—sank deep into the floor. My arms tingled with the stroke, tingled with hope for survival. With that swinging nozzle Cap could back up APPs, and I could move in from the side and start amputating.

. . . A lot of eyeball on *both* of us, we began to notice. We'd need to watch out for fellow extras. . . .

The transport bucked into a climb. A section of the ceiling slid back and sunlight poured in ahead. Jump time. You could almost feel all the sphincters tightening.

We surged up out of the lawn of a little city park.

"Please exit in an orderly fashion. You will have six minutes before the APPs are released and the air-battle begins. The port we have just emerged from will be an APP release point. Good luck to you all." The doors hissed open, and people spewed out like a human geyser. We hung back, getting armed. I gripped the ax handle overhand at neck and heel, set to punch out with both ends, not expecting any room for a swing. Cap paid out just enough hose to use the nozzle like a sap.

"Go out like a cannonball," Cap gritted, and we did. I led with a heel kick, which someone dodged. He grabbed my leg, slamming me down. I flopped over and shoved the ax's spike into his foot, rolled, and jammed the head up into someone else's groin, then wrenched around and swung the bit at some legs. I heard Cap grunting and bones cracking as I scrambled to my feet. We were standing back to back, three wary goons crouched at a slight distance. I was one big torch of adrenaline. I screamed "Die!" and went for one of them. No feint. I was trying to chop his leg off. He saved himself with speed, though I did bite a bloody little divot out of his side as he dodged away. Two others still hovered, the ax too good to give up on, until I heard the crack of the fire nozzle behind me, and someone shrieked, "My knee! You fuckin' broke my knee! How can I *run* now?!" The rest took off.

We sprinted down the street and turned up the first narrow cross street we came to, where the robot cars were sparse. The sidewalks swarmed, people trying every door in sight, some trying doors of parked cars for the magic few that would run. The near silence was eerie, a city full of silence around all this fever of movement.

"Spears," I said. "Long stabbers to kill 'em as they rear up. Impale them as they strike down at you, remember how they struck downwards?"

Cap said, "Yeah! We need a refuge with strong wood in it, door frames, floorboards, that we can chop out and make into spears."

"What's that?"

People were clustered at a shopwindow, and kicking at the glass. The crowd grew like fire, every new arrival launching furious side-kicks up at the glass. "It's some kind of eye-grabber, likely to be a trap," I said, but we were both sprinting toward it, no *time* for second-guessing, each heartbeat gnawing away the seconds till APP release.

A gun shop. The plate glass shuddered and splashed down before we reached it. The people poured through. We jumped in after them, sliding and teetering on the slippery shards. Various improvised clubs were exploding the display cases, people wrenching rifles off the wall behind the counter, people flicking out cylinders, working slides, thumbing clip releases, the words "empty" and "ammo" rising from the hubub. The silence of the streets outside was like a drumbeat, a tolling bell, and our babble of voices began to struggle for coherence, teamwork. "There's the cases on the wall!"

"Don't smash too hard, don't scatter the shit!" Tough, wired glass, frosting and dimpling with the blows, not giving.

"I got an ax, lemme in!"

"Let him in, he's got an ax!" I chopped right near the frame, shearing through, blinking away glass dust. Hands grabbed at the ragged flaps and ripped them out bleeding.

"Call it out and throw it, first ones loaded stand the door!"

"Call it out and throw it! Twelve-gauge!" People were pulling out boxes and others making room for them. We were becoming a team, Cap had a shotgun and thrust a forty-five auto at me, heavy and real. The slide worked. No clip. The ammo-grabbers were calling out calibers.

"Thirty-eight! Twenty-two! Thirty-eight! They're *all* thirty-eights and twenty-twos!"

New turmoil, people diving for the smaller pieces they'd scorned at first, others pouring into the big back room to search for more ammo caches, everyone shouldering and elbowing, hands scrabbling amid broken glass, a few people squirming out of the melee here and there clutching pistols and shouting "Thirty-eight, here! Here! Twenty-two! We'll stand guard!" Ammo boxes were sailing, fingers fumbling shells into cylinders and clips. I'd shoved the forty-five in my belt, taken the ax to the pine-paneled walls, and bit into real wood. It was tongue-and-groove. I tried to split it at the grooves, use the axspike to pry planks out that Cap could grab and wrench free. We were getting nothing but big splinters, but with one plank out I could get behind and lever the next one from the studs. It came off with a groan. I split it at one end, Cap wrenched the splits apart with a twist and got a long sharp piece, gripped this and propped the other piece on the floor so I could chop the narrower end to a point.

Thoom-whack-crackle

Thunder boomed in the sky, and the robot cars out on the street went into motion. It froze us all for an instant, then a kind of ripple went through us. Like one compound body we all felt the same rush of baffled adrenaline: *run*— but where? We were a potential team, but could we defend that gaping window frame with a few pistols?

A scream and a tumult came from the back room. Five people tried to bolt out of its doorway at the same instant, jammed tight in the frame, and sank under the weight of a spider crawling out over them. It bloomed out of the upper door frame like a hideous blossom of fangs and crooked, furry branches. It took a short leap from its human launching pad, and pinned a guy who had turned to bolt but slipped on glass and fallen—pinned him right through the chest with a crackly sound of pierced ribcage. The guy's scream trailed off to a squeak as his midsection swelled. Above the polished, pumping fangs, eight black eyeknobs glittered at us. Camera lenses, taking us in. Taking in just Cap and me—everyone else who could move was gone.

Behind the feeding APP, more people came squirming into the door frame, mindlessly jamming it, climbing each others' backs to fill the frame right to the top, but not before we glimpsed other spiders at work behind them, coming in through a hatch that had opened at shoot-start.

Cap and I looked at each other, and agreed that here was opportunity, one monster with its fangs engaged, the others blocked . . . but I was paralyzed and didn't dare lift my ax because it was *watching* me. Death itself was watching me. Who dares attack Death?

A battle cry at my side, and Cap launched himself, ramming his plank point right into that eye cluster. It sank in a foot, and all the spider's legs spasmed and pulled inward. That broke my trance. I screamed and stepped in with ax at full swing—*crunch*—sheared its front section half off its abdomen, releasing a spew of green fluid. "Jackpot! Jackpot!" Cap crowed as he tore an eyeknob off. "We gonna rip the snot outta these bugs!"

The people jammed in the doorway were screaming for help, their hands reaching out. I reached a hand to the one on top, hauled him free, and he immediately grabbed my ax and started fighting me for it. We wrestled over the floor, both with a death grip on the handle, then Cap's nozzle crunched against his skull and I struggled to my feet, as other people squirmed free of the door frame and hit the ground running for the window. And from the space they left a second spider sprouted, climbing over the human jam.

Its abdomen was wedged. It wriggled with a terrible machinelike strength, freed a fourth leg, then a fifth. . . .

But by that time, we'd reached it with our stakes, piercing its fore-section through the underside. "Hold it!" I shouted, taking up the ax. Cap hugged both planks impaling it, pushing upward to keep the fangs out of reach while its legs flailed like whips, raking us with their clawed tips, clubbing my head and shoulders, tearing my scalp. I got the ax up and swung the bit in between two of the joints. As I sheared halfway through the fore-section, the legs died.

I got all I had behind a second swing, and sheared its thorax clean off. The eyeknob I plucked and pocketed felt like ice, like solid diamond.

A glassy scrabble behind us. An APP swarmed in from the street through the window frame, sunlight flashing on its fur, on its eyes so greedy for our images. In the seconds it took us to wrench our stakes free, it was upon us. We were both off balance, and stunned by its speed. My stake caught a leg joint and Cap's caught another, just enough to tilt it and twist its lunge aside. With a swerve and a rippling of legs it was launched again, now at Cap. My thrust caught its abdomen as it passed, but the plank was snagged and torn from my hand.

Cap was stumbling back, his stake point parrying but getting no purchase. I got my ax, swung wild, and sheared off one back leg.

It wheeled on me and I jammed my ax between its fangs, barely fending it off. Cap jammed his stake in its bulb and roared, "Run!" I didn't understand. We'd slowed this fucker radically. But my body, more alert than my brain, hit the floor and rolled hard as a new APP sprang in from the street, its back legs grazing me as it overshot. I was up and we were out the window before it even wheeled.

Explosions in the sky! Shards of blown aircraft like huge crooked sabers whanging and sparking off walls, cart-wheeled down the asphalt, dismembering two extras too slow to dodge. Chunks of cannon-blown building added a stony hail to the mix, a big one killing the APP that was leaping out after us, but right behind him came our other robotronic acquaintance, not as slowed as we thought by his bleeding abdomen. Cap tried the door of a parked car, and—it opened.

We piled in and slammed it shut. It was a big old sta-tion wagon, but had no pedals, no ignition: a dummy, but shelter. Our APP crawled onto the roof, scrabbled and scraped, rocked the car as it planted its legs for leverage. The roof dimpled at two points, there was a *ping*, and two fangs sprouted down through the metal. The fangs pulled, and peeled back a shred of the roof.

"Oh shit. This thing is like *foil*!" Two more pulls had peeled a hole as big as our heads.

We looked around us. Everywhere on the sidewalk lay people trapped by thorny legs, their outflung arms twitch-

ing, tremoring, and swelling up. A jet exploded not ten stories up. Its burning steel knocked the corner off an office
building that crushed two men and the APP that was feeding on one of them. A woman with a spider on her heels
ran straight into the traffic and was hit by a delivery van
that launched her like a rag doll through the air. A robot
sports car ripped past, its driver's face gaping with precrash
horror, and it collided with an ambulance in a geyser of
flaming gas. Metal squealed as the spider peeled another
flap of roof off us.

"We've got to get inside," I said. "Get a wall at our backs
and a fucking *door* we can defend—let 'em through just
enough to chop 'em up."

Another spider reared up from the sidewalk, embracing
Cap's door, and working on his window with its fangs. Fracture stars appeared in the glass. "Your side's the only way
out," Cap said to me.

I looked at the cars whipping past on my left. The traffic was thick and fast, but there were intervals. If I rolled
out at the right moment, I could get across. The traffic was
lethal, but chewing the glass out of Cap's door was the
alternative.

I shouldered out the door and rolled hard, the street mauling my knees, elbows, hips. I hit the centerline and hugged it
as narrow as I could make myself, tires shrieking past both my
ears. I looked up and saw the spider launching right off the
roof for me, and a panel truck smacking it broadside, crunch-
ing its legs and carrying it past. I got to my feet, dove past a
Caddy and down between parked cars as *whack!*—a collision
sprayed metal past my ears and *wham!*—a gas blast blistered

the back of my neck and crisped my hair. I whirled left-right, ax ready . . . and found clear sidewalk both ways.

Cap vaulted over the crashed cars (for a blocky guy he could sure zig and zag!) and down to my side . . . and the second APP swarmed right on his tail, its hooked feet slipping a little on the metal. "Curtis! Fall in behind it!" he shouted. Dodging it, he drew it in, and spun away with it trailing after him, and me after it. I got a good swing, and planted the spike solidly in its abdomen. It wheeled to reach me but I stayed behind it, tearing it again and again, till I slipped in the green fluid it bled, and it arched above me for a strike. Cap came in from the side swinging the nozzle at its leg joints, cracking one, cracking another. I rolled hard right and found my feet, and as Cap slowed it with another cracked leg, I landed a full swing that sheared its fore-section in half.

"Payraft!" we started screaming. "Payraft!" Cap pulled the new tag and both of us waved eyeknobs at the sky.

The payraft came in a sharp dive right to us, bow canted down. We screeched, "Three tags! Three tags!" but when Cap lobs the first tag the paymaster, a buffed blond guy, is still holding the packet.

"Whoa there, cowboys—only one tag per APP!" We couldn't believe it!

"We killed three of 'em, asshole! Pay us!" We had new spiders coming toward us from everywhere, out of windows, one out of a gutter.

The raft pilot actually had a shouting match with the turkey before he dropped us three bonuses. We took off down the only open street.

"We split that third packet, Cap!"

"You bet, Curtis!" With Japh I wouldn't even have thought of saying it. It reminded me I didn't know Cap. The guy could hold the line and fight at your back though, and that was all I had time to know about him.

As we sprinted a whole stampede of other extras collected around us. A new wave of APPs was collecting behind us, jumping and dragging down the hindmost. A glance at the street we were fleeing showed spiders feeding everywhere, human limbs thrust twitching from between the hairy legs that jailed them. Then, ahead of us. No! An identical stampede on collision course. We swerved up a cross street, and slowed down all we dared to get some bearings.

Danger had opened our eyeballs to the max. Hell, in detail, lay down the next two blocks. At the farthest corner a pickup had collided with a fire hydrant. It sent up a big silver pillar of water three stories high, bright in the sun. The pickup's driver lay spilled out the door, a puddle of animatronic blood spreading on the pavement, and a bunch of live extras were hustling a grip on the hydrant, and hoisting its weight. They took it to where a bunch of people up on a fire escape were beckoning them, and lowering the street ladder. In the nearer block, a meteor of concrete blown off by the air-battle had flattened a stop sign, almost snapped its base. People had grabbed it and were bending it left and right, the whole sign moving like an upright pendulum. As we watched they snapped it off just in time and swung it like a big red ax right between the fangs of an APP already launched at them. The fire-escape crowd dropped the heavy hydrant like a bomb, crushing an APP climbing toward them, but not noticing three more APPs crawling down from windows above them.

"The things are pouring out everywhere!"

"It's the ones who hole up," said Cap, "that get nailed. Safer to stay in the open where we can fight and maneuver!"

"But we gotta get some woodwork, cut some more spears!"

"Inside for that then maybe, but just for that!"

Now spiders were devouring the balcony crowd, others on the ground catching those who jumped. "Big groups," I said. "Draw 'em like magnets."

"Let's go!"

We sprinted that block. More than twenty bugs filled it, but all had prey. New ones swarmed out of a cross street as we passed, but just then a chunk of air-battle debris zinged down and scattered them, and we raced past.

I looked back over my shoulder. That whole swarming scene happening around that big silver fountain flashing up in the early morning sun. . . . You had to admit, if you were just *watching* this, that it was a gorgeous shot.

Jool and Japh were a half block ahead of Kite, and Chops was having a struggle keeping them both surveilled, while at the same time watching his own back. They were in residential blocks, where the robot vehicles were fewer, and the first APPs came busy-legging out of the ranch houses or their garages.

Chops was all eyes, all his nerve feelers thrusting out—he would have looked like a bug himself if they had been visible. He saw the APPs cluster after people who ran in groups.

Those extras still clung to the instinctive monkey-need for other backs protecting yours, but that made a much bigger heat signal. Wrong way to go.

There went Kite, ducking into a two-story Spanish stucco house. Hadn't the moron noted these houses were APP ports into the set? Meanwhile down street there, Jool and her 'kick entered another house. They'd be looking for weapons. They had good moves, and the 'kick was definitely watching out for her. They had that double-ought. He hoped they'd thought of getting some kind of poles or planks, making harpoons. . . .

But this, right here, was Chops's golden window for revenge. If he didn't seize it quick, the fool Kite would surely get himself killed first.

Forgive me, Jool. . . .

He crouched by a car parked in the stucco's driveway. There was lots of activity hereabouts. A robot crack-up at the next cross street had flattened a young tree and way too many people had jumped on it, fighting to tear it free while fighting each other just as hard. Three spiders were bearing down on them right now, one overleaping a hurtling pickup and landing right on a guy. Everywhere APPs crouched feeding, on porches or down on the pretty lawns.

All this was mere background for Chops, its only significance that the stucco house seemed clear from attack for the moment. Mere minutes were all he needed. He had no defense against the spiders except agility, but was totally unconcerned with that. For his only aim was to kill Kite, and he knew just how to proceed.

His years in slam taught small, wiry Chops to be a sharp

reader of the machinery that imprisoned and tormented him—the machinery of other monkeys, of malevolent meat-frames with bigger bones and muscles, monkey machinery that could seize him and damage him at will. He'd already killed another of his tormentors while still inside—Trinidad, a *much* bigger monkey. It had taken Chops an eternity of patient planning to acquire the necessary tool. A broken blade from a safety razor. So little! But embedded in a piece of soap for a handle, it gave him a little half-inch steel fang. Quietly into the shower one night went Chops, to where Trinidad stood soaping. . . .

Such peace, such justice in that moment!

His reverie was shattered by noise.

More APPs, announced by the skitter of their hooked feet on the concrete, were pouring into Jool's end of the block . . . but rushing past the ranch house, several doors farther down where too many people had swarmed into a big two-story home. You could see the extras in the windows upstairs and down, rummaging chaotically for usable props, even as the spiders were pouring up the lawn around them. Watching the APPs move, it occurred to Chops that while their engines were undoubtedly down amid the leg joints, their hydraulics must extend up into the abdomen, to give those bulbs the flexible, powerful motion they showed. If he was attacked he would have to try to get on top, where his carbon blade might just cut through the join of fore-section and abdomen, deep enough to bleed the hydraulics and shut down their movement. . . .

He was already moving. Kite must not die without his participation. Chops darted across and up the lawn to the stucco's downspout, and shinned up it to the wrought-iron balcony of a second-floor window.

There was no gain in taking forever to finesse it—he shouldered the window to shards, climbed into a bedroom plausibly furnished, promising-looking floor lamp on a metal pole. He untaped his knife and sleeved it, checked outside the door, then rushed into the hall, down the stairs, shouting.

"Kite! Kite! It's me, Mumble! From City! I reconnized you! Kite! It's me! Mumble! Let's team, man! A tree down outside, Kite, a weapon! Help me get it before someone else does!"

As he reached the bottom of the stairs, he was answered by a voice with a cramped reverb, as if from a closet: "*Who? I'm down the hall here!*"

A utility closet, cautious Kite still inside it, the door pushed maybe a foot open, Kite's squashed-nose profile peeking out, bright and sweaty.

"It's me, man! Mumble, from City. Come help me quick. Tree got a trunk just like a ram, we could make kills widdit! I need your muscle, man! Come on!" Chops rushed right past him, beckoning him after, and out Kite came, pulled by the thread of hope, the presence of someone with a *plan*.

Chops rushed to the front door, opened it and waved him ahead. Kite paused on the threshold to scan the street, and—*snick-snack*—Chops sliced the backs of his knees to the bone: *one, two*. Kite collapsed to a kneeling posture, and Chops dragged him onto the porch.

"Hi, Kite! It's me! Chops! Guy who gave you that nose? How ya doin', big guy? Long time, no see!"

For an instant Chops was afraid he would be paralyzed with the joy of this moment, the perilous intoxication. But his hands, needing no prompting, went right to work. He twisted Kite over, and as Kite's arms reached for him with furious strength, Chops sliced the inside of his right elbow—careful, as before, to cut tendon, not artery. Only dealing with the left arm now, he found this a good extension to drag Kite, down the little flagstone path across the lawn, and onto the sidewalk.

He laid him on his back, stood on his left arm, put the knifepoint in the hollow of his throat, and gave him a big smile. "Isn't this great we ran into each other, Kite? See? It's me! Chops! The guy you fucked with in City? Know what I'm gonna do? I'm gonna feed you to a spider! Way cool, hey?"

Kite was totally bugshit now, screaming and weeping, thrashing like a boated flounder. Now that this was in the bag, Chops was getting worried about Jool—that house farther off than he liked, and every second adding dangers to her situation. He had to tie this up quick. . . .

And his need was answered, almost too well. Three APPs pumped across the street, coming straight for them. They had Chops flanked—his only retreat was back to the stucco house. "Well, enjoy the meal, Kite!" And he bolted, the lawn a blur under him, went up that downspout once again just like a squirrel, his ears savoring, as he did so, Kite's scream, and the crunch of fangs through his former torturer's ribs, even as spider claws climbed the wall beneath Chops's own foot soles.

He was over the balcony, and dived through the window,

to roll and come up by the lamp and seize it: solid metal, heavy disk base, and stout brass branches on top to hold the light bowl. He rammed first the base, then the branches in the wall, punching great holes in sturdy drywall. Both ends were solidly attached! He moved just in time to ram the branches up under the fangs of the APP that surged through the window.

He pinned the fangs up and back against the frame, the spider straddled over the sill, half its legs inside and half outside. He leaned all his weight, stretching the monster backward. Then he freed his right, brought up his knife, and slashed the hydraulic tubes in its midsection. The monster sagged, legs buckling.

He was on automatic: sheath blade; pluck and pocket tag; regrip pole and whirl, as a second spider powered up the stairs and in through the door. As Chops charged it, he noted a rear back reaction in the APP. Frontal assault seemed to cause a raising of the palps and two front legs, a parrying motion. This was very encouraging, if they all responded this way. . . .

The sanity Kate clung to was the piloting itself, the physics of vector and momentum, the swoop and swerve, the raft's mass around her like her own augmented body. She herself was simply Justice, swooping down with Virtue's reward.

She anticipated on the monitors, dove sharp at a tilt so her bows were an easy target for paytags. Looking down on their upthrust arms and shouting faces, she marked their desperation indelibly in her memory. Even when she pulled back to hover, she couldn't help tracking some of them. The bag lady who squirmed right out from under an APP, shedding several of her coats that had snagged on the fangs, bolted, made it clear for a block, still clear, then, acting unconsciously in character, swerved to climb into a Dumpster in an alley, as an APP came climbing down the alley wall the next instant and jumped into the Dumpster with her. . . . The cop who nightsticked an old man running with a cane, stole the cane and ran off with his two slender clubs, cane and nightstick, and left the stunned old man to the APP that had been right on his heels. The cop made the next corner at a wide swing and had a head-on with a robot van jumping the curb.

And here Kate was diving to a double payout, two guys waving tags, and she knew them: the two black guys who had found a wall holo on run-through. The stocky one tossed up his tag shouting that he had two. Here came the first tag into the raft, the scanner blipped it good, and Rod still hadn't dropped the packet. Instead he shouted, "Whoa, cowboy, one tag per APP."

"We killed *three,* asshole!"

"What the hell are you doing?" Kate shrilled. "Catch and pay! They've got incoming!" Rod was unbelievable. He was standing there, still hesitating, not liking the way people were talking to him! Sulking over harsh talk from guys who were an inch from dying! At last he paid out, and the other tags came up, and he paid those out too, still managing to be a half-second slow with each move. Kate, pulling back up to hover, was almost tearful with rage.

"What is wrong with you, Rod? These people are dying

down there! If you want to sulk like an infant, do it after the shoot!"

Rod stood glowering Byronically down on the set. She could tell from his look that he was thinking that from *Kate* he didn't have to take orders. She struggled for a grip. "Rod. You've got to grow up fast or you're going to start killing people. Just give *them* a break for the next few hours."

This swung him around. "Where is your mind, Kate? You're talking like some tech drone, like a *jumpsuit*. We do not *belong* down here. We are assistant directors! This is an instructional *tour* for us, and we are to be treated—"

"Get a grip! You are *not* a director of any kind! You never *have* been! Your *dad* is a studio VP! This movie is *your* concept, Rod!" Here, for a flash, because it came as an indictment, his eyes denied this—telling the truth for just an instant. "It's your pitch, Rod, and these people are dying your way, so just—"

"You have gone completely—"

"Hi, guys! Val here. You riding that raft sharp? You look pretty good from up here."

Kate was already going for another pay-dive toward two guys who'd found a running car and smashed an APP to a wall with it. Feeding APPs were all around them, one nearly done with its shriveled husk in a baseball uniform. The extras had only seconds to cop and run. "You bet, Val! It's exhilarating! It's real!"

Rod was Mr. Clockwork with this packet. The guys sprinted clear just as the one APP finished its meal and swerved after them.

"That's good to hear, kids. Our cast is depending on

you, and I know you're giving them your best. I'll be checking in."

"Bye, Val." And Rod called it too, from the bow—"Bye, Val!" Kate jammed them back up to hover so fast Rod's knees buckled and he swayed in his harness. But their rise was not fast enough for her to escape a photographic imprint on her brain of the image of that shriveled husk in the baseball uniform, the sleeves and legs far too big now for the blackened twigs that sprouted from them. . . .

LET'S JUST DIVE IN, HOMES!

The stars of *Alien Hunger*, Raj Valdez, Megan Ali, and Stone Fox, were in the HQ tower—at the tip-top of it, in the VIP lounge. The floor-to-ceiling windows, only faintly colored by their masking holos, gave them a breathtaking set-wide view. Raj and Stone stood before one of them, while Megan lay on a divan, nervously nibbling canapés. A voluptuous Arabian beauty, Megan's eyes avoided the surrounding turmoil, while the two men stood confronting it a bit self-consciously. Clearly, they were trying for the manly enthusiasm of guys enjoying a bloody fight.

"Whoa!" said Raj. "Look there! Three on two! Ouch!

That had to hurt!" For them, the shoot had been over for a week, the star footage already in the can, so broad-shouldered Raj had already gone back to his half-Zoo look, a tat of a rose on the left side of his face, the ear incorporated in the blossom, which shed one large drop of blood. He wore silver spandex, designed like a skintight version of a pilot's jumpsuit. Stone, taller and more lithe, was black, with beautiful Nilotic eyes. He wore a gold earring, dreads, and tailored leathers. "You got that right," he answered. "Jesus! What a way to die!"

Stone's unconscious sincerity struck a wrong note. It articulated what all three of them were feeling. *What a way to die.* They'd all been shot in close-up struggle with these APPs, the spiders programmed, of course, for a nonlethal choreography of attack, always to end in their own deaths, not their victims'. Even so, all three of them had been under those fangs, jailed in the bristly turmoil of those legs, and for all three of them, never-mentioned nightmares had followed.

They all met, and then avoided, one another's eyes. An uncomfortable silence filled the room, in which the muted air-battle outside, the distant shouts and screams, grew louder. A fourth party had joined them in the luxury suite: Shame.

"God damn it!" erupted Raj. "I want to give them something. Out of my own pocket. I want to give them . . . a *mil.*"

The others didn't need to ask who "them" was. It was the extras, of course.

"OK," said Stone. "Me too. I'll do the same. But . . . how?"

"We're scheduled for an overflight, right? But let's do it in a payraft. And let's do it right *now*! Let's just dive in, homes!"

It took the others a moment to absorb this. Raj and Stone—Megan had declined to be a part of it—were to be filmed in a raft with an attendant cam-raft, overflying the set just before the shoot's end, and for a half hour during its aftermath. It was for the Director's Cut, a revolutionary idea of Val's in its inclusion of a few moments of actual shoot time. The actors would record reminiscences of their making of *Alien Hunger*, following a preprogrammed safe route amid the last phases of the air-battle, then roaming at large, scoping the turmoil of the aftermath.

"Think about it," Raj urged. "Val wants a groundbreaking Cut. But what about us making almost an hour of actual payouts, dodging cannon fire, taking *real* risks."

There was balm for their shame in that last phrase. "Man," Stone mused in awe. "The Cut will go fucking *plutonium*!" But his real awe was for the risk, and the measure of . . . atonement in the deed. "I'm down with it! Yes! Megan?"

"I've already told you all—I'm not going down there. I don't want to *see* what's happening to them. You *know* I never even watch my own vids!"

"I didn't mean that. I meant would you—"

"Kick in a mil? Yes! Yes, I will! And guys? It's brave. It's so brave of you!"

The men laughed, embarrassed. "Com Payout to get the money ready, Raj," Stone said. "I'll com Val."

Val Margolian, one of the great multitaskers of his generation, actually abandoned the orchestration of his monitors to listen to Stone's proposal. It captured his imagination in an instant. He saw it at once as a megaton concept. He'd already considered it an inspiration to include a few moments of actual shoot in the Cut. But this! Almost an hour of payboat-level cinema. The vid's exoskeleton, the vast engine of its production put onscreen, with countless glimpses of the narrative itself seething just below. . . .

The POV alone would be a breakthrough phenomenon, and pure adrenaline for the audience—one cam-raft trailing the stars' payboat, rocketing the audience's eye through dizzying payout dives and giddy up-swoops, with freeze-frame scenes of street-level mayhem as the cash was dropped to desperate demon slayers already fleeing new demons as they reached to the sky for their wealth. Not just Val's vid, but the colossal construction that created it would be the star—the full scope of his genius exhibited.

The subplot would be irresistible: the honor and generosity of the stars making risky reparation for their exemption from danger *as* stars, would at the same time underscore the philanthropy of the live-action vid biz itself. That it lavished millions on the desperate poor was known, but for the first time the actual payouts would be *seen* on camera.

But of course the whole notion was impossible! Outrageous! Such self-exposure would be absolute catastrophe to Val's entire career! Every fiber of him recoiled in terror from the whole wild scheme.

And that was when he knew that he absolutely must go through with it. For this was the terror of genuine inspiration. It was that holy dread that fills you when a whole new horizon suddenly yawns before you. He'd felt precisely this when he first resolved to shoot *Last Gasp*. Then he had steeled his nerve and run with it, and had become the colossus he was today.

Yes. This was absolutely the next frontier. As he had invented this new and greatest genre, now he would invent the next—that genre's breathtaking self-revelation: the full reality of live action. Three months after *Alien Hunger*'s release, while the buzz was still hot, he would release the Cut, unleash the New Wave. It would triple the gross of the vid itself.

Not a second must be wasted.

For an instant, he weighed putting the stars on Devlin's raft. No, that would surely prevent his unmasking her, putting a cam-raft on her tail. One of her coconspirators then. Luce Harms, Devlin's lover.

"Val?" Stone, still on the com. "I think it would really—"

"It's a fine idea, Stone. Your raft and its cam-boat will be at Payout in five. Pick up the cash and go. Time is of the essence."

"Roger that, Val. Thanks."

Margolian commed Trek and Lance in their sector boat. "Hey, guys. You tracking Devlin nice and tight?"

"Tighter than a tick's ass, Val. Five cams on her," Trek said. "So far, all we're seeing is that she's definitely the fastest payout on the set."

"Stay on her. Send Luce Harms down to Payout to pick up a new paymaster—two of them: Raj Valdez and Stone Fox. And the cam-raft for their Director's Cut is now assigned to Harms's boat."

"Serious?"

"They want to share some of their own money with the extras. The Cut starts filming now, and I mean ASAP."

"Roger that, boss."

"Whoa," said Lance to Trek after clickoff. "Way slick! Nice to know Valdez and Fox got some real balls on 'em." He checked Harms's screen as Trek moved to com her. "Hold up a sec. She's diving." Visible just above her bows were a running APP and fleeing extras down on the street she dove to. . . . "Hey! Damn!" he said—and there was her raft settling to payout, one of the extras pulling a tag from a crumpled and squirming spider. Trek looked a question at him, and then commed the pilot.

Luce Harms didn't like her new orders. "Has Margolian gone batshit? I need fast pro payouts. There are lives at stake here!" Luce looked like an Iowa farm girl—even wore two short braids—and had pale green, very decided eyes.

"Orders, Luce. Whaddaya want? He writes the paychecks." She'd clicked him off before he'd finished, and rocketed off to Payout. He turned to Lance.

"What?"

Lance hit replay on Luce's screen. "Watch close."

". . . I don't see anything."

"Look again, up here, just under her bow."

"Like . . . a tiny little flash?"

"Yeah. And look—that APP was pumpin', and five seconds later, she's down and payin' off its tag."

"So you think . . ."

"Damn straight. Don't you?"

A silence followed. Lance thoughtfully stroked his shorthorn. Trek said, musingly, "So whaddaya wanna do?"

Lance looked at him. "You mean . . . whaddaya wanna *not* do?"

Slowly, Trek smiled. "Yeah. That's what I mean."

"Man," said Lance after a moment. "How are they *doin'* it?"

"I dunno, but check the readout—APPs are bitin' the big one sector wide."

"Can those numbers be right? So early?"

"There must be a lotta people in on it."

Sandy Devlin was keeping a bank of twenty screens on open link with a special group of her fellow pilots, and had monitored Luce's talk with the sector-boat. As Luce swept toward the deck at Payout, she looked into an open-link screen of her own, and straight into Sandy's eyes.

"Well?" she asked Devlin. "I'm gonna have a cam-boat on my ass from here on out. When can I fire without being seen?"

"Hey, Luce. Do we really give a shit at this point? We already know how we're getting out."

"So be it, girl. Let the chips fall where they may."

When her paymaster jumped out and the two actors approached, she held up a hand to forestall their greetings. "Just listen, guys. Congrats on what you're doing here, but listen hard. There's your harness. Split it so you each have one strap on your waists, and keep one hand on the grip at all times. You're both a little tall for paymasters, and you're gonna be whipped every which way at high speed. Don't fall out. Second." She pointed at the bulging satchel of extra cash they'd brought on board. "If you're gonna drop extra packets, bind 'em together tight, and drop 'em true. You don't want your gifts killing people by making them scramble for the pickup, right?"

"Right."

"Here's our cam-raft. Here's some ties for the packets. Lemme check that harness . . . OK then. Hold on tight!"

Jool and Japh went warily into the house, her micro twelve-gauge leading, but not by much, Jool keeping well spaced from him, Japh noted, in case he made a try at taking it. Japh approved, she was *alert*.

There were full furnishings in the rooms, but it was all ersatz when touched and hefted, lamp stands all brittle plastic, ditto pole lamps, the promising thick arm of an armchair that tore free as easy as snapping celery, and as light to the hand as a whiffle bat. A knife rack by the kitchen cutting board held only plastic knives; broom closets and utility room were bare. They searched stealthily so they could listen every second, hear the whole hidden interior, for they'd seen how some of the houses were entry ports for APPs onto the set.

When he glanced at Jool she looked so much smaller than he'd taken her to be, as if their danger had compressed her. She had tight moves, as quiet as a cat. Adrenalized, her up-tilted eyes looked bigger, as if they gave her wraparound vision. Her caramel face, sharp little chin foremost, radiated multichannel attention. She was the best kind of 'kick for a big, relatively slow man like himself. He trusted her—she had sold *books* in the *Zoo*. He didn't blame her for not fully trusting him yet—a 'Riser who might not be hard core enough to stand true in a clinch.

On impulse, as they came back through the living room, he tested the one thing they hadn't tried, a slender oval coffee table—and found it *was* wood, light but solid, with stout legs. When he gripped them crosswise, he could thrust the tabletop forward like a tilted shield, a good blocker in a tight place.

"Me first through doorways," he murmured, and she nodded. They moved toward the rear of the house, past two bedrooms, Jool ducking in to check them out while Japh stood the doorway with the table, his senses probing the house. Outside terrible sounds assaulted them—the whip-cracking, zinging thunder of the air-battle; the screams of fleeing voices; the shrieking of tires and the bangs of collisions—struck the house like erratic hail, fierce then light. Japh concentrated on hearing every least sound from the interior. At first this seemed silent, until, as they approached the rear of the building, he began to think that the rooms ahead *weren't* quite silent. An elusive murmur teased his ears . . . When Jool finished with the second bedroom—a head shake—he pointed to the door at the end of the hall and gestured caution.

They pulled that door open with exquisite slowness, and the sound became a faint hum. Jool crouched low, Japh above and behind with his shield at the ready, and they peeked around the door.

A large, sunken den. Two APPs feeding there. The hum was the sound made by the operation of their fang-pumps, pulling liquefied tissue out of a woman in a gardening smock that was rapidly growing too big for her, tenting over one upthrust knee, and a mailman, whose shriveled outflung hand still loosely clutched a broken chair leg.

For a heartbeat, four eyes confronted sixteen. Then the nearer APP, its mailman emptied, leaped straight off him. Japh had just time to think—*not much tissue left in the woman either*—when it exploded through the doorway. Japh had the table up just in time. The fangs punched through the wood. Japh, like a man closing a large valve wheel, wrenched the table a 180 degrees to the right, twisting the fangs in a knot just as they began to spout their paralytic solvent.

"Don't shoot yet!" he told Jool, and pinned the table to the floor with all his strength.

The great crooked legs were like storm-lashed trees, but with its fangs lodged nail-tight through an inch of oak, the spider was pinned, could not quite torque its body free. "Get the tire iron from my belt!" he shouted. "Stab the shit out of its head! The motor's gotta be in there!"

She was already doing it with her knees planted amid the eyeknobs, she was plunging the tire iron, prying and tearing as the APP's struggle swayed and jolted them both. It lurched and shuddered, its movement still violent, but now disorganized.

"Got the tag!" Jool said, scrambling off. "Free the table! Here comes the other!"

He twisted, splintering the fangs free from his shield, and lifted it again as the second leaped for them. But the wounded spider, circuitry tweaked, was no sooner free than it jumped and intercepted its undamaged comrade, unresponsive to the peacemaking gestures of its palps. Locked in combat, they tumbled back into the den in a commotion of legs. Jool said, "Block for me if they come back," and took the tire iron to a door frame, the stout planks of which promised stakes or pikes.

The undamaged spider was backpedaling, trying to disengage, twiddling with its short legs as if attempting some negotiation, but the other, copiously bleeding, was epileptic in its onslaught. It overswarmed the peacemaker, fanged it deep in its eyes.

"They're locked together!" Japh called over his shoulder. "Hurry! We can kill 'em like this!" The noise of creaking and splintering wood increased at his back. "You stand my side and block"—she was beside him now—"and we can save a shell." She had two formidable splinters.

"Find the pump for its hydraulics! The bulb, maybe!"

And her first thrust into the second monster yielded a spout of fluid. She was quick as a jackrabbit. A delirium of movement, and the floor was slick, while the APPs battled slower . . . and slower. Japh grabbed the tag off number two. Silence filled the house now, the traffic and aerial battle outside growing louder.

From the front door they peeked out. The full holocaust had boiled into these residential streets. Next door a caved-in house was like a flaming nest for a crashed jet. The sidewalks and the streets were littered with the shrunken dead and there were APPs in all directions . . . though none within a hundred yards or so.

This suburban zone, in the patchwork layout of the set, was walled in by strangely contrasting neighborhoods. In one direction, bristling 'Rises. Just as close in the opposite direction, shabby projects.

"Deciding where to go is wasted time," said Japh. "Everything's totally disjointed."

"Right. We gotta get out in the open and flag the payboat. Run where we have to when the APPs home in—I still got three shells!"

"Let's go, girl!

They burst out, Japh's iron and his stake in his belt, the table held at guard for both of them, and Jool with her stake in one hand and their tags in the other. They ran shouting and waving at the sky . . . and a raft was streaking down, maybe prealerted by the in-house cams—a raft that, oddly, had two paymasters, both of whom looked too gaudy for that role. The boat had another one tailing it too, riding about two lengths above and behind it, what looked like a bank of cameras in its bows.

"Two tags!" Jool shouted, lofting them up, but a little inaccurately. The pilot seemed an ace, though, gave the boat a dip and a twist to snare the arcing black gems—though the paymasters seemed a little less expert, both reeling dangerously in their shared harness.

"Here's some extra!" the one in silver shouted—and tossed down the two packets they had coming, and another, much thicker! They caught the first two OK, but the heftier one was tossed a little too hard—missed their reaching hands, and broke into *three* packets on the pavement behind them. In leaping for this incredible bonus, Jool kicked two of the extra packets, and they skittered away before her—just as she saw two new APPs closing fast on them from their left.

They scooped up the bonus, but Jool stumbled doing it, and was going to sprawl headlong when Japh's hand hooked her arm and *yanked,* and they both fell sideways as the lead APP, already launched, soared over them. Still down, they rolled hard left again as the second APP nailed the pavement they'd just vacated.

Then they were up and sprinting, dodging, holding just half a heartbeat's lead, with just a splinter apiece in one hand—Japh having lost the table in saving her—and their packets in the other. And heard, as they booked for their lives, one of the paymasters above them shout, "God *damn*! Great moves! Sorry about that throw!"

But they had less than two meters' lead, the scritch of pursing claws so close, when here—ye gods!—came a *dead guy* rushing toward them!

Not a dream! The spider-shriveled corpse of a man was sprinting toward them, his flat, flimsy legs flapping in the breeze! Some guy just drained! A hurrying husk!

Then they saw that a living man carried the corpse before him like a shield as he sprinted to intercept their pursuers.

"Break left! Break left!" he shouted from behind his cadaverous screen. They did it just in the nick as the lead APP launched for them, but encountered instead the corpse-bearer, who snagged his leathery trophy on its descending fangs, somersaulted up still gripping the dead arms, landed on the spider's back and hauled upward on its snared fangs. "Stab its belly!" he screeched.

Jool thrust her spike up amid the APP's hoisted under-joints, while Japh with his own parried the onrush of the second APP. She freed her point from the crumpled attacker, and turned with it to help Japh, who was desperately backing before his still unhurt adversary's thrust. Their corpse-bearing savior—by god! It was Chops!—leaped down from the first, and onto the back of the second APP, trying to use his leathery ally to snare its fangs in turn, when two new APPs came pumping toward them.

"God damn!" shouted Stone and Raj. "God damn!" Both were awed by the delirious footwork, the surreal contrivance of these struggling three.

"Grip your fucking harness, fools!" shrieked Luce—this warning not a microsecond too soon as she kicked the raft back into a near vertical climb, apexing in a backflip that the trailing cam-raft recoiled from with just centimeters to spare. So tight was her flip that the centrifugals kept the actors' feet still pressed to the raft floor through the instant they stood upside down, and then the craft shot out of the flip so fast their knees buckled while their grips on the harness almost tore free.

Luce streaked over that little battle at a hundred klicks—and whooshed right on past. But when the stars looked back, they shouted with astonishment. "They killed 'em!" Stone crowed. "They killed 'em all!" And the two of them crowed, jubilant to see the three extras amid four arachnid corpses, legs all contracted into crooked bouquets by their death spasms. They were pulling tags like crazy, but not waving them. Instead they were devoutly hauling ass from the scene of the carnage, with three new APPs closing fast on them.

"I got 'em now," said Luce's com as she sped away. She

looked back. Sandy Devlin's boat was dropping down in her wake.

"Roger that," Luce said. "These three deserve some special attention. Check out the corpse one's carrying." As she flew on, surveilling her sector, Luce told Raj and Stone, "You guys are doing pretty good for beginners, but watch your fucking *tosses*. Put that cash in their *hands*, guys!"

"I'm sorry, *really* sorry," moaned the contrite Raj.

"Hey," said Luce, showing a bit of a rare smile. "You boys are OK. Just stay focused. Practice makes perfect."

THE PLOT THICKENS

Val hovered about fifty meters above the air-battle ceiling, his fingers poised on his com switches, his eyes distributing their restless attention between his multitude of monitors, and the naked-eye reality below him. His wondrous multitracking brain sifted the turmoil below for glitches, fires to put out. He felt what he always felt in mid-shoot, an anxious jubilation. He felt he was buoyed in the air—not by his raft's engine—but purely on the wave of vital energy that welled up above his creation, as if his talent were a kind of sea on which he sailed. It was madness and majesty, to feel this!

He commed Auto Traffic. "Sammy, I want the pace stepped up in south Q around the Mutual Beneficial Building."

"Roger that, Val." Pileups there had intensified, and were compounded with collisions of several extra-driven cars. A dozen APPs were crippled in the wreckage and a riot among the extras was starting to spread from fierce competition for the downed APPs' tags. A wonderful scene. With minimal editing, the extras' fury to get the tags would screen as a spontaneous mass attack on the aliens.

But even as Val orchestrated, his brain gnawed away at his Director's Cut inspiration. His stars were already airborne, Harms expertly dodging them through the cannon fire. What was he *missing* about this Cut? Here was Harms swooping to a payout. Here was Raj Valdez dropping—and dropping clumsily—bonus packets to a pair of extras. That bad toss was going to kill them, new APPs closing on them as they scrambled up the cash, some wild footwork . . . and what was this intercepting them? Another extra carrying . . . an APP-killed corpse? Good lord. As the struggle cohered, Val tagged the clip—this *had* to go in the final print. Incredible inventiveness! But now, more APPs, and they were surely doomed . . . ? Then Harms threw an incredible backflip that nearly downed the cam-raft. That woman could fly—was nearly as good as her fellow rat Devlin. . . .

A moment later Val sat stunned. She'd swept over the new predators and left all dead, legs contracted. *Had* to have fired something right into the nexus of their hydraulics, to fold up their legs like that. By god, he had them now!

And then dawned the added inspiration that had been knocking for admission to his mind. Though awed, as it unfolded for him, he never ceased directing. He commed Holo. "Zachary? Sunlight on the wall holos isn't quite in real-time sun-sync. Make 'em look a half hour earlier."

"Roger that, Val."

He commed Robot Air. "Sylvia? Let's have some more cannon fire at about floor thirteen of the Mutual Beneficial building. I think it would be a great touch to have the top half topple down across that parking structure later in the shoot."

"Roger that, Val. How hard should we hit it?"

"Weaken it. We'll actually bring it down in the last quarter."

"Copy that."

Ye gods, why hadn't it struck him at once, the moment he'd decided to show so much of the shoot itself in the Cut? Hunt out the conspirators and film them in the act! Film their sabotage and their arrests in midshoot by Metro!

A natural crime-and-detection thriller, just handed to him. The Cut would indeed be a whole new vid in itself, with *Alien Hunger* swarming beneath every frame of it, shot at whole different angles, centering the viewer in the seething stratum of the creation of a classic.

Again punching up APP mortality, and finding it 23 percent higher than ever recorded, he felt this time like a man striking gold. The rats in his walls were swarming, were in a feeding frenzy of APP slaughter. Sabotage in climax mode. Now was the perfect time to film them, *take* them. They were flinging him down their gauntlet, and the challenge thrilled him.

He commed Properties to send up all the rest of APP reserves. Then he commed Thecker, chief of Metro Surveillance. "Paul?"

"Yes, Val?"

"Paul, this is code red, get-it-done yesterday. You listening?"

"Yes *sir*."

"I want eighteen Metro, unmarked, your top pilots, full cams mounted in the bows. I want them tailing and camming the following payboats—you copying?"

Val's fingers flew on the keyboard, dumping his list of suspects onto Thecker's screen, speaking as he typed. "Your boats are looking for some kind of projectile fired by these payboats to kill APPs. They're to tail at minimum three hundred meters, avoiding detection if possible, with cams on zoom and on ultra and infra too. We want good footage of shots fired and APPs killed. Once they have it, arrest at once, full cams on the arrest as well. You copy?"

"Copy. Orders going out as we speak."

"As you know, contract allows lethal force on saboteurs. Shoot 'em down if they resist or evade, and don't worry where they fall in-shoot. Cam the shoot-downs too. You copy?"

"They'll be airborne and tailing within fifteen or less, Val."

"I want detailed sit-reps and uplinks here from all their cams in *ten*, you copy?"

"Yes sir. And about time, if I may say so, sir. APP mortality is—"

"I know, Paul. Just do it."

Val's whole body was tingling. He'd given Thecker neither Harms's nor Devlin's names, and he was tingling because of what he had just decided to do next.

He commed his chief assistant director, Mark Millar. And saw, when Mark's rugged face came onscreen, that tension of hope that Mark could never quite mask when Val called him during a shoot.

"Mark, are you ready to do this old man a favor he'll never forget?"

"Always, Val. Always."

"Come up and take the chair, old buddy. Come up in a payboat and have them throw full cams on it, please. And bring me up a jumpsuit. Five minutes."

"You've got it."

Val's nerves and muscles hummed with readiness. A marvelous sense of adventure filled him. In the early days, when anti-grav was far more risky, he had punched raft himself during his own shoots. He had payboated, sectorboated, even flown Metro pullouts of downed payboats, and had stood on ground zero of sets and dodged his own APPs—had worked every part of a dozen shoots, run every risk while inventing the art form itself. He *owned* live action, at every level, and now he was going to take back this vid of his with his own two hands.

Editing would be crucial, as with all art, but the saboteurs at work, their conquest and capture, would be irresistible social realism. The shoot-down footage, and especially the crashes, must be most artfully selected. He blessed his legal acumen gained in live action's formative period. Contractually, all studio personnel were studio property on-shoot.

The implications of the art form he was creating unfolded swiftly before his eyes. The windfall of Raj and Stone's impulsive generosity was the Cut's flagship. Their beauty and charisma, their philanthropy ennobled live action's whole enterprise, underscored its mission of social service. The richest, soaring through cannon fire and explosive debris, to endow the poorest!

Meanwhile, the elements of class struggle implicit in the saboteurs' more subversive "humanity"—how that would tantalize the vid-lovers of the world. They were already eating up the drama of folk but one class lower than themselves being eaten for cash. To see these rebel rafters taking up arms on the Zoo's behalf, how seductive that would be to the viewers' lurking guilt. It didn't matter that studio Metro would be the bad guys of this subplot. They were just doing their job for the status quo, so the vids could keep coming, and the viewers could keep watching them. Might it outrage their humanity? Yes! Like live action itself! In Viewerland, outrage was merely a spice. . . .

"**Hey, Curtis!**" **Cop** said. "That library!" He pointed at a small branch with a glass street wall, and an entry on the side whose door looked strong enough to defend. "Wood shelves!"

We dragged one shelf over to block that door from inside, and went to work emptying the other shelves. It was disorienting. The books were real! Tons of texts! Titles I'd only dreamed of holding in my hands! And here we were scooping them onto the floor like trash, because yes, the shelves *were* wood, and splittable into stakes and lances.

Ankle deep in dumped texts, we split ourselves lengths of the tough planking, my eyes flicking down toward the titles sprawled around us, my heart longing almost unbearably for a different world where I could be with the books hour after hour, in peace and silence. . . .

Beyond the glass wall was a small park, kind of an Old Town district surrounded by brick apartment buildings. As we were getting points on a pair of crude lances, a square of the park's grass flipped up, and APPs started pouring up out of this hatch, radiating at top speed, swarming up the building façades and breaking in through the windows, and four or five beelining right for the library door, so drawn by our heat signal that they jammed up there in a thorny cluster, all trying to get through at once, knocking over our shelf barricade, but blocking each other's entry—their palps twiddling each other like mad, but unable to disentangle, compelled by their drive to get in and suck us dry.

We attacked the glass wall with ax and nozzle, and praise god it exploded. We bolted into the square, spotted a clear street radiating off its far corner, and ran for it, getting a lead while our own APPs had to back out of their tangle to come after us. . . .

And just then, the world exploded. Straight off our legs we went, two chunks of flying debris in a blizzard of bricks like meteors filling the air. Dust blinded us, and the hammering of our bodies on the pavement stunned us. . . .

A vast moment of after-silence . . . or maybe it was just my own deafness. We staggered to our feet in an altered landscape.

Something big must have come down. The square was filled by dunes of bricks and debris. One of the apartment buildings was now a cutaway, its whole front wall collapsed, leaving a bunch of floors visible in cross-section, with half a dozen extras dazedly climbing down from their broken hive—moving faster already though, as it began to dawn on all of us that protruding from this great spill of bricks— along with broken people and broken cars—were *spider legs* here and there, some twitching feebly, some moving more strongly, and some dead still.

Hot damn! We ran for the nearest one, and started digging it out. We heard some gunfire, but figured it was some of our fellow survivors clocking APPs. We uncovered our squashed trophy's "face," and as I plucked its tag, I heard another gunshot. Something hammered my head and knocked me on my ass.

I staggered up with Cap's help. "Back off and give me that tag!" Here was a big guy dressed like a jogger. He was holding a pistol on us. He'd grazed me with a god damn bullet! And an even bigger guy in a loud Hawaiian shirt, pump shotgun in one hand, was taking another tag from the dead hand of a guy he'd just killed! "Every fuckin' tag in this square's ours, it's our fuckin' square!" shouted Jogger. "We Death's Head, an' we claim it!"

"Death's Head!" raged Cap. "This ain't the Zoo, you fuckin' turf-monkey! We work together, we can strip a shit-load a these bugs an *all* make out!" Shotgun killed another extra, which scattered all the rest who had been converging on the same bonanza that had drawn us. Training the gun on us, he went over to take the tag his victim had tried to bolt with. Jogger sneered at Cap, "You strapped, bitch? You got somethin' with some bark, or jus' that stick an' that hose? You bitches wanna live, you dig out that bug there, and gimme *its* tag!"

"Up yours!" I screeched. I musta been in shock. "You won't waste the ammo! You're a freakin' 'tard if you do! We gotta *unite* against this—"

Up came the gun, and he capped me—except that his feet went out from under him just as he squeezed it off, and he was pitching backward, and the APP that rose behind him, shedding bricks, buried its fangs in his back. Hawaiian Shirt saw this, pocketed the tag he'd just killed for, and rushed over and shotgunned the APP while it was engaged on his partner, plucked *its* tag, and pocketed that along with his partner's pistol, turning his pump back at us. "You bitches dig for me—get that one there."

Without even a signal between us both Cap and I, first bricks we took off the spider, we flung at him—missed him, but his ducking backward tripped him off his feet. He slammed into a pile of bricks, shifting it, and suddenly he spasmed and lay there tremoring.

Cap grabbed the shotgun from his now epileptic hand, and we got to either side of the spider that had fanged his spine and was now beginning to rise from its burial. As soon as its midsection showed, Cap shot it. He jacked out the shell and shot again, but clicked empty. "Shit!" But the APP wasn't moving.

"Let's get his tags and search him for more shells."

Two tags, no shells. His partner's pistol was also empty. We ditched the guns and started waving and shouting "Payboat!" at the sky.

The mass burial of bricks was beginning to shift and twitch here and there, protruding spider legs moving more strongly, bristly black bodies shedding bricks. Pucker time. We were right near that clear street stretching off to safety, but the dunes of brick hid plenty from our line of view, and the noise of the air-battle would hide the sound of fast-approaching claws.

"Payraft! Payraft!"

I found myself picturing that jam of spiders in the library door, all their palps twiddling. It gave me a notion. I let Cap wave and shout while I rolled Hawaiian Shirt off the bug that killed him. I cleared the bricks off its palps, and chopped one off. It was light, and a little more than half the length of my arm. I tucked it in my belt behind me, and just then, heard the suck-vent of a raft settling down above us. Good. Time to get paid, I chopped off the other palp and tucked it behind me.

"What the hell are you doing?" someone bellowed above. "You're vandalizing studio property!"

There were our tags, thrown by Cap, already arcing up into the raft, and standing there in the prow of the raft was that same buff asshole who had balked at paying us last time! He was holding the pay packets and brandishing them like a stick he was going to beat us with.

"Who *are* you?" I raged. "Pay us for our tags!"

And the pilot, that lean dark woman, was shouting at him almost as hysterically as we were: "Rod! You asshole! Pay them, there's APPs coming there!"

That galvanized us—*we* couldn't see them, but she had the vantage. We raged at the guy, but he ignored us. Told me, "You just put those APP parts right down! All you take is the tag!"

"What the hell you *saying*?" Cap howled. "We allowed to tear these bugs *up*!"

The enraged pilot took action—the raft dropped thirty feet straight down to hang twelve feet off the ground, and she shouted, "I will *crash* this boat if you don't pay them *now* Rod!"

But the guy was unflappable. He just hung there in his harness, noble and stern. "Go ahead. But I'm not paying out until he puts down that studio property he's stolen."

But now I was hearing something besides what he was saying. Something I had been noticing about all our voices: they all had just the slightest bit of an echo. . . .

I looked down those long blocks of street that were our escape route. The nearest fifty feet of this block looked fine, but from that point on it didn't look quite right. . . .

We were in a cul-de-sac! That escape route was a wall-holo!

"You pompous ape!" I shrieked. I had a floating feeling, I was so enraged. APPs were coming fast, and we were being forced to dicker here in front of a dead end. I grabbed a brick. "You gray meat booger!"

And I flung the brick at him with all my might.

It was a bad throw. It went low, and punched straight through the screen of the suck-vent in the bow that was part of the raft's cooling system. It siezed the engine up so hard the raft flipped like a coin in midair.

It slammed down on the bricks right-side up, but so powerfully that the whole raft buckled amidships. Part of the paymaster's harness had snapped with the force, which whipped old Rod forward, and broke his head on the bricks. He slumped there, bleeding down a spill of brains, while beside this mess poured out a spill of *bonuses*—smaller green bricks of cash strewn over the red bits of masonry: a stone fortune disgorged from his payout satchel!

It was stunning. Time seemed to stand still. All reality was here in front of us, maybe three million clacks like fruit fallen from a tree.

We were all hands, weapons dropped, seizing and stuffing our pockets, our fingers hitting those bundles like striking hawks. My life, Auntie's and Japh's and Jool's lives—they were all being transformed second by second as I *pocketed, pocketed, pocketed*. A completely different world lay before us if I could only stay alive from this moment. I took up my ax and my spike.

"Time to run," I told Cap, "and not down that—"

"Help! Wait! Help me!" It was the pilot, belted in and so mostly unhurt, now dazedly crawling from the wreck.

"Help you how?" Cap said, taking up his stake, paying off some hose to swing his nozzle like a mace. "We can hardly help ourselves!"

"I . . . I know the set! I know good refuges near here! You can't go that way—it's a wall holo. We've gotta go that way!" She pointed back down toward the library. "And there's APPs coming, almost here!"

"Make that *here!*" I said, grabbing her arm and sprinting, for here came four spiders swarming up over the bricks.

"You better be able to run," shouted Cap, grabbing her other hand. "Lead fast, or we'll leave you!"

"A cache of weapons . . . serious loaded weapons . . . not far off . . . Mutual Beneficial tower . . . real firepower . . . lots of ammo." She had no breath for more. And then we were all running for our lives.

The Star Raft came over an air-battle crash zone—half-gutted buildings, a square heaped with bricks and debris. "Hey! There's a downed raft there!" shouted Raj Valdez.

"Looks too late for that paymaster," said Stone. "Look at his head!"

"Hey, Luce. Look there!" Raj was pointing to a jump-suited figure fleeing with two extras and hotly pursued by bristly death. "Can we pick her up? Man, those bugs are close!"

"Negative." Luce Harms had just whipped them into a steep dive. "We're max weight already. Her crash beacon should alert Metro. Hold on!"

She came down fast and low, straight across the group. The rearmost of them, a guy in a guard's uniform, had barely a fifteen-foot lead on the foremost APP.

As the raft streaked past, the actors thought they felt muf-fled pulsations of the raft's undercarriage. Looking back, Stone shouted, "Hey! They wasted those bugs! They wasted all four of 'em! Look! How'd they *do* that?"

The APPs, great cratered wounds in their bulbs and midsections, lay spasming. And the extras, however they had done it, seemed dazed by their own accomplishment, and they were slow, at first, in turning back for the tags.

DEUS EX MACHINA

Mark Millar, chief assistant director to the creator and greatest living director of live action, was a lean and watchful man. And though he loved and honored Val Margolian now no less than he had ever done, he was still, after eight years, just an assistant, and he was getting no younger. Thus, Val's com had caught him on the phone with Holly Zimmer.

" 'Take the chair, old buddy,' eh?" Holly smiled from the screen on Mark's cell. "What will this bring your career-long chair-time to, I wonder?"

Though now striding toward the flight deck, Mark took

care to give all his attention and charm to their interrupted chat. Holly, her hair all stylish silver quills, an exquisitely groomed and elegant woman of a certain age, was his lover. She was also the CEO of Panoply Studios, Inc. "My career total now stands, as I believe I've told you, dear, at fifteen hours and forty-three minutes in the saddle. Not enough shoot left to make seventeen, I fear, even if he gave me the rest of it."

"You think it's our saboteur problem?"

"I think it is. I think Val is going down into the set to kick some saboteur ass."

The pair of them had been monitoring APP mortality rates every bit as closely as Val, had indeed been ghosting all Val's coms throughout the action.

"Well," Holly smiled, "here he is starting to film a police action on his suspects in midshoot. Hands-on guy that he is, he'd surely want to go down and direct that little subplot personally. And please get what you can of *that* footage."

"Roger that, dear. Here's my raft. Signing off."

"Kiss kiss."

"Kiss kiss."

Mark and Holly shared a knowledge about this shoot that even its great creator lacked. Val, some weeks ago, had ordered a minute inspection of his suspects' rafts. Holly had suborned the chief of Properties in a private interview during which a handsome sum had changed hands. What Margolian learned from the Properties chief was that nothing had been found during this inspection. What Holly and Mark had learned was that *almost* nothing had been found.

Removal of the keel plates of these rafts had revealed only

one minor anomaly in their refrigeration conduits. A small universal union had been let into the main conduit right above one of the keel vents. "Something," the chief reported, "something not very large, mind you, could be screwed into those unions."

"Could be attached to the union right above the vent."

"That's right."

Mark and Holly had kept this revelation to themselves because they shared a dream. It was an inspiration Mark had unfolded to her one night in bed, about a year ago, in the early days of their relationship.

"I actually ran this by Val last year," he began, "and he just couldn't see it. I think maybe it was just too simple a concept for a man of his complex talent. Just picture this." An awe and a tenderness came into his voice as he shared it, his vision, his breakthrough inspiration: "*The Battle of the Somme*. Or, *The Battle of the Bulge!*"

Holly sat up, hugging a pillow—still a little self-conscious of her recently augmented breasts. "World War One. World War Two . . . I don't follow you."

"Think of it, Holly. Live war. Two armies of uniformed extras. *No APPs.*"

Now she shared his awe. "No APPs. My god. Oh my god . . . ! Even if we tripled their bonuses, we'd save . . . a billion! And the concept! A real war fought for the viewers' hearts and minds! Oh my god!"

All through the construction of *Alien Hunger*'s set, the two of them had fashioned *The Battle of the Somme*—the logistics of its set; the motivational structures that would cause extras to cohere as opposing armies (tiered bonuses based on enemy kills tabulated by laser-camera tracking of all shots fired, and gunboat-rafts to discipline defectors); the degree to which augmented extra mortality could offset the cost of augmented bonuses; the cost of bulletproofing rafts. And all the while, with the passion of artists blazing a new frontier, they polished Mark's screenplay, already multiply drafted over the two years since he had conceived his opus.

And while they developed their oeuvre, Holly delicately felt out, one by one, Panoply's board of directors. Her tact had been exquisite, but her findings, as they accumulated, still paralyzed their plans. Margolian bestrode the industry like a colossus, and should he take umbrage, and offer his creative captaincy to a competing studio, Panoply's stock would surely take a savage beating. Not one of the board members showed the least inclination to fund a project that lacked his full approval.

Now, Mark Millar was atingle with premonition. He sensed his master was on the brink of a major misstep. He risked delaying by two added minutes his swift response to Margolian's summons, the time it took to uplink his raft's cameras to the command console over which he would soon preside, and to attach a spy-eye—an omni-directional micro-cam—to the boat's bow.

He sped skyward. Never had his years-long reverence for Val been greater than it was at this moment. That he had, in eight years, spent only a fraction of the time in the saddle that a chief assistant director had a right to expect for the training that was due him, he utterly forgave. Had forgiven it all along. Genius claims its own, and cannot share—he understood!

But genius was a form of madness, and unless Mark's instincts were awry—for he too had the divine spark—Val's creative power was approaching critical mass. He was abandoning his masterwork at its hour of birth. He'd asked for a jumpsuit and was going in undercover, to detect and apprehend.

He overtopped the air-battle, and docked at the command raft. "Permission to come aboard, sir."

"Permission granted! Always! Thank you from my heart, old friend." Val's handshake was warm, powerful. And in his eyes . . . yes, a spark of reckless glee.

"You honor me, Val. I'll always do my best to deserve it."

"Take the throne, Mark. I don't know how long I'll be. We have some extra Metro on-set, mostly in Sector C. Leave them be, even if you see 'em firing on payrafts. You copy?"

"I do indeed, Val. Rats in the walls, eh?"

"Precisely." Val was getting into the jumpsuit, zipping it up. "What else? Oh yes. In case I'm not back, they're bringing down the top half of Mutual Beneficial across the parking structure."

Val was rubbing his palms together, the youthful zest of combat filling him—old Zeus, feeling his oats. He spread his arms. "So. How do I look?"

"Fit as a fiddle, and ready to kick some ass. Please be careful."

"Don't worry. You know, Mark, you get to a certain point in your career, and you can afford to indulge yourself." A wink, wild and merry, and Val was at the payraft's controls, diving down into the heart of the shoot.

If this was to be grand tragedy, Mark thought, how

perfect was that wink! The mad king, winking sanity good-bye.

He got to work, scanning monitors. Commed Proper-ties. "Billy? Pope Street in Sector R. Small riot over tags on some downed APPs. Send in a dozen more from around the corner of Cardinal."

"Roger that, Mark, but APP reserves are way down—less than fifty left."

"OK. Make it six, then."

"Roger that."

Mark smiled, cracking his knuckles. Directing again! But he'd already directed a key part of this flick, hadn't he? If he'd shared with Val what they'd found under those pay-boats, the king wouldn't be down in his own set now, looking for it. Result: Mark was now directing a far more interesting flick than the king had left him—a flick starring the king himself.

Mark noted three screens on the center of his array that were all devoted to Sandra Devlin's raft. Hmmm. He up-linked the raft he'd given Val, and there in its cams was De-vlin again, shot from the rear. Val was already tailing her, maybe three blocks back. . . .

"Chops, you sonofabitch!" Jool shouted as they ran. "Why aren't you home taking care of everyone!?"

Chops ran slightly behind her, still carrying the useful husk of Kite, so tough and bony-leathery. He ran ready to shield their backs if their pursuers should pull close enough for a leap. "Wrench is covering them! Just run, Jool!" he shouted.

No more suburbia. Here it was old brick warehouses, streetcar tracks, truckers' stations. From one of the warehouse rooftops a man leaped into four stories of thin air, the APP chasing him soaring down after. The man was dead on impact, and the spider broken, but there was no going for its tag because their own pursuers were tight on track and coming at full pump.

Chops heard a crisp concussion behind him, and a shadow strafed across them, the payraft throwing a tight, slick one-eighty and shooting back toward their rear, the pilot shrilling down from overhead: "Keep running!"

No problem there! When the raft recrossed them, there was another thumping concussion, and the pilot shouted down to them, "Turn and stand! Kill it!"

They wheeled. Behind them were two broken spiders and just one oncoming. Jool spiked its underside, and Chops with his Kite-shield leaped astride, stabbing through its midjoint, while Japh stabbed its bulb with the tire iron. Thirty seconds later they had it bleeding out.

"Tags, tags, tags, come on!" The payboat was at hover above them. "Stand ready to pay, Radner!"

The extras scattered for the three new tags. Suddenly a bonanza of tags: these new three, Chops pulling others from his pocket, and Jool and Japh with two more. . . . At a bark from the pilot, the eight packets were tossed down before all the tags had hit the raft floor. Then, as the extras turned to run, the pilot called, "Wait!" and the paymaster tossed down eight more! "Now listen. Down that cross street there's a parking structure next to the Mutual Beneficial building. The top level is full of working cars—the studio hiding its quota out of reach, right? Watch the stair-wells and ramps, but get to the third level, and you can kill APPs for the rest of the shoot with those rides!"

Jool was staggered. Gifts rained down on them all day! That makeup guy. Finding Japh for a 'kick. Then suddenly, Chops at her back. And now this cash, all she'd come for already in pocket! Oh, please, let her get herself, her friends, and her pockets out of these walls alive!

"Chops! Will you *lose* that corpse?!"

"No way! This's my pal Kite—he draws their bite and snags their fangs."

Five minutes later, and there was the parking structure crouched beside its skyscraper. Inside the first level, all in shadow, they viewed an acre of cars, half of them peeled to shreds like tinfoil toys, and shrunken corpses every-where.

They went in crouched and ready. It was echoey in there—a good thing, for the scritch of spider claws on con-crete would be magnified. All was silence now, which some-how made them hear the cries and chaos that must have filled the place at the shoot's start, when the hordes had flooded in for the rides. The poor extras had imprisoned themselves inside them, only to find no power, and no pro-tection when the spiders flooded after and peeled the chas-sis off them like banana skins.

"So many dead here," Jool said, "might keep people from going higher up." Not so, it seemed, for when they crept up the nearest ramp, they found it half-carpeted with the leath-ery dead. But they found level two was less littered . . . and the ramp up to three was clearer yet.

They reached the roof level, bathed in sun. Not a corpse was in sight, and they beheld perhaps three dozen rides, parked in a well-spaced array. Some big debris had come down from a cannon hit halfway up the skyscraper and crushed a couple of the vehicles, but practically the whole level was wide open for defensive maneuvers—if in fact these rides had the power to move. The air-battle loomed much larger from just fifty feet up: dogfights, screaming pursuits, air-to-airs streaking, and cannon fire flashing—no early warning from echoes up here. The trio looked down from the parapet.

They beheld unabated frenzy on the streets: a riot of APPs, extras, corpses, and traffic collisions. Japh said, "If they come up the ramps we got no way down. We gotta get in working rides ASAP. Let's see what runs."

They scattered to promising vehicles. Jool selected a beefy pickup. She touched a button on the steering wheel's shaft and it fired right up with a healthy roar of power.

Mark Millar watched Sandy's flyover of three hotly pursued extras, then her turn, and her second flyover. Voilà! Two flyovers, and two dead APPs. And damn! She paid out twice! And then still hovering, she seemed to be giving directions! Val, likewise at hover, was back there watching her. He must surely be going apeshit.

Mark, fascinated, had to shake himself out of a mere spectator's mode. Time to show due diligence. He commed sector-boat C.

"Hi, Trek. Lance. Have you guys been screening Sandra Devlin?" Was that a hint of guilty surprise in Trek's face? A careful blankness showed there now, his bright orange 'bones making Mark think of an animal face looking warily out from its forest cover.

"Hey, Mark. That's an affirmative. Val wanted us to scope her close."

"Did you see what I just saw? A double payout?"

"Roger that, Mark. We, ah, didn't see any tags go up for that second pay-drop."

"Well, don't call Metro. Val's on this personally."

"Roger that, Mark. We're screening him too. Why's he in a jumpsuit?"

"I can't say. But from here on, he wants you to leave Devlin to him."

"Roger that, Mark." They clicked off.

Now why had he told them that? His sense that they were already on Devlin's side had prompted it. He was directing. A good director lets interesting developments *develop*. Leave Devlin to Val . . . and Val to Devlin?

Back to the bigger picture. Scanning set cams, he happened to notice Devlin's three overpaid extras. They were just going into the parking structure next to the Mutual Beneficial building. Oh ho. Here was what Devlin had been tipping them to—all the working vehicles on the structure's top level. She wouldn't have known of Val's little brainstorm, and that the top half of the skyscraper would soon be coming down right where she'd sent them.

There was potential for a fascinating scene here. Those three particular extras—two lean street types, the third one sizable—had moves, had nerve. Under attack, they could stage a real automotive ballet up there—great long shots possible from the cams in the surrounding buildings. Then, at the height of the action, *splat*—half a building swatting the whole thing flat in mid-dance.

Mark commed Properties. "Billy. Sit-rep on reserve APPs."

"Down to twenty-five, Mark. They're taking an ass-kicking."

"Six more then, to the top level of the parking structure. Then override me another six from the vicinity and send them up too—got a major scene developing there."

"Roger that, Mark."

Hmmm. Millar was in the saddle at an auspicious moment. The studio had never finished a shoot with fewer than a hundred fifty APPs in reserve. . . .

Trek and Lance shared another stick of tobacco, brooding. Trek burst out, "Hell with it! Listen. *I'm* doing this. If they check the com log, I take full responsibility."

"No way, man. Do it. I'm with you."

Trek commed Sandy, who was just pulling up from a payout and shearing off to another one, Radner gripping his harness for dear life.

"Yo, Sandy. Just keep flyin' and listen. Mark's at the wheel upstairs—he copped to your double payout—and Val's in a payraft tailing you. Also, we've screened at least ten extra boats flying your sector, cams mounted but pilots unknown and likely Metro, all scoping your squad's moves."

"Thanks, guys." They watched her dip to pay out to a heavyset meter maid who had just speared an APP with the steel pole of a speed-limit sign. "You boys must think I'm pretty cute."

The two young men grinned. Lance said, "We think you're pretty hot for an older broad."

"You ain't seen nothin' yet. And I want you to report everything I do—it won't hurt me and I don't want you losing your house in the Hills."

"We're gonna play it by ear."

"I've got your number. Don't look for me after the shoot—we'll find you." She clicked off.

"What does she mean, don't look for her after the shoot?" Lance asked. "*Duh!* You think she's stickin' around after what she's pulled today?"

"Truth. And I don't think she's finished doin' it either."

"Got that right. Hell, what she's shown us just up to *this* point's already the best vid I've ever seen."

"Still . . . ," Trek said after a pause. "Once she's done, how's she gonna get *outta* this?"

Val Margolian had her now, by god. A double flyover, and two dead APPs, untouched by the extras they pursued. And then, a double payout. He could Metro her to the ground right now, except that he still didn't know how she was *doing* it.

He followed her, telling himself to anticipate, think with and ahead of her. A couple orthodox payouts followed, extras unendangered, regulation drops. And then, a more imperiled pair ahead: on a fire escape, third floor, two women trapped by climbing spiders were waving their tags desperately, on very short time. And Val saw what she would do just before she did it.

Yes, there she went, throwing a wide sweep at a ninety-degree tilt—Radner clinging desperately to his harness—her keel presented to the fire escapes as she shot across just below the waving extras. Then she threw another wide turn, shot back at payout height, and hit hover. Two dead APPs were smashed against the railings of the fire escape just under the extras, dangling from their legs' entanglement with the bars. And as she was receiving the women's tags, a fragment of something dropped from one of the defunct spiders: a shard that flashed as it fell, like glass—or ice.

And it came to Val. As he watched Radner toss the women two packets each for only two tags, and yes, again shout something to them—more survival tips, no doubt—he experienced the fierce joy of the hunter who at last nails his quarry.

Ah, the dour bitch! The studio's humanitarian impulse—its expenditure on higher performance rafts for quicker payouts—had created the beefed-up cooling systems that Devlin was surely exploiting. Refrigeration, pressure pumps, coolant—graft on a few short branch pipes and you could create a little parasite on the cooling system, a small ice-cannon that wouldn't even protrude past the keel plates, firing projectiles that would be melted away by the end of the shoot.

The essence of a criminal like Devlin, of all her little helpers, was envy. They were the archetypes of a mythic drama that was as old as the history of humankind. The slayers of Socrates, the crucifiers on Golgotha—time and again they enacted their shadow drama, its storyline always the same: the hatred of the mediocre mind for those with the talent and stature to achieve greatness. Inevitable, that they should be drawn here. Of all the artists of his generation, who was more likely than himself to become the focus of their busy little worm-work? But also, who more likely to defeat them? To *film* them at their work, and capture them within his own triumphant creation? To reduce them to being merely his *material*?

Oh, this was priceless—his nemesis pierced and wriggling on a pin, a part of his collection.

Devlin soared away on her maggot's mission, and Val Margolian steered his course that shadowed hers. He'd film her almost to shoot's end, and then have Metro shoot her down.

CONVERGENCES

The fifteenth floor of the Mutual Beneficial building—that was what Kate, the downed rafter, told us as we ran. Fine, but just reaching the place near killed us three times over. Traffic got thicker as we got closer, and we found the big boulevard it fronted just boiling with mayhem.

"They leaked word," she panted—we'd crouched in a fire-gutted storefront half a block down and across from the seething entry—"among the extras. Studio plants on the transports. Rumored the gun cache different places all along this block. Wanted big action here—huge APP releases, major traffic smashes."

She had *that* right: the boulevard six lanes wide, smashups everywhere, crushed APPs heaped amid their prey, new extras dodging traffic after their tags and new APPs ditto after them, with robot rides roaring through it all on whatever clear asphalt was left.

"But they're up *there*," she said, pointing up the skyscraper, and then said, "Shit."

"What?"

"Cannon-fire hits—halfway up there, see? That's not planned. . . ."

"What floor are we—"

"Two floors higher than the hits. It looks OK. You guys still game?"

Cap and I looked at each other. We had millions in our pockets. Part of our brains were saying get down in a safe hole quick, lie still as stone, and walk out rich.

But another part of us said fill your hands with firepower and spend the rest of the shoot blowing the *shit* out of every one of these bugs that fronts you. Our limbic lizard brains, pumped on terror, said *Trust no hidey-hole* and *Crush bug ass*.

"We want those guns," I said.

"OK. We've got to get to the fourth floor. We—"

"You said the *fifteenth*—" Cap began.

"Shut up, please! *Trust* me. I'm scared shitless—I barely have the nerve to do this, so just listen. *Major* APP port in there, on the fourth, but by now they're all out and hunting, most down here now." She pointed to the seething lobby, visible through a big glass wall. The glass doors were jammed with dead, both human and animatronic, but over these still more of both were swarming. "If you can get us up to the fourth, I can get us to the fifteenth from there."

Cap and I were studying. The whole lobby boiled, as did two grand staircases sweeping down like parentheses from a mezzanine . . . but the staircases boiled somewhat less.

"Are those walls really glass?" I asked.

"Thick, but yes—just glass."

Cap and I traded a look. "Come on," he told her. "Stay *with* us."

We jumped out onto the sidewalk, and as it happens sometimes, the instant to move came exactly then. We each grabbed an arm of her and leaped into the roaring street—I think she screamed, but run she did. One, two, three robot body-smashers grazed us behind, in front, behind—and we were across the raging boulevard.

We attacked the glass near its corner—the chaos inside didn't quite fill the lobby wall to wall. I got every ounce of me behind the first swing. The impact seemed to crack every bone I had, but the axspur made a little star of cracks. *Whack* went Cap's fire nozzle, with twelve feet of hose for centrifugal force. The little star branched a bit.

Demons we were, crazed with the work, while Kate watched for bugs—fumbling out some kind of keypad, but not seeming to use it.

Suddenly, big ragged cracks! *Whack, whack*—a big hole exploded, and an APP exploded right out of it. We hammered it down simultaneously, impaling it on a fang of glass, and climbed in across its spasming body, dragging Kate after us.

It was worth the work, to come in at the edge of the riot. We kept the wall on our flank as we ran for the stairs. Our timing was lucky, climbing those stairs. Every bug we encountered was fighting or eating as we dodged and darted upward to the mezzanine.

"Fire stairs to the fourth!" Kate shouted, leading us leftward. We found that stairwell empty, save for the dead of both species. Up we sprinted. Came out careful in a fourth-floor corridor. Kate ran in the lead, pointing to the hall's distant end, saying, "There's—" when we crossed a transecting corridor, and saw four APPs not thirty feet off, pumping right for us.

"Build a lead!" Kate screeched. "We can't rush through that door!"

It amazes me now, that we still had that much sprint left in our legs. The bugs slowed slightly making the corner, and we hit that door with fifty feet of grace. I tore it open, she and Cap slipped through, me after, just getting the door shut when *wham*, a spider impacted it, nearly launching all three of us out into sixty feet of empty air. We were on a narrow balcony, railed to waist height, and barely containing us. I braced with all my might, the spider-thrust trying to launch me into space. "Where now?" I gasped. "This thing won't latch, I gotta hold it!"

"There!" she pointed.

A window washer's lift dangled just beside and above the end of the little balcony. Cap hoisted Kate up onto it. She steadied it while he more precariously got his greater mass aboard. *Wham, wham, wham* went the door, threatening to crack my straining spine. "I'm starting it up!" shouted

Cap. "Brace it with this!" He tossed me his sharpened plank. I butted it against the railing, and lodged its tip against the door. The lift was slow, had risen maybe three feet when I reached for it.

Wham, wham, crack! The plank dislodged, the door slammed open, and a spider launched out so furiously it sailed into the sky. But here came the others, just as I scrambled aboard. They seethed in the narrow platform, struggling to extricate themselves from one another. We'd risen just barely out of their reach before they disentangled . . . and started to climb the wall after us.

Their weight made them slow. Half the time their claw tips slipped, but they each had eight to work with, and none of them fell. One body length behind us, relentlessly they climbed as we crept upward. The air-battle flared and crackled, and rafts knifed the air around us. We rose at a leisurely matched pace, as if we and the spiders were just taking a casual vertical stroll together. . . .

"Look!" we all said at once. For now we could gaze out over the top of the set wall. Out there stretched a vast, smog-tinted vista, beyond the foothills, the endless plain of the L.A. Basin, all threaded with freeways and bristly with powerpoles and trees. The Real World. The reason we were here, or Cap and I at least . . .

Floor after floor we rose, vaster and vaster the view, just lazing upward together, us and the spiders, while cannon fire sizzled and walls spat shattered bricks and the roar of voices down on the streets grew fainter.

At last, "There's the window!" cried Kate. "In quick—it won't close after us, we'll have to block it!" As our eyes cleared its sill, we glimpsed a luxurious living room, with a glassed-in gun rack over a gas fireplace. We hoisted Kate and threw her in, and in we rolled after. "Go for the guns!" I told Cap, and grabbed the couch to lift it up against the window frame. And nearly tore my arms out. Bolted to the floor! I wasted no time on other furniture, heard glass smashing but dared not turn. I grabbed the first spider claw that hooked onto the sill, and tried to unhook it. It was like grabbing a piece of moving machinery. Two more claws hooked the sill and the one I held kicked and threw me backward, breaking my grip. As I fell, a second bug started climbing in around the side of the frame, as the first one poured through.

"Stay down!" shouted Cap, and *WHACK!*—the first one's fangs and foresection blew to tatters. In came number two, and received the same. "Wanna try it?" Cap said, grinning, racking the next shell and tossing me the shotgun. I greeted number three as he rose to the sill and oh, what a feeling! I blew it right off the wall.

We shotgunned the legs off the couch, and propped its mass to block the window. With a twelve-gauge apiece, went out into the hall and checked every corridor for lurkers. Then we went back to the suite to arm ourselves more thoroughly. At last, something like security!

Secure now, and suddenly the thought of Japh and Jool was torture. Now I could protect them for the rest of the shoot, and make them rich after. I had to try to find them.

A Glock semi-auto forty-four with a shoulder rig. Extra clips in with my cash in one pocket, extra shotgun shells with my cash in the other pocket—thank god Costumes had made these pockets sturdy! More clips and shells in my button-flap shirt pockets . . . Cap had just asked me something.

"What?"

"I axed, you keepin' those?" He meant my spider palps. I thought a moment. "Yeah. They feel . . . lucky. Good souvenirs, if nothing else." I resecured them in my belt at my hip, and my ax at the other hip.

Cap asked, "You got something on your mind, Curtis?"

"Yeah. I do. My 'kick is on the set . . . and a girl I know. I've gotta try to find them, help them. You understand?"

"Yeah. I do."

"Will you look after Kate?"

"That I will, Curtis. That I will. Just don't you go getting hurt. Remember you got a lot to lose now. And we got some good times to be havin' together, up in the mounains, you hear?"

On impulse, I hugged him. It surprised him, but pleased him too. "Whyn't you do some scopin' before you go down? There's a parkin' lot on the other side—should give you more view of the streets."

"Good thought. Kate? You watch this man's back now."

"Roger that, Curtis." She hugged me, her eyes wet. "Exit port C—that's where we'll wait for each other."

"Good. Exit port C."

"Try the suite directly across the hall. It has the same layout as this, and the view you want."

"I'll see you two outside."

The opposite suite was the same, except that it had a glass case of swords and sabers instead of guns. The window showed me some exciting action on the top parking level fourteen stories down—a kind of automotive ballet in progress.

There was a scattering of cars parked here and there, and three vehicles were in motion amid . . . eight, nine, ten APPs in full pursuit of them. A red pickup, accelerating madly with one on its roof and one in its bed, jammed on its brakes, dumping the one off its roof, then accelerating, not quite in time to kill it, but managing to crush three of its legs, the second APP meanwhile already taking the first one's place, and peeling the roof off the cab with its fangs. A big black sedan threw a power turn and front-ended an APP against a parked van, definite kill there, the sedan's windshield drenched with green. It hit reverse but wobbled backing up, its front end torqued by the impact, and another APP jumped its roof and tore a huge section off right above the driver's head. The next fang-stroke would nail him—a big guy in green punk spikes—so he accelerated, jammed the brakes, throwing the spider off balance, though it held on, and rolled out the door. Torn metal snagged his spikes as he rolled out, and the latex glue wig base peeled off him as he hit the pavement. Close-shaved black hair with chevron sideburns and ritual cheek scars. God almighty!

"Japh!" I bellowed it out, but the window was between us—lucky, I realized, because he didn't need distraction. Japh was sprinting now for another vehicle for shelter, two APPs tight on him.

I threw up the window. A damn long downhill shot with a twelve-gauge, pretty desperate. I fired at the one closest to him, but it was the one behind him that flinched and staggered—and even that one kept running. Not enough punch from this distance. I pumped down five, the last two finding the one behind Japh, slowing it, the bulb leaking fluid.

Panic threatened me—they were almost on him and my help couldn't reach him. I ran to the wall, smashed the glass, and started grabbing swords and sabers, and throwing these down like spears. They all started to tumble as they fell, but the first had crazy luck on it. It end-over-ended, and planted itself to the hilt in the fore-section of the spider on Japh's heels.

God bless his quick reactions, amazed though he was. While the other swords were still jouncing and clattering down around him he jumped up on the APP, pulled out the saber, snatched up another, and sliced both fangs and both forelegs off the second one as it reared up over him. Then he jammed to a parked van, and jumped into it. You could see it surge as the engine fired up. He had a second to thrust his head out the window and look upward. . . .

He saw me! I could see his grin from way up there. He waved, and gunned the car forward at two oncoming, while the third car in motion, a gnarly SUV, angled in to help him. I bellowed down, "I'll come right down to help you!"

Lord, how true that was! That part about coming "right down."

Even in the delirium of action, Japh savored a moment of wonder and glee. A rain of swords out of nowhere! Who else would do a thing like that but Curtis? Curtis, right above him! Alive and unharmed!

Japh had two spiders coming head-on, and saw Chops's

SUV coming head-on behind them. The guy had moves, but could this work? They braked just before colliding, crushing the two APPs between their high bumpers. Though braced against the wheel, Japh still hammered his head on the glass, left cracks in it, but not in his skull at least. He hit reverse, they backed apart, and went after Jool, Japh's front end crooked now but manageable, and no time for a change. Jool's truck had two bugs on it now, and one in chase.

Japh gripped the wobbly wheel and ran shear alongside her, his cab crushing three legs off the spider on her roof, then, as she pulled ahead of him, swerved tight in behind her to crush her pursuer. But Chops, swooping in from the opposite side, had the same idea, and though they seriously squashed that APP, they slammed side-to-side doing it, and Japh felt his front end wrench and go lame.

"Get aboard!" shouted Chops. Japh swarmed aboard with both swords as Chops swung around to catch up to Jool. At the far end of the lane she threw a one-eighty and came straight back at them, accelerating for another dump-off maneuver—hit her brakes and the five-legged spider pitched right off, came tumbling under the wheels of the SUV. . . .

As they crushed this APP, the whole parking structure trembled beneath them, and a spew of concrete came meteoring from the Mutual Beneficial building—where Curtis was! A *big* chunk of concrete, which cracked the pavement and smashed three cars before it came to rest. A flying fragment of it tore the head off Jool's third APP, and peeled it right off her roof.

Their vehicles idled, no APPs left in evidence, but their eyes now riveted on the towering structure, on the amazing great chunk now punched out of its lower-middle floors—in fact, just below the window Japh had seen Curtis in. The impact would surely have stunned him.

A blue streak from the sky, and again the towering building shook, and shed more hurtling frags from its wound, whose impacts made the whole parking structure hum to its foundations.

"Cannon fire!" screeched Chops. "They're blowing that building to shit! Jool! Get in here with us!"

"Curtis is up there," Japh said. "I've gotta help him."

"I don't think there's time! Look at it!" And just as Jool piled into the SUV with them, at a point just above its great wound, the building's topmost twenty stories began to sag off the vertical.

"That's it!" shouted Chops. "It's gonna fall! Everyone buckle up. No time left to get offa this structure!"

Three more cannon blasts tore at the skyscraper's wound. Its upper two hundred feet cracked free and, with immense deliberation, began to fall. Chops slammed the SUV into reverse.

The tires screamed as they backed from under the giant's line of descent. Tilting . . . tilting . . . and here it came, windows flashing as it plunged. The SUV hit the guardrail with its rear bumper, and Chops kept his foot on the gas, rubber smoking to press their rear bumper against that railing, as far back from the impact zone as possible.

The colossus slammed onto the structure. The SUV

rocketed into the air, did a complete flip, and crashed down wheels-first onto the pavement, pavement that now sloped sharply down to the fallen giant, buckled by its impact.

They all thought they had broken their necks as they shot upward, then broken their backs when they slammed down, but through his daze, Chops realized the engine was dead, and they were rolling backward. He pulled the hand brake and stopped them from rolling back down against the top-pled titan, where all the other cars were now clustered. The three of them all staggered out, and stood on the tilted pavement in a cloud of concrete dust as thick as smoke.

Most of the toppled half-building was still hinged to the standing thirteen-story stump by folded but unbroken girders, but its top dozen stories had snapped at the point of impact, lying flat on the buckled pavement and protruding beyond the parking structure's rim, so that the flagpole on its apex hung over the street below.

Dazedly they gazed up the steep slant of the main column—a hundred and fifty feet up to the smoking stump that still propped it.

"Curtis was just above the cannon strikes," Japh said. "If he survived those, then he hardly fell at all."

"Bent like that," said Chops, "it could snap any time. Hey, look there."

Fangs and a foreleg protruded inertly from the debris. He kicked at concrete rubble, and plucked an eyeknob.

"Here too," said Jool. An APP crushed between two cars. She pocketed the tag. Like an Easter egg hunt. A strangely peaceful moment.

Then Japh looked up along the huge cracked shaft slanting up into the sun. "I think it'll hold if they don't cannon it again. I've gotta go up and find Curtis. I'm sorry. Will you guys be OK?"

Chops looked up the building, and looked at Jool—clearly he did not want her going up there. Jool stared at Japh, and after a moment said to Chops, "We got a tidy sum in our pocket right now, got two more tags and the survivors bonus still coming. Enough to take care of everybody. . . ."

Chops was shaking his head, but then froze, and cocked his ear.

scritch scritch scritch scritch . . .

All three looked up at once. Twenty feet overhead, spider legs thrust from one of the windows of the toppled tower. The whole APP came twiddling out, and before it had reached the corner and launched itself down upon them, was followed by another.

THE KING IS DOWN

Sandy Devlin exulted. Never had she been on a shoot where so much APP ass had been kicked! A 30, even a 35 percent survival rate was already in the cards, with just a little more Help from Above.

Twenty-two rafts throughout the shoot, including four other payboat chiefs like herself, were icing APPs left and right. The Defectors, they called themselves, with wry, secret smiles, and this, for them, was the Last Shoot. Their houses were already converted to cash, and their bags packed. They'd all been afraid that they were too few to strike a hard enough parting blow, but it was turning out better than they'd dared hope. Ice-cannons were trimming APP density just enough to let the Zoo-meat gut APP-meat six ways from Sunday.

She'd never flown faster from payout to payout, nor tracked the safety of so many individual extras—some really brave ones this shoot!—and through it all, she had even kept Kate on screen, and seen her get safe to Mutual Beneficial, as close to a haven as the set offered, if she could make it to the upper floors. Talk about multitasking!

She hoped she was giving old King Val back there a good show. She knew he was filming her, knew he was bent on getting her whole act in the can, trying to figure out how she was doing it, before he called in Metro to shoot her down. Let him try. There wasn't a Metro pilot in the fleet that could outfly her.

Then, as she pulled high to scope for more payouts, she saw something missing from the skyline. It was the top half of Mutual Beneficial! The sonofabitch had gunned it down, with Kate Harlow inside it!

For a long moment, Sandy's mind hung in a kind of limbo. *You're not a killer,* she mused. *You try to be just the opposite. Do you really want to make an exception for Val Margolian? . . . No, you don't want to kill him outright, I guess. . . . But how about dipping him—dipping him as deep as he'll go—into his own shit?*

Her thoughts roamed the set, sifting possibilities. Trying to think like a director, searching for the perfect scenario. She had him under her control—that is, he was going to follow wherever she led him. . . .

And suddenly, she had it.

She began to lead him, meanderingly at first, bringing him around to the neighborhood she wanted, calk-ing distances and speeds to a whisker.

In position now, her target ahead, time to put on some speed, make him accelerate, yes, a bit more, twenty klicks faster, yes. . . . "Hang on tight, Radner," she said. "Tight now! Tighter than a tick's ass!" And she kicked her raft into a towering backward arc—Val would lose her for just a second, and that was all she needed.

"Jesus Christ!" squealed Radner. "What are you doooooo-ing!?"—as they curved high, high through a canted three-sixty (get the angle just right, now . . .) and came whooshing back down on Val from above and behind. He was staring up at her as she meteored down across him, keyed lightly on her console, and pumped two iceballs right down through his console keyboard, blowing it to frags in his face, annihilating his navigational control. . . .

Yes! As she pulled up past and above him to hover, she watched his raft sliding inexorably along the course it had held at impact—no braking action, no sign of steering control, sloping along at a smooth eighty klicks, and punching straight through the third-floor windows of a ten-story, old-fashioned office building. . . .

She could just detect the noise down there of his raft smashing its way deeper and deeper and deeper into the building—flimsy walls and doors in that set, she knew. . . . It was a sector of "older" brick office buildings—was very densely APPed, and torn up inside by air-battle fire and debris. It should be a real nightmare, surviving in there, if Val could manage to do that.

Sandy scooted back to work, smiling faintly with the thought that Mark Millar was at the helm, and musing on just how quick Millar might be about pulling Val back out of there. . . .

I should have run straight down to help Japh, but I couldn't tear my eyes from the wild fight they were waging. The first cannon hit threw me back across the room, and knocked me silly. I was lying on something soft, seeing stars. Another hit, like the building had blown up right under me, dust and broken glass blizzarding around me and then, more terrifying, a deep, creaky tremor running through the bones of the skyscraper.

I struggled off the futon couch I'd landed on. I had to find my shotgun and get out of this fucking building now, see if the blasts had hurt Japh down there . . . and then came three more blasts in succession, world-enders all, one right after the other. I was on the floor again, swimming through sharp debris, my whole body humming like a tuning fork . . . and the world began to tilt.

I stayed on all fours, scrambled back to the couch, crawled into the futon and wrapped it around me length-wise . . . *tilting* . . . *tilting* . . . I began to float, the couch frame slid away from me and I floated toward the floor as the floor rapidly became the ceiling.

I clutched that futon around me like life itself, like a pair of wings because I was hanging airborne along with all the furniture in the room. And as I floated through that long second, a universal roar surrounded me, and I howled without hearing my own voice. An avalanche crushed me, and I was gone. . . .

. . . I came back, and I was a living bruise lying blind in a padded coffin. The pain slowly clarified: a multitude of crushing pressures all along my front. I tensed, tested my legs and arms, and felt nothing broken, though there was a sharp pain in the small of my back. I found just enough room to work my hands up alongside my face.

I braced myself, and bench-pressed hard, felt some give. Massive, alarming movement, a big, complex mass began to teeter, *fall*, dragging me sideways. My head, and then my shoulders, were sliding out over *emptiness*! And then I felt big, bulky forms falling off me.

I could *see* my situation then, because I could turn my head. My head and shoulders stuck out past the edge of the window frame, and I watched the couch's wood frame and a table and chair or two falling, and there was my shotgun falling with it!—everything falling, and smashing to splinters on the parking structure a hundred feet below. I realized then that the pain in my back was the spur of my ax, and I straightened it on my hip.

Most of my body was wedged in the angle where the ceiling joined the wall just above the window—just *below* the window now. A jumble of furniture had piled on top of me in this same corner, and just now fallen off me. The room, the whole building, was maybe forty degrees shy of straight upside down.

With maneuvering I was able to sit up. I carefully climbed past the window and a little ways out across the ceiling, and paused to assess.

The building was steeply propped, still joined at one edge to its stump. I was on the wrong side of the building to get out. I had to climb through to the top side, the one we'd climbed in by, and go down the exterior wall, if I wanted to get to Japh in time to help him . . . if Japh was still OK.

A steep, scary path it would be, but a clear, quick one, one I could survive if I didn't go down it *too* quick.

So what was I waiting for? No shotgun, but I still had my Glock and my ax. . . .

I began to climb carefully the rest of the way across the ceiling to reach the upside-down doorway into the hall. *Carefully* because of our tilt, making the ceiling a steep floor that was just waiting to slide me straight back down and out the window.

I reached up and got the doorknob. The heavy door swung open, knocking me halfway back down the ceiling as it came. I gripped the plaster with my whole body and managed to stop my slide. Wormed my way up to the top of the door again and got a grip on the frame. Crossed over that, and then across the hall ceiling. Pushed open the door to the opposite suite, and climbed through.

There was a pair of slender hands gripping the lower (formerly upper) edge of the window frame. Cap's voice floated up from somewhere outside and below those hands:

"You got friction! Lotsa cracks! Use your fingers an' toes and inch on down!"

The hands released their grip and sank from sight.

Good. They might not be sure I had left yet, but Cap was seeing to Kate's safety first. And great! Here was a shotgun on the ceiling near the window—had a strap, so I hung it off one shoulder. Poked my head outside.

So steep! There was Kate, maybe fifteen feet down, her cheek pressed to the concrete like a lover, her arms hugging stone, her hands starfished to it, apparently frozen with fear. Cap was two windows below her, one foot planted on the corner of the window frame, trying to talk her down to him.

And far below them, was a radically altered scene. The parking structure's top level was V'ed down onto the level below it, all the vehicles collected in a jumble along the building's flank. Only one was moving, a dusty black pickup with Japh in the bed of it swinging a pair of swords at a bug that was climbing over the tailgate, struggling, as he fought, for balance against the slope and the truck's motion, because it was driving a wild pattern amid a pack of APPs chasing it on all sides. Good driving, but it wasn't Jool doing it because I saw her lean from the passenger window and cap a flanking bug with her derringer twelve-gauge. She blew its bulb to a green slick that the truck—veering from a leaping bug on its other side—got its tires in, going into a slide that nearly threw Japh from the bed. The driver was good, righted their course, hooked left, and crushed the APP that had just missed its leap. . . .

I had to move, had to get down and help them. Gripped the frame, fed my legs outside and down the wall, and gave my ass to the air.

There was barely enough slope for gravity to stick me to the wall. What gravity *mainly* wanted to do was peel me off, set me bouncing, jouncing, plunging down. Reluctantly, I released my grip.

The drag of the shotgun, the bulk of all I carried tugged me down. My hands starfished to the wall like Kate's, I tried to be all friction. My left foot touching the next window's glass, I wriggled sideways till my toe found the narrow ledge of its frame. Gripped the frame's side with one hand, and then dared to lift my head from the wall and look down on Kate, who was clutching, frozen, to the window below me.

"Kate!" I called. "Listen. We've gotta get down to help my friends! I'm gonna slide past you to the next one down. Then you can let go and I can catch you!"

"OK!" Her voice was a quaver.

"Yo, Curtis! Glad you could make it!" Cap from below. "Stay with the window line an use the frames like a ladder!"

Fine, but it was a long slither between rungs. And the air-battle was still hot, splitting the sky everywhere. Where was it I'd read that if you heard the shot, it wasn't going to hit you? But it didn't have to hit *us*, just this building. Down I went. Curving out past her, wriggling back to the window line below her.

But I got going too fast—almost missed the window, and just reached up in time to catch the bottom of the frame with one hand. But I felt I had discovered the balance of gravity and velocity now. "Cap! Go on! I've got her now. That's my 'kick down there. Join forces and we can kill 'em all!"

"Roger that!"

"Let go, Kate! I've got you!"

She did it—and was coming too fast. Got my hand up to her foot and, straight arm, just managed to hold her. "OK now, we've got it. Together now. Keep hugging the wall and I'll catch the next frame."

Holding her shoe, I found I could press her toe to the wall, like a brake for us both. We bellied down another window. Another . . . another . . . two more.

"Shit!" shouted Cap—quite a ways below me now he sounded. "Grab window! Back to the wall! We gotta shoot!"

"One more down," I told Kate, and dragged her, while Cap's pistol started barking, barking. I set her foot in the next ledge down. "Stay here!" I slid down one more, planted my heel and turned onto my back.

Shit indeed. Cap halfway down the building, and two bugs climbing not three windows below him—one leaking fluid, but both coming fast. Unstrapped the shotgun and shouldered it. Oh please let me not blow my foot off! "Lean left!" I shouted, and fired, nearly breaking my shoulder.

No hit. Racked, and fired again. Lead APP took it in the fangs, while his pal kept climbing. Cap tore some bulb off it, but on it came, and his pistol clicked empty. I racked and fired, racked and fired. It sank, bulb gushing—and down below, two *more* bugs were climbing onto the building.

In the same instant that I heard a roar behind me, the rim of my right ear was sliced off, and as the stars cleared from my eyes, a shotgun came end-over-ending down the wall past me.

"I'm sorry!" wailed Kate. "It jumped out of my hands!"

"Let's go!" I shouted. "Come down!"

Thank god for adrenaline. I went sliding right down on

my back, threading new shells in the magazine. I passed Cap, who had just finished reloading, and started down after me. . . .

What a sequence! What a *pair* of sequences! And for both, Mark Millar had his directorial instincts to thank. Sending the extra APPs up to the parking structure had perfected what Val had begun by toppling the 'scraper in the first place. And what a payoff. What a wild automotive ballet on the structure itself, and what a white-knuckler up on the slope of the fallen colossus.

But he'd put cam-rafts on the structure from the get-go, not a frame of that wild battle would be lost, and so he had to tear his eyes from it right now, had to focus on his second and even bigger windfall, a much trickier and darker opportunity.

This one Mark had created by withdrawing sector-boat surveillance on Val Margolian's raft, making his single-handed pursuit of Sandy Devlin a truly incognito affair. And he had *further* contributed to the scene's potential drama . . . by giving Val a jumpsuit that lacked both a belt-com and an APP driver.

Of course, Val had wanted to take down Devlin *personally*. And as for the belt-com, well, it was an understandable omission, resulting from Mark's haste to answer his master's summons.

Mark himself smiled at these pretexts. The hard fact was that Val had demoted himself to the status of an actor in his own epic. Mark was merely embracing his own new responsibility: that epic's director. This was Mark's sixteenth hour in the chair—his sixteenth hour in *eight years*. He was going to make the most of this moment, wherever it led his career. He began screening the interior cams of the building that had—not three minutes ago—swallowed Val's raft. He felt as excited as a kid opening a treasure box.

A good deal of air-cannon damage within the top five floors, and half the cams blacked out by it. The ones still functioning revealed dimness, shattered walls, leathery corpses half-covered by broken-down doors. It was an old-fashioned office building—here was a busted-up dentist's suite, a print shop, doctor's office. . . . Deceptively solid-looking carpentry in here, and a big APP release, for the structure's basement was the portal for a block that featured two hardware stores, and a pawnshop full of gun racks, and where extras had concentrated in abundance.

Down to the third floor now . . . more surviving cams down here. He keyed them up in sequence from the street side . . . bingo. A string of dead cams marked Val's crash zone. From the cams just offside of these, he found a tunnel of ruptured walls two . . . three . . . four rooms deep. And there, he found the raft nested in broken furniture and drywall, having come to rest in what looked like a conference room with a big table. The ceiling of the room had half-collapsed down onto the table, which explained how Val had exited the scene, for the raft was empty.

An image came to Mark: Bach, fingers poised above the keys of his organ. What notes next? The sequence was critical.

Commed Properties. "Billy?"

"Mark, please! We're down to exactly nine reserve."

"Hey, Billy—that's showbiz! I want four of 'em sent up the Battery Street portal in Sector C, but I want you to hold them on pause in the portal and I want their cams and their overrides uplinked to me here. Copy?"

"Copy that, Mark."

"ASAP please, Billy."

"Roger that, Mark."

Mark waited. *Everything* could wait until . . . here they were, the four new screens, with on-screen keyboards for the APPs' control.

One more detail now. He commed Sector F. "Hey, Streak. Speedo."

"Hey, Mark. In the chair for a spell?"

"Yes. And I've got a situation, guys. Val's down in-set—I saw him last in your sector. He's in a payboat with bow-mounted cams, wearing a jumpsuit. One of his incognito things. He doesn't like to be bird-dogged on his private business, but I've lost contact with him and I'm worried. I want you to look for him, just in case."

"Roger that, Mark. We'll send in six Metro, comb the sector."

"Thanks, guys. If you spot him, just let him know I've lost touch. The blame's all mine if he's miffed."

Val Margolian, shedding glass and plaster dust, crawled out of his raft. Stood up, and struck his head against the half-collapsed ceiling of the room. Staggered to a spot with more clearance and stood swaying for a few moments, letting the shock drain out of him, his body groping for its equilibrium.

There was daylight far behind him at the mouth of this ragged tunnel of punched-through walls. . . .

He knew exactly where he was, and as his thoughts cleared, realized how well that homicidal bitch had chosen this for his crash site. Its flimsy inner structure would permit his deep burial upon collision, and this building was an APP outlet.

Battery Street had been wreckage-strewn, and pretty quiet as they'd overflown it, so the first release of APPs had done their work, and dispersed set-wide. But since her cabal's APP slaughter meant that reserves were being called up everywhere, new death might emerge in here at any time.

Val's hand went to his belt for his crash com—and found it absent. Ditto his APP driver. Ice branched through his nerves.

Mark Millar might have overlooked the gear in his haste to assume the chair. And Mark could not, in any case, have foreseen Devlin's assault.

But Mark did know that Val was coming down in-shoot, to trail and maybe tangle with renegades. . . .

Well, survival first, and retribution after. A second check of the raft's console reconfirmed all communications to be dead. First order of business: Get far as possible from street level—get to the roof and flag a raft. Seize again his scepter and his thunderbolts, and annihilate the little Celtic bitch who'd shot him down.

Get to the roof fast, because the APPs here came in from the basement. Of course the fastest way to the roof was up the stairwell at the far wall of the structure. Unfortunately, the stairwell started from the basement, and was itself the very conduit of APP release. But it ended at the roof with a stout metal door that locked. Seven floors up from here.

The fewer flights he climbed in the stairwell itself, the better. This half-collapsed ceiling, dangling onto this conference table, could put him on the fourth floor, and maybe the broken-up interior offered further shortcuts. Mounting the table, he got a knee onto the sagged flooring of the room above, gripped its splintery edges and hauled himself upward.

This was agonizing work. Astonishing, the hardship of wrestling with matter physically, without the mediation of mechanical devices! Slivers lanced his palms and fingers, broken glass bit his knees as he floundered into the exploded room overhead. The tongue of flooring sagged steeper with his ascent and he had to scramble, grabbing and clawing with his bleeding hands. He almost slid back down, exhausted. Then the dread dawned that his noisy exertion might summon APPs to him. This sent a flush of adrenaline through his limbs that lifted him more swiftly, and he gained the higher room.

Gasping, he leaned against the broken wall. Six floors to go. This was not a "set" to him at present. It was a maze of blocked halls and perilous doors, all shards and splinters and shadows. And as he struggled through it, his exertions were steadily increasing his heat signal.

What if the com and driver were intentionally missing from his belt, Mark handing him a cement lifesaver? A just-in-case thing, assuming that Mark couldn't know Devlin would down him. If that was so, then couldn't Mark be sending more APPs up here right now?

No. Val must not think like that. The crash would have destroyed his onboard cam-links to Mark. If Mark had missed the moment of Val's crash, then he wouldn't know where Val was, unless he happened to check the interior cams of this building, just one among many hundreds.

Don't dither, just move! OK, but his hands felt terribly empty. He recalled the big splinters he had seen extras using for weapons.

Here was a loose plank of trim around the frame of a hall door. He worked his bloody fingertips under, and pulled it. With a shrill squeak of nails, it came halfway off, splintering at the end—good!—giving it a point. He hauled on it again, and had it free.

Now lay it nails-down and stomp their points flat. He did so . . . and thought he heard a distant after-concussion, but not like an echo. . . . His stomach roiled, but all was silence.

And then—was it just one floor below?—there came a faint, vigorous *scritch scritch scritch*. Climbing. Toward him.

His legs came alive, stumbling down the littered hall—and now, the scrabble of claws up the sagged bit of flooring he had just climbed! A door! A stout door between him and it—between him and a thing that was going to eat him *alive*! Found a door and plunged through—it latched, but felt so light, so flimsy as he thrust it shut. *Scrabble scrabble* outside and *wham*, a great weight hammered it and two of the panels cracked. *Wham*—the top half erupted and spider legs thrust clawing through.

He stumbled backward, collided and fell against . . . a dentist's chair! Got behind it, and as the spider, amid a spray of splinters, poured through, seized the heavy-jointed metal arm that bore the drill mount and swung it toward the onrushing nightmare. The spider, forelegs reared, batted the arm and swung it back at him. He staggered back and raised his plank.

It swarmed around the chair, driving him back, and then it reared up again and flourished its forelegs at him, twiddling its fangs and presenting, in that instant, its underside. Val thrust up with his spike. Felt a moment of despair as the metal in the monster's leg joints seemed to foil the thrust, but then saw the spider crumple, all its legs contracting, and fall lifeless.

Still clutching his spike, Val sprinted for the stairwell. Damn the portal, he must make the roof! Reached the stairs. Up flight after flight he pumped his way, but not halfway up, there came the click of following claws. Gasping, he climbed another flight, but his wind was failing and he heard it right behind. He whirled around and here it came . . . seemed to miss its footing, and paused a moment scrabbling for traction just three steps down. Val roared, and plunged his stake, buried it deep among its eyeknobs and pierced the hydraulics.

The monster spasmed and died.

Silence above and below him. He had won! His heart exulted. He had beaten his enemies mano a mano. Treachery had thrust him down into the Inferno, and he'd clawed his way back up by main strength!

He paused on the last flight before the rooftop. He felt

like the mythic Man of Power about to reveal himself—like Odysseus shedding his rags, and stringing his bow before the suitors. He stripped from his waist the useless pilot's belt, and ripped off his pilot's jumpsuit. He would display his undisguised Identity to the open air and rafts would dive to his will. And then he was going to blow that Devlin bitch *personally* out of the sky.

Now came the *scritch* of new claws—and there was the APP, just four flights down. No matter. Here before him was a door it could not break through. He walked up to it. Stepped through, out onto the roof, closed and bolted the steel portal. Swift spider impact from within. A powerless rattling and clawing.

Val stood gazing over the rooftops, once again the master of this model world! Now to call down vengeance.

XVII

THE LOST ARE FOUND

Sliding fast as we were, firing as we went, we'd taken some legs off the two new bugs, but they were still climbing toward us when we hit the hydraulic slick bled out by the first two we'd killed. Suddenly we were sliding much faster. I had just one shell in the chamber and no chance to put in another, when here was the lead bug, rearing as I closed with it. I jammed my muzzle into its fangs and let go, the blast lifting it as I crashed in among its legs.

Its claws tore me, but my impact dumped it sideways into its partner, and all three of us went sliding down on the blood of the one I'd just killed, the live one still trying to reach me as we all skied faster and faster in a tangle of legs and hydraulics and claws, and crashed onto the horizontal stretch of the broken building.

"Roll right!" I heard Cap call. I did, and heard him firing as he came down, but I hauled out my ax as his pistol clicked empty and he hit the pile. Lucky I had. The surviving bug was just rearing up at him when I split its eyes with my bit.

"Help Kate!" I shouted, as she came sliding down. Reloading, I looked down at the parking structure just in time to see the black pickup throw a turn, with four bugs in pursuit, and stall out. No—run out of gas! Jool jumped out with a saber—must be out of shells—and the driver, a wiry little guy, did the same at the other side, because all four bugs were trying to climb into the bed with Japh.

I let fly at one, and tore its bulb enough to slow it. Lord! There's nothing like a twelve-gauge! Then I jumped off the building onto the roof of the highest car in the heap at its side. Tricky footwork, jumping from car roof to car roof, but now I was close enough to draw one of the bugs after me. Let him get closer, and killed the shit out of him. Made it down to the pavement, and joined my friends in the pleasant work of extermination.

The mayhem on the set hadn't quieted a bit, but when the six of us stood at ease, gathered down there on the pavement, it seemed that we gazed at one another in a beautiful silence. Then I was hugging Japh till there were tears in both our eyes, and then we were all laughing and high-fiving like maniacs.

All of us were crazy—a sense of happiness that felt like an indestructible bubble. We made introductions like we were in some historical costume drama. And this is Kate! How do you do, Kate? Cap, have you met Jool? Allow me to present Chops, Kate. We were all drunk on . . . being alive.

"I can't believe you two," Jool said to Japh and me. "You crazy fucking 'Risers! Yesterday you roar in and bust my business up. And today, here I am, and here *you* are again, and . . . we're all rich."

But her eyes had lingered on mine, and there was a glee in them that was about something besides being rich.

"Isn't it amazing?" I answered her, trying to answer her eyes as well. . . .

"The foothills of the Trinities," said Chops. "I'm gonna have a pond. A big one. Reeds growing around the fringes. Egrets and herons. And man, I'm gonna *swim* in it."

"What about fish?" asked Japh.

"Man, I'll stock it with trout for ya."

"A big black dirt garden," said Jool. "My mom would think it was paradise! She can make anything grow any-where, but with deep black dirt . . ."

"Maybe she could teach my auntie," I said, surprised by the thought. "Her hands are all twisted from the keyboard. Maybe gardening would—"

"People. Friends. I'm sorry. Listen." It was Kate. Her tone brought the real world back around us. We cringed at a roar of the air-cannon, and scanned around for APPs. "Lis-ten. We should all get back up on that building, where we've got some vantage. Payout's easier there and you've got more tags. We don't have long to go. I . . . think we shouldn't start daydreaming yet."

"It's a good idea," I said. "And they can pick you up when they pay us out."

"No. I'm staying on-set. I've got something that might help us, in case there's trouble before the end."

We didn't ask her to explain. We liked that "us," coming from a studio tech who could just wave her arms to be snatched back up into the air.

We then enjoyed a kind of nightmarish Easter egg hunt. From the parking structure, we plucked a dozen APP tags. Up on the building, we plucked four more. Then, resting up there, we signaled a payraft. Cap and I, grinning, explained why we insisted that the other four take all the payouts. Kate, offered pickup by the pilot, called, "Thanks, but I have something to do down here."

I gave Kate a bunch of twelve-gauge shells, gave Chops my Glock and clips—Japh insisted that he preferred his sabers.

Val Margolian could not believe what fury and vengeful pride had done to his wits. He had burst triumphantly up here onto the roof, burning to summon down rafts by the naked power of his Identity. In his vengeful wrath, he had loomed too large in his own mind, had failed, as a director, to see the scene he would be a part of; to see his own actual dimensions within that scene.

They took him for a damned Extra! All the rafts were working at full sprint in a payout frenzy, thanks to Devlin and her cronies pumping APP mortality so high, and all they glimpsed was a silver-haired guy in slacks and dress shirt, arms raised like Lear, screeching at the sky but with no tag in his hand.

"I'm Val Margolian!" he raged at them. "I'm the director! I'm the author! I'm VAL MARGOLIAN!" It was a torment of humiliation, as if he were some mad impostor, some wigged-out Zoo-meat trying a desperate ploy. He stood here center-stage, *trapped* on stage, a fictional character who couldn't shed his role.

Why had he shed the jumpsuit? Put him in *that* role—fallen pilot—and the next raft that passed would swoop down for him. His fury at his failed ploy, at Devlin's spotting and nailing him, had goaded him to that brainless gesture. And now, with that damned APP still hammering at the steel door, he couldn't go down to retrieve it.

But . . . why was that bug still persisting? Why hadn't it wheeled away, seeking another access or other prey . . . as it was programmed to do when blocked?

That first APP he'd fought. Why had it reared back like that, as if threatening him, trying to terrify him? It was programmed simply to spring and feed at first opportunity. And that second APP, slipping on the stairs . . . they were designed for flawless ascent of stairs. . . .

That reared-back APP. Something almost comic, mocking in that self-presentation. Like . . . *BOO!*

No. Oh no. Someone was overriding these APPs. Puppeteering them. One of the rebel rafters must have hacked in. Giving him a taste of his own medicine they would be thinking, and making hay on the APPs while they had him down here scrambling and dodging. And he had helped them! Stupidly delayed his own pickup by shedding the jumpsuit!

Or . . . Mark Millar could be doing it. Surely, only he could be running them with such detailed control.

A fine cold sweat bloomed on his body.

But no! If Mark had wanted Val dead, he would have killed him inside, not driven him to the rooftop for pickup. It had to be the rebels, having some filthy fun.

But what was this? At last! A payraft slanting down . . . Hallelujah, people who knew him by sight. It was the Director's Cut raft, with Valdez and Fox in the bow, and their cam-raft tailing them. Val would make sure that *this* footage was edited out, but lord he was glad to see them! They were still some distance out, the two actors waving at him energetically. He had to smile at their youthful enthusiasm— gaily waving like they'd run into each other on a day at the beach!

No . . . It wasn't that kind of waving. They were making urgent signals, pointing at something. What were they . . . ?

Mark Millar was rapt. His mind hung on a condor's wings. By god, *this* was the true creative delirium, an exaltation of unfettered invention that had been Val Margolian's private property for so many years!

From the moment Mark, in the body of an APP, had erupted through that door, reared back above Val, possessed his cringing shape in the red and violet light of its infra and ultra eyes, he knew he would have to devour his master.

For he quickly grasped that a priceless narrative had been born the instant Val's raft had plunged into that building. The disguised director shot down by the rebel rafters! For their work had already been caught by the Metro cams tailing them—several clear shots of ice-cannonballs striking APPs were already in the can. With this plot on-screen, Val's heroic struggle up from their treacherous shipwreck *had* to be filmed. The whole conflict, so irresistably gripping: a guerrilla war between Creator and Anticreators.

The Creator struck down! And assailed by his own monsters! And then, of course, the Creator striking back . . . and slaying one! No! Slaying *two*, at least!

Even as the narrative was born in his mind, Mark's left hand was keying APP One's pursuit of Val, keying it through the door of the dentist's office, while his right hand was positioning APP Two . . . here, and APP Three . . . here, and APP Four, the pièce de résistance . . . here. Fleet thought fleetly blossoming into the solid machinery of fate.

The Tale, not Mark, was going to kill Val. The spontaneously generated Tale Val's vid, and his own fierce impulse, had set in motion, and Mark's own blossoming genius was smoothly guiding to its climax.

Never had Mark loved Val more than he loved him now. The man, like Atlas turning into a mountain to uphold the sky, had sunk his very life into the greatest action sequence ever filmed. What a closing scene: The King, his valiant hands stained with the inhuman blood of two of his attackers, overwhelmed and devoured on a rooftop by a third.

And thus Val Margolian, at his apotheosis, would have

brought near completion two epochal vids: *Alien Hunger*, the greatest sci-fi live action ever shot, and a Director's Cut that would rank as the greatest true crime thriller of the era, *The Sacrifice of the King*.

And then, with Holly Zimmer flanking him, Mark Millar would make live war upon the industry, would become the colossus of live action's next phase, a string of blockbuster military historicals.

Whoa! No need to fake APP Two's death—Val actually *killed* it! "You *are* the King," Mark said softly, sadly smiling. "You *are*, Val"

And, still all unconscious, Val put a perfecting touch on what he'd set in motion. Stripped off his disguise, and strode onto the rooftop in his own defiant identity! Oh, this next scene was going to be a gem.

Its final element had already come to Mark, all the marvelous ingredients still just leaping to his hands. He commed Luce Harms and ordered her to the rescue. Let the Star Raft, with its trailing cam-boat, preside over the conclusion.

All right, they were just a couple blocks away. Mark made APP Three declare its continued presence with a renewed assault on the steel door . . . and then he awakened APP Four—clinging to the building wall just below the parapet—and brought it up onto the rooftop. Released his control, and let it do its thing.

Val was hyper-alert. Though his eyes were on the approaching raft—answering their vigorous waves, still not getting it—when the APP leaped, he dodged. Damn! The old man could move when he had the motivation. Dodged just in time. Slipped doing it, but the bug had to scramble through a turnaround after overleaping him, and he gained his feet and sprinted—*away* from the raft, but that was smart, drew the bug across the roof and then hooked sharply back—magnificent! Tricked the bug into a second overleap! Gained precious seconds to build a lead, and now the raft was angled right down in above the edge of the roof, Val sprinting, sprinting for it—what a sequence! The spider was turned and already closing fast.

Look how Valdez and Fox cheered him on! They had fallen completely into character for derring-do, Valdez leaning way out from the raft in his glittery silver spandex, reaching his long, ropy arm down from the bows, his buffed neck straining as he shouted—you could almost see the words he was shouting: *Come on, Val! We got you! You can make it!*

Both actors were radiant, transported by this moment, vid made life and themselves really *being* the heroes they played!

And here came Val sprinting, reaching for Valdez's arm, the APP Four's foreleg actually touching his heels—this was incredible!—and now Val was leaping up, grabbing the startled Valdez high up on his arm, seizing his shoulder, and, in his mindless fervor, giving a mighty pull that, at the same time that it toppled Raj out of the raft, hauled Margolian aboard it!

Mark watched in awe. Fate had just given him a scene beyond anything he could have conceived himself. The noble actor—nailed right there, writhing even now under the spider's deep-sunk fangs! And the fallen angel, the director, there, standing in the raft, in the safety he had so tragically purchased with the life of bold, self-risking Raj Valdez! And what was Val doing? He was furiously demanding the pilot's chair from the woman who held it, so intent on seizing his stolen scepter and smiting his enemies that he seemed not even to have noticed the shriveling, blackening star on the roof below!

Humbly, Mark sat a mere spectator now. This priceless drama was its *own* creation. Harms, one of the key conspirators, was arguing furiously with Margolian. Suddenly she turned the raft on its side, and Val had to hug the floor to stay on board. She rocketed the raft away, still flying at tilt, showing Val who was in command. She zigged and zagged to drive the message home, and then shot away, the camboat flying breakneck to keep up. Mark was certain that Val would not escape that raft until shoot's end, and the camraft would catch all of the King's airborne captivity.

Absently but efficiently, Mark returned his attention to all his other screens—had indeed already conceived another little touch to be added to his work on the Mutual Beneficial scene. But still he allowed part of his mind to muse upon his future.

Val had absolute creative control over *Alien Hunger*. The Director's Cut, as publicity, was studio property—front to back, editing and all.

Val lived—and Mark was glad of that! Was overjoyed!—but the era of live war was still at hand. With this Cut in the can, Holly Zimmer would see to that. The board of directors would gladly bank the immense profits that the Cut would reap, but they would also see the wisdom of developing the career of a second star director, one with a new genre to unfold to the world, and one who had never been seen by the whole vid-watching world throwing his savior, *Raj Valdez himself*, to the jaws of a spider.

XVIII

TOTENTANZ

We were arrayed in an outfacing perimeter on the fallen building. Not talking. Trying to keep our ears focused for the small sounds of claws amid the roar of the streets and the air-battle.

Another payboat came down over us—the pilot a wiry, bright-haired woman with quick icy eyes, and the paymaster a truly exhausted-looking little guy. Jool, Japh, and Chops saluted her, and the pilot smiled.

"You guys sit tight," she said. "I didn't know this was coming down when I sent you here"—nodding at the building—"but what more can happen here now? You're armed, stay here off the streets. Every last APP's up, the whole reserve. Hey, Kate. What's up?"

"We're good, Sandy."

This made the pilot grin. "Riding it out, hey? I knew you had it in you. The end's not far off. Stay put." She rocketed the raft back to work.

After a moment, Kate said, "She didn't know it was coming down, and I didn't either. . . ."

Something in the tone of that. "*You* didn't either?" Jool prompted.

"I was an assistant director." She didn't sound happy saying it.

"So why were you payboatin'?" Cap asked.

"I was demoted. But what I meant was, bringing this down was an in-shoot inspiration of Margolian's. And if so, it would be just like him to push it that last extra step."

Cannon fire obliterated our ears. White lightning, whistling concrete crowded the air. Great chunks exploded out of the tilted part of the 'scraper, the bursts marching all the way up to its juncture with the vertical stump of the building. And then the fire settled in at that juncture, beginning to smash the top right off that stump. The huge tilted part was already trembling for a fall.

"Run for the the tip," screamed Kate through the din. "That falls the rest of the way, the rest of the parking structure will collapse under us!"

Run? You better believe we did. Huge cracks sprouted through the building under our feet. That flagpole at its far end, still a good fifteen feet above the street, was wagging like a tail, but we sprinted for it like a safe haven compared to the giant coming to pieces right behind us.

"Shotguns down first!" screamed Cap—meaning we could hold a perimeter for the others to come down in. Passing Kate, I saw her pluck something small from her toolbelt. As I neared the tip, out over the street, it was like running on an earthquake—I hung the gun on my neck and dove for the flagpole, got my arms around it, hung jittering like a fish on a line, and dropped. Hit pavement, unslung, and came up barrel out, had to fire right then into fangs so close I saw the drops of solvent hanging from their tips.

Pretty quick it was me, Cap, and Chops, jacking out buckshot and forty-fours as Jool, then Kate dropped down in our perimeter. Then an atom bomb went off—the propped piece of skyscraper toppling, and the whole parking structure under it exploding down onto the street, blasting a sleet of dust and debris in all directions that backed off our predators for the moment. But suddenly there was Japh, sprawled way out midstreet, in spider land, struggling to get his legs under him, not managing. He must still have been on the flagpole when the building collapsed and the pole had catapulted him out.

"Jool!" I screamed. I grabbed my last handful of shells and shoved them in her hand, then sprinted to Japh, blasting spider meat as I ran.

Reached him in time—*almost* in time—blasted an APP just as it brought its fangs down at Japh's uplifted arm, blew that APP almost away, but one of its fangs connected, pierced Japh's wrist, and swelled it with venom before slipping out again as the APP collapsed.

I dragged him back as Cap came with covering fire. "Don't move!" I said. "Don't circulate the poison!" Because his hand was puffed like a huge purple glove with the venom, and the swelling was pushing up into his forearm, swelling out an inch a second.

"No!" I screamed, dropped my gun and pulled out my ax and said, "Hold it out! Hold it still!" Because my ax already knew what it was doing, the only thing it could do, we could do, I was gripping the haft, the bit swinging up, arching high above my head, then my right hand shortening its grip for extra pull on the downstroke. If I had thought about this half a second before my ax hand thought of it, I could never have done it. My arms obeyed the ax, and I chopped clean through his forearm just where it tapered to the wrist.

"Hold on!" I was undoing my belt, tying him off with it tight, *tight* just above the stump, all the while knowing we were in for it now, hearing Chops's gun click empty, hearing him take up my twelve-gauge, fire that once, and *it* click empty, only Jool's derringer and Cap's gun roaring now. . . .

A clear moment—nothing left close for that moment, but spiders everywhere and closing fast. I picked up my ax, which had fallen when I took off my belt, and saw something else, black and crumpled, had also fallen . . . and picked up the palps. I stood straddling Japh. "We can't leave him, guys! How long to shoot's end?"

"Five minutes!" cried Kate.

"Jool reloads after every shot. You stand by her side Cap, and you with the ax, Chops."

He laughed maniacally. "I'll Chop 'em!"

"What you got, Kate?"

"Let's find out." And she stepped out to meet an on-comer, her fingers tapping a little keyboard. Confusion in its legs. The back ones kept coming, but the front ones were backing. She held the thing twitching, not coming or going. Jools sawed-off went off behind me, and here came a bug straight for me and Japh.

I stepped out to meet it, waiting for its fangs to go right through my chest, praying I hadn't gone insane without realizing it. The battered, crumpled palps stopped it cold.

The spider got instantly down to a vigorous palp-wiggle with my battered prosthetics—a thorough investigation.

It wheeled as it twiddled, checking me out from different angles, left and right, right and left, and I wheeled with it, trying to imitate its rate of twiddle . . . but I couldn't get it to wheel *away*, satisfied.

The spider found me . . . inconclusive. It seemed to think there was something unusual, perhaps intriguing, in this palp-job I was giving it.

Then here came a second one. I heard a shotgun blast behind me, heard the whistle of the ax, saw Kate still holding her APP tangle-footed . . . I was on my own. Here was my new partner, and I whipped one of the palps up to it. It stopped it, but only just.

They both set to twiddling furiously on one palp apiece. I definitely wasn't giving good palp now. They inspected me fiercely, wheeled in opposite directions, and I straddled Japh again, arms stretched to the limit to keep contact. They wheeled back together, then turned to twiddle each other—a reality check.

Ah! This was more like it! Rich, full-bodied palp, the way it should be! They wheeled back on me to check out this gimp with the half signal once more. No! I was definitely not good palp, and seemed to be giving off the wrong kind of heat signal too. . . .

They were nearing some kind of frustration crisis, really mauling my palps now, crowding in on me. Desperate, I whipped both palps on one, twiddled, whipped both on the other, twiddled. It bemused them—bemused them, detained them just a beat. Then I wheeled hard, crowding the one I was palping sideways into the other. The other scuttled around and came at me again, and once more they had me splitting the palps at full stretch, directly between them.

I was losing it. The mad dance was lifting my brain away from me. I wasn't me anymore, I was just this crazy detail in this mad movie. When the closing music came up, as the credits rolled, I would dissolve away. . . .

Both spiders reared up on their back legs and froze, reaching for the sky. Then they performed a crude, ghastly bow, bending at the midsection, salaaming with their forelegs. Then they turned, dropped to all eights, and sped away from us. I turned around. Jool, Chops, Cap, and Kate stood stunned. Their APPs too had backed off, and were reared on their back legs, waggling their forelegs at the sky.

"How 'bout a chorus line!?" a woman's voice called. "Let's line 'em up and dance 'em around!"

Two women and a smallish guy were rushing toward us, holding little keyboards like Kate's, fingering them with off-hand mastery. The shoot raged on, but we stood in a clear zone. The guy had a punk wig of red spikes, and surfer bag-

gies with loaded pockets. The women were dressed in jogging gear and the pockets of their shorts also severely
bulged. One had a screaming red wig on, and the other,
though she was white, a huge Rasty do. "Come on! Hoist
him up," said Rasty, rushing up to Japh. "Next street's part of
Amnesty Corridor, the Medic station will be open for business in seventeen, sixteen, fifteen, fourteen . . ."

Chops, Cap, and I were hoisting Japh by his thighs and
arms, getting him into a sitting carry, rushing him over the
pavement toward the intersection.

". . . six . . . five . . . four . . ." Our heavy-pocketed new
friends intoned it in unison, trotting at our sides, their
drivers held ready to defend our flanks. . . .

And then—high above the set—a golden, mellow trumpet solo sounded, majestic music that filled the phony city,
and that stilled all other sound, for now the aircraft froze
in the sky, and the traffic whined to a standstill, and spiders
everywhere were stopping, sagging, freezing where they
crouched.

And that noble, amped voice that had started the shoot,
addressed us once again. It uttered mellow words of mercy,
of reward—it billowed out over the silent buildings. The
shoot was done! We had done well. We were to follow
the directional flashers of the Metro rafts now coming to
hover above our exit routes from the set.

"All extras now possess as their uncontested, unexam-
ined, untaxed property any and all cash on their persons. All
extras will collect the survival bonus at their exit gates.
All extras will be given the services of armored Metro transports and armed Metro escorts to convey them and their

earnings from the studio to any destination of their choice. All extras requiring immediate medical treatment will find surgical facilities on every block of every exit route marked by the rafts' directional flashers. Panoply Studios thanks you for a truly outstanding performance. Have a great day, folks."

A big med-raft was parked just past the first corner—it had six cots, state-of-the-art life support. They had Japh on the cot, IVed, shot with meds, and two surgeons prepping his stump under the light, within thirty seconds. "We'll do full sutures," said one through his mask as they worked, "smooth off the bone, sew him up. The call's already in—the transport takes him straight from the gate to Panoply General for a first prep in prosthetics. A bio-electric hand, state of the art, already paid for."

A little guilt there, behind that doctor's mask? He was a healer working cleanup for a meat-shredding machine, after all. But I was grateful anyway.

"Thanks. I'm riding with him."

"We all are," said Jool, Cap, and Chops together.

Rasty smiled at us. Icy blue eyes on that little woman, and I think I glimpsed red hair beneath her wig. "You guys are one hell of a team. I was catching your act whenever I could during payout. I am telling you here and now, officially, that with all my years of watching extras, I dub you guys Most Bitchin' I Have Ever Seen. I hope we all run into each other somewhere. But right now, my friends and I have to mingle. Good luck."

Then she took her APP driver, and waggled it in front of the medical team at work on Japh, and flung it against the wall. The little guy and the other woman did the same, plastic frags flying. The two surgeons met their eyes for a moment, and Rasty gave them a wink. The surgeons went back to work, and our three saviors melted into the stream of surviving extras.

All those extras! They were limping and dirty and battered and torn. They walked still astonished through the trashed world that had been their only universe for the last two hours. They threaded through the rubble, and the torn machines, and the corpses shrunken into eloquent pantomimes of the moment of death. What stunned them most was not so much the hell itself that they had lived, but that it could be switched *off* like this, with a casual flick of the wrist. They looked up as they walked, at the air still busy with silent rafts—looked up into the realm of the studio gods who had run this show. There was as much amazement as rage in their eyes. But as they looked up, the sun fell on their faces, and you could see the first flashes of wonder, of release, of dawning hope there too.

"Notice that raft there?" Cap was beside me, looking up.

"Yeah," I said. It seemed to be on auto-avoid, just cruising along, threading through the other traffic and dodging whatever approached it. The pilot had no head. Was just a crudely stuffed jumpsuit strapped in the chair. Ditto the paymaster in his harness.

"All right!" said Jool. "I guess we know whose boat *that* is."

We watched all those rafts, got a glimpse of some others that just might be dummy-driven too.

Kate was sitting by Japh's cot, talking to him. She saw us watching the sky. "That's unusually thick traffic up there, guys, a lot of unmarked Metro, and they're just cam-ing, not busting. It's something in-house, the studio filming itself at work. Whoa! Look there!"

Here came a payraft cruising at a sharp tilt, with a silver-haired guy hugging the floor amidships and Stone Fox in the harness. Close behind it was a big cam-raft, all its cranes and booms, bristling like spider legs, extended to light and film the lead raft from every angle. And right under it, care-fully matching its speed, came another raft, with techs and suits in it. These people helped the two men down from the tilted raft—while half a dozen unmarked Metro rafts, clos-ing in from all sides, got their own footage of the whole operation.

"My oh my," said Kate. "That's the director. It looks like he hasn't been directing this shoot for some time. It's defi-nitely not him who authorized all these close-ups of his rescue. . . . Listen, guys." She stood up, though she was still holding Japh by his surviving hand. "Thank you. Thank you, guys, for my life." There were tears in her eyes.

"Hey!" said Jool. "You fought for us. You stood our backs. Thank you for *our* lives. Our casa is your casa, any time."

"That's right," I said—and I looked at Jool, Chops, and Cap and we looked at Japh, and we all knew we meant *our*. Kate bent to kiss Japh. "I've got your address now, big guy. I'll be seeing you before you change it."

She commed a Metro raft, and as she got into it, Japh called to her, "You tell the studio I'm suing if this prosthe-sis compromises my career as a concert pianist!"

"That'll be *their* worry," she said, smiling.

Japh blustered and swore he wanted to walk—to *run* out the gate—but they put the four of us in a med-raft, Japh on a gurney, and we glided our way at walking height amid the last of the extras filing out. We traded jokes with them as we went, Japh waving his stump—to the flusterment of the medic with us—and roaring out crudities at the sky: "Hump my stump, Panoply! I'm going *fishing*!"

And the happy, battered, sunbathed extras roaring: "You tell 'em, 'Riser! An' tell us if you need a hand with the pole!"

Here was the gate in the set wall. Here were the Metro handing us our survivors packets as casually as parking chits. How blithely I tucked mine away—amid the obese nest of its fellow packets.

Arrayed out there on the runway surrounding the set wall were the transports. Big squat brutes, practically bomb-proof, built to carry new-made fortunes into the Zoo. The loading was slow, multiple destinations being co-ordinated for each vehicle.

"They help you get it home," said Cap wryly, "but they don't help you get out of town with it. So here's what we do. Don't take the transport home, it's a red flag. We take it to Scarfield's Wreckers, buy a shitload of some good weaponry, and some rides that look beat up but have some juice and tires on 'em."

"A lot of other people be heading to Scarfield's already," Jool said.

"It's a big lot," Cap told her. "He got plenty for every-one."

Jool and Chops conferred, and Chops announced to the rest of us, "We're gonna have to get at least one truck. We got tanks, pipe, wiring, generators, tools—stuff that'll get our new houses set up faster. You 'Risers, an' you Cap, you got stuff you're takin' to the mountains, we'll all truck together—whaddaya think?"

We all liked it just fine. "We'll come visit you," I said. "Start getting coordinated. Couple days, when Japh's got his hand."

"No," said Jool. "We want you to meet our folks, but first we'll visit *you*, and then you'll let us *escort* you back to our place. We come this far, we don't wanna lose you guys now. That Zoo is *dangerous* for 'Risers, boy!"

Man, did we all laugh at that one. We laughed and laughed, looking back up at the set wall, at the shining structures towering within it. . . .

XIX

A PROFOUND IDEA

The new set was taking shape. Mark Millar had established his offices on the top floor of the HQ high-rise even before it had been enveloped in its new outer identity—one tower of a huge old, half-destroyed cathedral. Mark watched the tech-rafts outside hosing concrete foam into the forms enveloping him. The years, it seemed to him, arced away before him like a rainbow bridge, a technicolor trajectory of groundbreaking vid.

Val had gotten *Alien Hunger* in the can within a month. To Mark, the board had given co-director's credit on the Director's Cut. A monkish assistant all these years—a reverent presence hovering helpfully at the elbow of Greatness—now he was coequal maker of a Cut that had already, just two weeks released, matched the earnings of *Alien Hunger* itself since its release two months ago.

The media were ablaze with Raj Valdez's death. Stills of poor Raj's kitelike remains, tautly sheathed in silver spandex, had somehow been obtained by the press. The public was afroth—was still gobbling *Hunger* like it had just hit the shelves, while the Cut was raging on every talk show on the planet.

"Hi, Mark!" Holly Zimmer's silver quills and loving smile on his screen. "I just can't stop *gloating*, dear. Panoply with *two* star directors, blazing new frontiers in all directions!"

Holly's mood these days ran to the rhapsodic. Panoply stock was stratospheric. The corporation had just acquired a competing studio of no small stature, and had a second almost landed. The first of its two star directors was currently in the south of France . . . evolving his next vid. The second sat amid the burgeoning set of *Battle of the Somme*, whose word-of-mouth ran everywhere like wildfire.

"New frontiers in all directions," he echoed her affectionately. "You're an artist, Holly. That's the artist's creed in a nutshell."

"You make me very happy saying that, Mark. And in fact, a new direction has just come up. A good friend of mine just showed me a screenplay."

Mark tensed, though not a tremor reached his smiling face. He'd assumed it was already agreed between them. Next for him would be his *Gettysburg*.

"Just listen, Mark. It's one of those golden insights that's glowing right there in front of everyone, too obvious to notice, and then someone wakes up and says, 'Wa-a-a-it a minute!' A live-action vid *about* the extras!! Big names to play the key extras, of course, with the shoot *itself*, of course, the whole apparatus included. We take the bottom shields off the rafts, get all the high-tech on screen, exsetera. But it's a drama about the *extras* themselves, the extras who also are *real people* that we come to *care* about. It's about their life-and-death struggles against, and ultimate *triumph* over, the horrible machinery of the shoot. It will go fucking *plutonium* in Zoos around the world!"

Mark Millar, for all his careful self-control, had not quite hidden his exasperation. "Holly. That's wonderful. That vid is *inevitable*. But *Gettysburg* should follow *Somme* immediately—strike while the iron of *Somme* is hot. And I have to say, bringing the audience behind the camera, don't you think we should do that a little more sparingly? I mean not just start doing it vid after vid?"

A shade of frost in Holly's still smiling eyes. Mark saw he might have torn it, slightly. "Mark, you're anxious to get your trademark established, I totally understand, but you don't want to glut the audience with *your* breakthrough either. I think another behind-the-camera, especially with *this* script, would set a nice offbeat pattern, keep the viewers keen to see what we'll do next."

Mark didn't want a standoff with Holly. Not right on the threshold of his career. He resorted to candor, bared his doubts. "I'll be honest. I don't mind waiting for anything at all you want to shoot first. My real qualm is that too much behind-the-camera, brilliant though it can be, could wear the mystery off vid and yes, sophistication aside, hurt the magic."

Holly regarded him for a long moment, appeared to be looking for the right words to answer him.

She smiled. "Even you, Mark, young—youngish Michelangelo that you are. Even *you* miss the same point that Val, for all his greatness, has always missed. Disclosures, *revelations*, make no difference. People don't give a shit about what they know, or don't know! As long as it's new, they'll watch *anything*! They've got nothing else to *do*!"

Mark was amazed to realize that he was shocked by these words. That he was actually indignant. Of course. Because he was a true artist, and Holly was not. He smiled at her. Henceforth, he would keep his own counsel, gracefully and skillfully shoot what she wanted shot, and wait his time. "You're wonderful, dear," he told her. "Us pompous types in the chair think we're masters of perspective, but your eyes are keener by far. I can't wait to read that script."

"You're a darling and a genius. I'll give it to you at lunch."

XX

OK, THEN

Well, we went back to L.A. again last spring—it was the soonest we could manage it. We had the two new houses framed by winter, camped in the little cabin for three months—and man, we had some fine time for reading then, read a quarter of the way through the whole new cache of books that Jool brought with her—and that was a pickup-bed-full. What bliss! Then we got the houses roofed, floored, and sheeted by May. So it was time to retrieve furniture and more materials from the houses in Jool's compound.

Millie and Rick, Jool's neighbors, stayed here in Sunrise to help Japh and Chops work on the pond, and their charming irrigation system. As for Japh, he wasn't just working on the pond. He was expecting a visit from Kate. He was also locked in a battle of wills with his parents. He'd paid off their mortgage, but he won't visit them again till they've come and visited us here first. His dad's a dour but decent old hombre, and Japh's mom is chewing his ears off about it on a daily basis. We'll get them out here in the end.

So I, my Auntie Drew, Jool, and her Momma Grace went back. We took that smaller truck of the two we came out in. That stretch of the Five near Redlands, right? Pirating our produce outbound, and our bring-back from the city inbound.

Jool and I sat our rear-mounted thirty-cal on the roof of the truck's van. Momma Grace and Auntie Drew rode up front behind top-quality bulletproof.

Jool and I were the muscle, Auntie Drew was the map specialist, and Momma Grace was the driver. Momma Grace is still pretty plump, but she could haul *ass* behind the wheel. She knew she could drive like that before we started running the Five.

Of course when you're *dressed* to dance, you barely get a waltz. We got just one chaser in the bandit stretch, and once Jool and I had removed its tires and its radiator and part of its engine block fifty-cal, it desisted from pursuit.

It's a thrill, like high voltage, to reenter the megalopolis, to ride fast, twisted freeways over oceans and oceans of Zoo, to see the high, gorgeously plausible 'Rises, rank on rank, on their gently rising ground toward the Hills, and to see all those high storybook castles on the heights beyond them.

What mad grandeur! I'll always go back now and then to swim around in it a little. I've even started thinking I might track down my mom someday. The Zoo is vast, but hey, I found Japh on that set, didn't I?

But also, as I looked at it all streaming by us, I got down in my heart, and I thanked god that we no longer lived here.

When we pulled up to Jool's compound, there was honey-colored sun all over that fenced mass of foliage. I'd first seen it in the dark, and always remembered it that way. I was always surpised by how it blazed with flowers in the daylight.

Jool had lived here all her life, Jool had *made* this place through years of hard, tricky work. I could see, behind her cunning, impassive little face, that it moved her to stand in front of that gate. All she had put into this home-stead, all the little victories she'd brought back here, mak-ing this little garden of security sounder and safer, a bit at a time. . . .

Hugs for the block guards—and long-time neighbors—that Jool's group had given these houses to. Hell, I hugged them too, old Wrench and Ray—they'd stood our backs with shotguns here during the long, dicey load-up of be-longings for our first caravan out.

Since she had given them the houses, they now adamantly refused Jool's cash wage for today's work, till Jool threw a cat fit in the street and danced and screeched and flung the money at them. Big remonstrations, loving protests. Then more big hugs for them, especially from Momma Grace.

She and Auntie Drew now put on the stout, practical, multipocketed gardening smocks that Momma had taught Auntie how to sew, and they carried trowels and spades and pots and potting soil. They went right to work. They went from bush to sapling to flower to shrub, all the things Grace had planted over the years, taking something of everything for transplant.

My auntie, in emulation of her beloved Gracie, had become a passionate gardener. Auntie would say, "Oh my that's gorgeous! Now that's a hy*drangea* if I'm not mistaken, Gracie?"

And Momma Grace would say, "It's very remi*niscent* of a hydrangea, dear—it's a tiger lily. I remember when Jool brought home the bulbs. She was just fifteen, and we were having a *painful* disagreement about her being on the streets so late, and the next night . . ."

It was the best thing I'd done for my auntie I realized, watching her move through the greenery, practicing her horticulture, and learning Gracie's past. I could see in her crusty little monkey profile how she enjoyed it. Having a friend.

Wrench and Ray had occupants in two of the houses already. They were going carefully, searching out good people, friends of friends they knew something about. They helped Jool and me load the furniture—all neatly stacked and tarped and ready for us, and then they caught Jool up on the neighborhood.

"Looks like it's time to lend a shovel," said Wrench after a while. The ladies were starting to get down to the digging.

"Don't let 'em talk you into taking the sycamore tree," said Jool.

"Child, if she told me to, I'd dig that thing out and carry it up there on my back for your momma." Wrench looked like he could do it too. When the overwhelmed half-staffed high school had failed them, Gracie had taught his daughters to read and love books.

Jool stood looking around her, printing it in her memory.

"A lot of time here," I offered, "and a lot of it sweet time."

She half-smiled and nodded, still looking around.

"But if you could build this *here*," I added, meaning the Zoo, "think what you're going to build up there."

"Hey. I don't need any peptalk, 'Riser-boy. I'm gung ho. Except I've gotta tell you that *snow* shit is no bowl of cherries!"

"Hey, are you illiterate? You never read about winter—never read Annie Proulx?"

"She write about the Trinities?"

"She writes about everywhere, and half of it's colder than hell."

We stood there a moment, looking around us at her former home. In the silence we heard, from somewhere deep in the garden, my auntie's voice.

"Now wait a second, don't say anything—this is a holly-hock, no, it's *heather*, that's what it is."

"Well, the three of them are commonly confused, because *hydrangea* also begins with an 'H.' "

"Hydrangea! That's what I was *trying* to say."

"Isn't it lovely? I remember Wrench brought me that, it was five, no, six years ago. It was actually raining that day, or half-raining . . ."

I said, "You know, there's something I think I gotta bring up, Jool."

"What?"

"As soon as we get back, we've got to invite Jill Coombs over to dinner."

"Silly Jilly?"

"She is truly *funny*, and you know it, and she would like to eat Chops for breakfast, lunch, and dinner. I've seen her make Chops *laugh*. On *three* different occasions! Do you hear, sort of *get*, what I'm saying?"

Now she gave me the gimlet eye, with that unpleasant little smile twitching at her mouth corners. "What is this about, Curtis? What are we getting at here?"

"Jool. Look. We both know I'm gonna put this the wrong way, so let me just get it out and get it over with, OK? I am *honored*—and I mean it!—*honored* to share you with a man like Chops. I love that man. He saved my life, and I would give mine for him. I don't *want* you to stop being with him! I'm talking about *Chops* here, *his* feelings. I think we should invite Jill over to dinner."

I'd seen this before. She stood there listening to something I wasn't actually saying, ignoring my words and somehow reading a whole bunch of *different* words in my face.

There was a pause while she studied me, during which her eyes somehow got greener, and a little more tilted. Whatever she was adding up seemed to total out OK. She smiled.

"You're right. Jill is truly funny."

"OK, then."

"OK, then."

"Jool," I told her, "you're something else."

ABOUT THE AUTHOR

Michael Shea is the World Fantasy Award–winning author of *Nifft the Lean* and other novels. He has also written many short stories for major fantasy and science fiction magazines. He lives in the San Francisco Bay Area, where he is working on *The Siege of Sunrise*, a sequel to *The Extra*. His collection *The Autopsy and Other Tales* has just been released by Centipede Press, as well as his collected Mythos stories, *Copping Squid and Other Tales*, from Perilous Press.